scott westerfeld

MIDNIGHTERS

vol. 2 TOUCHING DARKNESS

An Imprint of HarperCollinsPublishers

Acknowledgments

Kathleen for air conditioning,
Niki for the Scrabble dictionary,
Ron, Iain, and Eloise for assorted tridecalogisms,
and Justine for helping Rex find his inner animal.

Eos is an imprint of HarperCollins Publishers.

Touching Darkness
Copyright © 2004 by Alloy Entertainment and Scott David Westerfeld
Midnighters symbols by Scott Westerfeld

www.harperteen.com

Produced by Alloy Entertainment
151 West 26th Street, New York, NY 10001

Library of Congress Cataloging-in-Publication Data
Westerfeld, Scott
  Touching darkness / Scott Westerfeld.— 1st ed.
    p.   cm. — (Midnighters ; v. 2)
  Summary: As they continue to battle evil creatures living in an hour
hidden at midnight, Jessica and her new friends learn about Bixby,
Oklahoma's shadowy past and uncover a deadly conspiracy that reaches
beyond the secret hour.
  ISBN-10: 0-06-051956-8 — ISBN-13: 978-0-06-051956-8
  [1. Science fiction.] I. Title.
PZ7.W5197To 2005   2004008716
[Fic]—dc22

❖

First paperback edition, 2006

To My Father

1

LAWS OF GRAVITY

At last, everything was *sorted out*.

Her clothes had finally found their way into the right drawers. Books lined their new shelves in alphabetical order, and her computer's tangled mop of cables had been subdued with rubber bands into a thick ponytail. The moving boxes were out in the garage, folded flat and wrapped with twine for Monday's recycling truck. Only one last box, labeled CRAP in black marker, sat in the corner of her room, filled with a dozen boy-band posters, two pink sweaters, and a stuffed dinosaur, all of which seemed way too childish for her new life.

Jessica Day wondered if she'd really changed

that much since packing the box in Chicago. Maybe it was getting arrested that had suddenly made her feel older. (Okay, officially she'd been "detained and transported to parental custody." Whatever.) Or maybe it was having a boyfriend. (Although that wasn't official yet either, come to think of it.) Or maybe it was the secret world that had opened up around her here in Bixby and then had tried so hard to kill her.

But everything was organized now, she told herself again.

For example: thirteen thumbtacks were lined up under each window in her room, and thirteen paper clips rested on the lintel of the door. She wore a thirteen-pointed star around her neck, and in a shoe box under her bed were Anfractuously, Explosiveness, and Demonstration (also known as a bicycle lock, a highway flare, and a heavy flashlight). All their names had thirteen letters, and all three objects were made of bright stainless steel.

Looking at her bedside clock, Jessica felt the flutter of nerves that always came at this time of night. Excitement, an anxiousness to get started, and a suddenly dry tongue, as if she were about to take a driver's test at a hundred miles an hour.

She took a deep breath to calm herself and sat down carefully on her neatly made bed, unwilling to disturb anything. Even taking a book down from the shelf might unbalance the whole night. The room's neatness felt precarious, though; it could only go downhill from here.

Jessica got that feeling a lot these days.

Cross-legged on the bed, she felt something in the front pocket of her jeans. She fished it out: the quarter she'd found in the closet while cleaning up. The previous tenants must have left it behind. Jessica flipped it in the air, the metal flashing as it spun.

On the third flip, at the top of the coin's arc, a shudder seemed to pass through the room. . . .

No matter how carefully she watched her clock, the exact moment of change always startled Jessica, like the jolt of the L train back in Chicago when it began to roll. Color bled from the world, the light turned cool and flat and blue, and the low moan of the Oklahoma wind fell suddenly silent. Suspended in the air before her, the quarter shone softly, a tiny and motionless flying saucer. She stared at it hard for a while, careful not to get too close and break the spell.

"Heads," she finally declared, then reached under the bed to free Explosiveness and Demonstration from their shoe box. She stuffed them into the big front pocket of her sweatshirt and crawled out the window.

Out on the front lawn, Jessica waited again. She didn't bother to hide, although she was still grounded for another two weeks (one result of the whole getting-arrested thing). The houses around her glowed with a faint blue light. No one was watching, nothing moved on the street; even the scattering of falling autumn leaves hovered motionless in the air, trailing from the dark trees like long dresses. The world was Jessica's now.

But not hers alone.

A shape grew against the cloudy sky, arcing from rooftop to rooftop, gracefully and silently bounding toward her. He hit the same houses every night, like a pinball following a familiar route down the bumpers. Just like Dess said she could see numbers in her head, Jonathan claimed he could see the angles of his flight, the most elegant path appearing before him in bright lines.

Jess touched the reassuring weight of the

flashlight through the sweatshirt's cotton. They all had their talents.

As Jonathan softly corkscrewed to the earth before her, Jessica's nervous energy began to turn into something more pleasurable. She watched his body coil, knees flexing and arms spreading, absorbing the impact of his scant midnight weight against the grass, and felt herself pack the last threads of her anxiety away in a box labeled CRAP at the back of her brain. Fear had been necessary for her first two weeks here in the secret hour—her survival had depended on it. But she didn't need it anymore.

"Hey," she said.

Jonathan swept his gaze around the horizon, checking for anything with wings. Then turned to her and smiled. "Hi, Jess."

She stood still, letting him cross the lawn to reach her. His steps carried him in soft arcs a foot high, kind of like an astronaut taking a stroll on the moon.

"What's the matter?"

"Nothing. Just watching you walk."

He rolled his eyes. "It's harder than it looks, you know. I prefer flying."

"Me too." She leaned forward carefully, not reaching out with her hands, gently closing her eyes. As her lips brushed his, gravity lifted from Jessica, a familiar lightness flowing through her body.

She pulled away and sighed, her sneakers settling back into the grass.

His long, dark lashes blinked. "You're in a funny mood."

Jessica shrugged. "I'm just . . . happy." She turned around, taking in the softly glowing houses, the empty sky. "This all seems safe, finally."

"I get it. So you don't need me to protect you anymore?"

She whirled to face Jonathan. He was smiling broadly now.

"Maybe not." She patted Demonstration again. "But we do need to study for that physics test."

He held out his hand. Jessica took it, and the lightness filled her again.

Flying with Jonathan had become like breathing. They hardly spoke, negotiating their course with a gesture toward an open stretch of road. Just before each jump, Jess tightened her right hand around his. She loved seeing the world as he did, looking down from the peaks of their arcing path onto Bixby's grid of dusty streets and autumn-thinned lawns, frozen cars, and dark houses.

They didn't head for downtown tonight; she tugged him into a winding course around the edge of Bixby. Without saying so out loud, Jessica wanted to test how close she could get to the bad-lands without attracting attention. Since she had discovered her talent (not as wonderful as Jonathan's, but far more formidable), none of the things that lived in the frozen time had dared to challenge her.

The badlands were visible from here, a dark bruise stretching across the blue horizon, but she and Jonathan were alone in the sky, except for a lonely, motionless owl riding the stilled winds.

The darklings and their kin were still very afraid of her, Jessica told herself.

"Need a break?" Jonathan asked.

"Sure. Soon."

It was hard work, flying. Jumping with all her strength again and again, wrapping her brain around the strange rules of Jonathan's midnight gravity. In physics they'd just learned about Isaac

Newton's three laws of motion. Jessica had four.

One: Jump at the same time as Jonathan. Otherwise you go spinning.

Two: Push off forward, not straight up. You want to get somewhere, not hang around in midair.

Three: Flat is good. Aim to land on rooftops, parking lots, and roads. Lawn ornaments can be painful.

Four: *Never* let go of Jonathan's hand. (She'd learned that one the hard way. Two weeks later the last bruises on her knees and elbows were just beginning to fade.)

"How about up there?" Jonathan pointed toward a gas station sign that towered over the interstate. A clear view in every direction, no possibility of a sneak attack.

"Perfect."

They landed on the gas station's roof, then pushed off at a high angle, floating upward to the edge of the darkened sign, their feet alighting softly on the rusty metal. When Jonathan released Jessica's hand, real-life weight pressed down on her. She swallowed and steadied her feet, a fear of heights returning along with gravity.

Something strange caught Jessica's eye. Half

visible in the open field behind the gas station, a hazy column rose from the scrub grass.

"Hey, what's *that*?"

Jonathan chuckled. "That's a real-life Oklahoma dust devil."

Jessica peered through the darkness. Motionless, glowing fragments were scattered throughout the apparition, suspended on a blurry, crooked tower of blue. "It looks like the ghost of a tornado."

"Dust devils *are* tornadoes, sort of. Really weak ones. When I first moved here, I used to go out in the desert and stand in them."

"Hmm." Jessica could see paper cups and a sheet of newspaper suspended in the vortex. "Looks kind of like a garbage devil, actually."

"Maybe here close to town. Not out in the desert, though. Just pure Oklahoma dust."

"Sounds . . . dusty." Jessica glanced upward. The dark moon was just visible through the patchwork clouds. She sighed. The midnight hour was half over already.

They sat at the edge of the sign, legs dangling over the precarious drop. With her arm through Jonathan's, his lightness filled her again, and the distance to the ground didn't seem so terrible.

Another beautiful view, she thought. The highway to Tulsa stretched out before them, dotted with eighteen-wheelers pulling all-nighters. She saw another owl high above them, balancing on the air currents that fed the dust devil.

Jessica pressed her shoulder against Jonathan's, realizing they'd only kissed once tonight, when he'd landed.

"We should probably talk about that physics test," he said.

"Oh, yeah. Sure." She looked at him and narrowed her eyes. "You actually *like* physics, don't you?"

"What's not to like?" He pulled a candy bar from his pocket and started to inhale it. Flying made Jonathan hungry. *Breathing* made Jonathan hungry.

Jessica sighed. "Uh, lots of formulas to remember, lots of homework."

"Yeah, but physics answers all the important questions."

"Like what?"

"Like if you're driving a car at the speed of light and turn your high beams on, what happens?"

10

Jessica shook her head. "Yeah, how did I survive without knowing that one?" She frowned. "And I'm only three months from a license. You think that'll be on the written?"

Jonathan laughed. "You know what I mean. Physics is full of crazy stuff like that, but it's also *real*."

"With you it is." Jessica pulled his hand to her lips. "Here at midnight."

She thought of the quarter suspended in the air back in her bedroom and smiled. "So, here's a physics question for you, Jonathan. When you flip a coin in the air, does it stop moving for a second right at the top?"

"That's easy: no." He sounded absolutely confident, annoyingly so.

"Why not?"

"Because it's on the earth, which is spinning and orbiting the sun, and the sun's moving through space at like six hundred meters per—"

"Wait, stop." She sighed. "Okay, let's say the earth wasn't spinning or any of that other stuff. Wouldn't the coin stop for a moment right at the top?"

"Nope," he said without any pause, staring into

11

the frozen vortex of the dust devil as if seeing the answer there. "The coin would be spinning around its own axis and would probably travel in an arc."

"Not *this* coin," Jessica said firmly. "It goes straight up and down and isn't spinning. So right at the top, there's a moment where it stops moving, right?"

"Wrong."

"Why the hell not?"

Jonathan said with maddening surety, "Well, there *is* a point right at the top where the coin's vector is zero. When gravity cancels out its upward momentum."

"So it's *not moving.*"

He shook his head. "Nope. The coin is going up, then the next instant it's going back down. Zero time passes when it's not moving, so it's always moving."

Jessica groaned. "Physics! Sometimes I think the darklings have the right plan. All these new ideas can only give you brain damage. Anyway, you're wrong. The coin does stop."

"No, it doesn't."

She reached for his hand, lifting him to his feet. "Come back to my room. I'll prove it to you."

He frowned at her. "What about—?"

She pulled him closer and kissed him. "Just come."

They sped straight across town, shooting across the dust-coiled lot of a derelict car dealership and down an empty stretch of Division Street. Jessica pulled Jonathan along in determined silence. She didn't care if she failed the test on Monday or not. She'd spent so much of her time with Jonathan in motion, running for her life or avoiding the winged things sent to watch her. Even when they rested, she and Jonathan were always balanced on some dizzying summit—the top of a building, a grain silo, or in the cold, precarious struts of an electrical tower. She just wanted to be somewhere *normal* with him.

Even if it was her bedroom. In twenty-five minutes he'd have to head home anyway.

The familiar sight of her street opened up below them, wide and lined with oaks scattering their last few leaves. They made a turn from the house on the corner (black tar paper shingles gave the best friction). One last jump would carry them to her lawn.

She pulled him close.

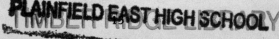

"Jessica . . ." His voice was cold.

"Just come in for a few—"

"Jessica!"

He twisted his body, spun them in the air, his free hand pointing at the ground below.

Jessica looked but saw nothing. Her blood ran cold. She reached instinctively for Demonstration and brought it to her lips, ready to whisper its name.

They descended to the grass, and he clutched her tight and pushed off again. She didn't know where Jonathan was headed; he'd taken over their flight completely, as if she were just baggage. Jessica scanned the skies for darklings, slithers, anything. But there were only clouds and the setting moon above them.

The jump was low and hard and sent them scrambling to a stop on the roof of the house across the street. Jessica felt a fingernail break as her palms rubbed raw against the slate. This was the first place Jonathan had ever flown her, she remembered for a moment, and like that first time, she was being pulled along like a balloon on a string.

They came to a skidding halt at the apex of the roof.

"Down there!" he whispered, pointing at the dense bushes that ran along the edge of the yard.

"A darkling?" A mere slither wouldn't have alarmed him like this.

"I don't know. It looked . . . human."

A midnighter? she wondered. Why would one of the others be spying on them?

They crept forward and peered over the edge of the roof.

The figure was crouched in the bushes, a human shape huddled in a long coat against the autumn chill, holding some dark object up to its face. Jessica counted to ten slowly; it remained absolutely still.

"It's just a stiff," she said aloud, then realized she had used Melissa's word. "Someone normal."

"But what's it . . . What's *he* doing down there?"

They rose together and stepped from the edge of the roof into a slow, graceful descent.

From the ground she could see the ghostly pallor of the man's skin, the unrealness of his frozen stance. He was young and handsome, but daylight people always looked ungainly here in the blue time, like the inexplicably dorky poses Jessica always managed to strike in photographs. His jeweled watch was frozen at midnight exactly.

The object in his hands was a camera, its lens jutting through the bushes like a long, black snout.

"Oh my God," she whispered.

The camera was pointed at her house. At her window.

"Jonathan . . ."

"Yeah, I see."

"He's some kind of stalker!"

Jonathan's voice grew soft. "Who just happens to be here at midnight? Watching *your* house?"

"He can't possibly know anything. He's a *stiff*."

"I guess." He took a tentative step closer to the man, snapping his fingers in front of his face. No response.

"What do we do, Jonathan?"

He bit his lip. "I guess we go see Rex tomorrow and ask him what this means." He turned back to her. "For right now, you have to go back in."

"What?" She looked at her window. She'd left it open, protected only by a gauzy curtain. "I don't want to go back in there with him . . . watching."

"You have to, Jess. Midnight's over soon. You

16

don't want to get caught out here. You'd be grounded forever."

"I know, but . . ." She looked at the man. There were worse things than being grounded.

"I'll stay right here," Jonathan said. "I'll hide and wait until midnight ends and make sure he doesn't do anything."

Jessica's feet were rooted to the spot, normal gravity heavy on her.

"Go on, Jess. I'll be watching him."

There was no use arguing. The midnight moon was setting, and she didn't want to sneak back in the window during normal time. Once the man unfroze, she was probably safer inside than out. She touched Jonathan's arm. "Okay. But be careful."

"Everything's going to be fine, I promise. I'll call you tomorrow morning." He kissed her hard and long this time, giving her one last taste of featherlightness. Then Jessica crossed the street and crawled in through her window.

The obsessively neat room seemed cold now, unwelcoming in the blue light. Jess ran her fingers along the bottom of the windowsill, feeling the thirteen thumbtacks. In a few minutes they would be useless. Number magic couldn't protect her from the man outside. Soon even Demonstration would be just a flashlight.

She shut the sash and locked it, then moved around the room, securing the other windows.

A glance at her watch confirmed that she didn't have time to check the locks in the whole house, not without waking up her parents or Beth. But she had to do *something*. She went to the neatly organized drawer of scissors, tape, and computer disks, found a rubber stop, and wedged it beneath her bedroom door. At least if anyone tried to come into her room, they'd make a lot of noise.

Still, Jessica knew she wasn't going to get much sleep tonight.

Sitting on the floor, her back against the door, she waited, clutching Demonstration in her hands. It might not do its flamethrower thing in normal time, but with its heavy steel shaft, it was better than nothing.

Jessica closed her eyes, waiting for the safety of the blue time to end.

The jolt came again—softer, as always when the suspended moment of midnight finished. The floor trembled beneath her, the world shuddering as it started up again.

A noise reached her ears and her eyes jerked open, her knuckles white against the flashlight. Color had flooded back into the room. There were hard shadows and bright, sharp details everywhere. Jessica squinted through the suddenly harsh light, eyes darting from window to window.

Then she saw what had made the noise and let out a sigh of relief. The quarter sat on her floor where it had finally fallen, bright against the dark wood.

Jessica crawled over and peered down at it.

"Tails," she muttered.

2 | 12:01 A.M.

FLATLAND

Normal time came down on Jonathan like a lead blanket.

He lay flat on the roof, just above the man with the camera. Jonathan's arms and legs were spread to gather more of the shingles' friction, but as gravity returned, he slid for a dizzying second down the tilt of the roof. A scraping noise escaped from under him, and he cursed silently.

Then Jonathan heard the whir of the camera below, a string of insistent whispers that jumped to life as normal time began. The man had been taking multiple exposures, across the *exact* moment of midnight. That was bad news. But at least the camera's whine had drowned out the sound of his slide.

Jonathan lifted his head painfully. It was hard even to breathe, squashed onto the cold expanse of slate by the suddenly crushing gravity. Below, the man lowered his camera and checked the time on his expensive watch, which glittered in the moonlight. He started to break down the long telephoto lens.

A shiver passed through Jonathan. The slate roof was cold now that midnight had fled, and the chill Oklahoma wind went straight through him. He'd expected to be home before the blue hour ended, so he hadn't even brought a jacket.

Damn, he thought, imagining the long walk home. Moving silently, he drew his limbs closer to his body and blew into his hands.

Below, the man had gotten his camera into its case. Drawing his coat tighter, he crossed the backyard of the house in a low crouch and gracefully pulled himself over the wooden fence. The sound of footsteps faded down the alley.

Jonathan edged himself to the gutter and looked down, wishing he hadn't picked the roof as his hiding place. A minute ago it had seemed the natural thing to do—natural when you could fly, anyway.

But here in Flatland, it was a nasty drop.

He lowered himself down, his fingertips clinging to the gutter, which creaked loudly. Then he fell like a sack of potatoes to the ground.

"Ow!" A sharp pain shot through his right ankle, but Jonathan bit the sound off, hoping it had been covered by the moan of the wind through the trees. The agony squeezed its way into his eyes, hot tears forcing their way out. He took a deep breath, ignoring the pain. The man had already gotten too far ahead.

Jonathan limped across the lawn and pulled himself up the fence to peer over. He could see a figure at the end of the alley, walking away fast in the cold. Jonathan hauled himself over, his muscles straining. It always took a while to adjust to normal gravity, mentally as well as physically. Midnight only lasted for an hour every day, but it was the only time Jonathan felt complete. For the other twenty-four hours he was trapped in Flatland, stuck to the ground like an insect in honey.

Dropping onto the hard-packed dirt on the other side of the fence sent another lash of pain through his ankle. He bit his lip again to keep silent, crouching in the shadows by the fence until the man turned a corner up ahead.

Jonathan limped after him.

A few moments later the sound of a car starting rumbled down the alley. Jonathan scuttled into a back driveway, barely escaping the headlights. In his mind he saw an easy jump that would put him just over the roof above and out of sight, but in Flatland it was all Jonathan could do to scramble into the shadows behind a parked pickup truck.

The car passed slowly in the unpaved alley, grumbling over loose rocks and gravel. Its headlights were blinding. Jonathan's eyes hadn't adjusted from the blue hour any more than the rest of him had. He tasted blood in his mouth, where a throb of pain beat in time with his frantic heartbeat. Great. At some point he'd opened up his lip.

After the car passed, Jonathan limped out from his hiding place and crouched in the red glare of its taillights so that he could read the license plate. Ducking back in the shadows, he repeated it to himself again and again, like some magic spell of Dess's.

The sound faded, and Jonathan allowed himself a sigh of relief. At least the man had gone. For the moment, he had only been spying.

But why? As far as Jonathan knew, no one who wasn't a midnighter knew about the secret hour. Silence had always been the unspoken pact among the five who had experienced the blue time.

But this man had to know *something*. What were the chances that this was just a coincidence? Did he pose a threat?

Jonathan headed down the alley, favoring his good foot. He'd have plenty of time to think about all this on the way home, in between trying not to freeze to death and looking out for Clancy St. Claire. The sheriff really had it in for Jonathan since busting him and Jessica for breaking curfew. *And* it was a Saturday night, Jonathan realized, not the best time to run afoul of St. Claire. He didn't care to spend two nights in jail, bouncing off the walls in the secret hour and waiting for Monday morning to come.

He limped to the end of the alley and peered out carefully, then took a few steps into the street. No car, nothing.

He glanced back at Jessica's house down the

road. Her light was still on. She was probably scared to death, watching her windows and wondering what lurked outside.

Jonathan shivered, thinking about skipping the cold walk home. On the weekend his dad would hardly notice, and Jessica's floor would be a lot warmer than some ditch. He could leave early in the morning, before anyone else in the house stirred.

Jessica had asked him to come home with her, he remembered. She'd wanted to show him something. Or maybe she'd just wanted to be with him somewhere safe and private. They'd hardly kissed each other at all tonight.

"Crap," he said softly, wishing he'd thought of this before sending Jessica home. She probably would have said yes.

She'd probably be glad to see him at her window.

After a long, cold minute Jonathan sighed and let go of the frustrating thoughts. This wasn't the secret hour anymore. This was Flatland. Even one tap on the window risked their getting caught, and Jessica would be blamed. Her parents would freak if they found him there. Jonathan was pretty certain that the cops had mentioned his name to them when they'd taken Jessica home. He doubted he'd be welcome at any time of day, much less in the middle of the night.

He turned and took the first few painful steps away. When he could fly, the trip home from Jessica's took less than five minutes, but in normal gravity (and with a sprained ankle, he was pretty sure) it was going to take at least two hours.

He huddled in his thin shirt, checked the darkened road ahead for police cars, and headed home.

3

GEOSTATIONARY

The dream came again, full of glowing wire frames, lines of fire forming spheres, like the doubled eights of a baseball's stitching or the twirl of peel left after an orange is stripped in one long spiral. The lines twisted around each other, bright snakes twining on a beach ball, performing new tricks every night. They examined their combinations restlessly, searching for one pattern out of many. . . .

Dess woke up sweating, even though her room was cold.

She rubbed her eyes with bitten-down thumbnails and looked at her clock. *Damn.* It was after midnight; she'd slept through the secret hour again.

27

Dess shook her head. This never used to happen. Even on those rare occasions when she did go to bed before midnight, the passage into the blue time always awakened her with its shudders and sudden silence. What was the point of having a whole secret hour if you slept through it?

But somehow she'd missed it again.

The fiery shapes of the dream still pulsed through Dess's mind, her latest project troubling her brain again, demanding answers that didn't exist yet in the scraps of data she'd managed to gather. The dream came every night now, her mind a renegade calculating engine clattering in the darkness. But she had come to understand what some of the images meant.

The spheres were the earth, this lovely ball of fun that humanity was stuck to, except for Jonathan in the secret hour, lucky prick. The glowing lines were coordinates—longitude and latitude and whatever other invisible geometries made Bixby important. (Now *there* were two words that should never go together: *Bixby* and *important*. Whoever had decided that this town should be the center of the blue time needed to watch the Travel Channel more.)

Dess frowned. Tonight's dream had conjured up a new image in her head: a circle of bright diamonds evenly spaced around one of the beach ball earths, orbiting it at a stately pace. There were twenty-four of them, her mind told her—a very darkling number. But what did the image mean?

Sometimes she wondered if this whole project had unhinged her. Maybe she was reading too much into Bixby's location.

Dess shook her head. Her father's oil-drilling maps were very accurate, and math *never* lied. The intersection of 36 north and 96 west sat a few miles outside town, dead on the snake pit. Those two numbers were stuffed full of twelves. That had to mean *something*; the snake pit was a source of Rex's lore and a major darkling magnet, squatting in the badlands like a giant spider in the middle of its web.

One thing had become abundantly clear to Dess: the geometry of the blue time was a lot more complicated than any spiderweb. There were asymmetries in the way the secret hour formed itself, subtleties in the way its lines reached across the hard-packed desert and into Bixby. Melissa sometimes complained about how her mindcasting changed depending on where she was, gaining or losing strength like a car radio fading in and out on a drive through the mountains. And now that Dess had bothered to map all of Rex's precious lore sites, a pattern had emerged there too.

And of course, there were the people who disappeared, like Sheriff Michaels two years ago. Darklings never seemed to bother stiffs, but they had to eat something. Rex said there were special places where the barrier between frozen and normal time was shaky. That was the real reason behind Bixby's famous curfew. If a normal person—or an unlucky cow or rabbit—wound up getting frozen near one of these spots, they could be sucked through the barrier for an unexpected trip down the food chain.

All this meant one thing: midnight had a shape, with ripples and rough spots. Maybe there were places where Dess's number magic was stronger or weaker, or where Jessica's flame-bringing would really kick ass, or where the darklings couldn't come. Maybe there were also places to hide.

Great theory, but the details were the tricky part. This math was *hard*. It was trig on steroids, and thinking about it wore Dess out all day and then mangled her dreams at night.

She lay there, staring at the notes scribbled on her blackboard, wishing she had some sort of calculating machine to untangle the numbers. Dess frowned again; she'd never used a mere calculator in her life. And the school computer that Mr. Sanchez let her hack around with wouldn't cut it either. What she really needed for this stuff was a NASA-grade, global-warming-predicting, doomsday-asteroid-tracking supercomputer.

Across the room Ada Lovelace stood on her little platform, staring at Dess, stoic as ever.

"Yeah, I wish you could help me too," she told the doll. But the real Ada was long dead (for 153 years, in fact), all that talent gone to waste before the world was smart enough to realize how brilliant she was. "I know the feeling, sweetie."

Dess rolled out of bed.

The big problem was *measuring* all this stuff. The blue time didn't come with street signs and trig tables, and you couldn't Google it for more details. When she pumped Melissa for data, Dess always hid her thoughts, not wanting to reveal her sudden interest in the mindcaster's reception problems. For some reason, Dess wanted to keep this discovery her own little secret. . . . Well, okay, she knew the reason. Rex and Melissa definitely had *their* secrets, after all, and Jessica and Jonathan were so far up Couple Mountain, she was considering sending a rescue team. This thing was *hers*.

But her secrecy didn't leave Dess much to work with, just midnighter gossip and her dad's oil-drilling maps. And those she had to borrow in the middle of the night.

"Speaking of which . . ." It was 1:25 A.M. now, a solid 16,500 seconds before the old grump's alarm clock went off, if he was working this weekend. The perfect time to do a little map math.

Dess swung her bare feet to the floor, feeling the wind pushing up between the ancient boards. She tested her weight against the wood—some nights were creakier than others. Her bedroom door opened silently thanks to her weekly treatments of WD-40. (Sometimes it was useful having a dad who'd wanted a son.)

The wind was fierce tonight, a low, insistent moan marked by the beat of a loose shutter somewhere in the trailer park across the field in back. Thankfully, there were enough random creakings throughout the house to cover any noise she might make.

In the middle of the living room was a big flat file, the metal top marked with rust circles the exact circumference of a Pabst Blue Ribbon bottle. Among the empties and bottle caps filled with cigarette ash was a row of precisely arranged remote controls that she rarely touched. Dess had done her parents' taxes and paid their bills for them since she was a kid, but she did *not* do VCR manuals.

Over the last week she'd already worked her way through the top three drawers of maps, so Dess carefully slid open the fourth one down. The dark smell of Oklahoma crude emerged, the scent that signified *Dad* to some part of her brain and brought to mind the black half-moons that never left his fingernails.

The edges of the maps curled up, as if they were smiling at the sight of her.

"Hello, my pretties," she whispered, then squinted in the dark. "What on earth are *you*?"

Weighing down the center of the maps was an unfamiliar little device, about as big as a package of cigarettes. It looked new, without the oil smudges and dinged corners that her father's stuff always acquired. For a moment she thought it was some new remote control, the sort of widget that might command an industrial-grade TV dish.

But then she picked it up and saw the compass logo above its small, blank screen, reading with one sweep of her eyes the multitude of tiny buttons underneath.

"Whoa." Her mind flashed back to the new image in her dream: the twenty-four bright diamonds in orbit around a wire-frame earth, evenly spaced around its equator and casting out lines of triangulation that hooked onto its surface.

She ran her fingers across the device and suddenly knew what the diamonds were—geostationary satellites, each forever suspended above one spot on the planet, sending out Global Positioning System signals all day long.

Dess pushed the power button, and the little screen came to life.

$$N\ 36°\ 16.41320°$$
$$W\ 96°\ 51.21380°$$

"Oh, *yeah*."

The coordinates flickered through Dess's mind, swinging a radiant *x* and *y* across a well-memorized map in the second drawer from the top. They were familiar but far more precise than anything she could figure from the little numbers that marched around a map's edges: the device was giving the position of her house. Her living room, in fact, down to a meter of precision.

Forget the supercomputer—*this* was the machine she needed. A little beastie that always knew exactly where it was, that would give her all the numbers she needed to crack the blue time's code.

Dess stared at the device, suddenly thirsty, her right thumbnail between her teeth. The only problem was how to borrow it. The thing wouldn't work in the secret hour—even if Jessica's flame-bringer voodoo sparked it up, a lone GPS receiver was worthless without those twenty-four satellites pinging away up in space. Dess would have to use it in normal time.

Which would be tricky, unless she just . . .

Dess swallowed. Certainly her father hadn't *bought* this. He wouldn't spend good beer money on a toy. He was a foreman now; the company must have just given it to him. He probably wasn't even using it. Dad hated all forms of fancy technology unrelated to football instant replays.

She looked down at the glowing numbers again.

"Pretty . . . ," she whispered. And damn it if *geostationary* wasn't a tridecalogism, thirteen letters exactly!

At worst, she'd have to hide the GPS carefully and listen to the old grouch rant and rave and turn the house upside down for a few hours. Like that didn't happen every time he lost his car keys.

No sense sitting here in the dark, Dess decided. She already knew what she was going to do. Her dreams had shown her what she needed.

But Dess paused a moment at that thought. Why *had* she dreamed about the Global Positioning System when her awake mind hadn't had any idea that her father owned one of these things? That was something to consider.

In the meantime, though . . .

She closed her hand around the device and whispered, "Mine."

4

CORIOLIS FORCE

"Morning, Beth."

"What's so good about it?"

Jessica turned to face her little sister, who was holding a piece of wheat bread in her hand.

"I didn't actually say 'good morning,' Beth. Just 'morning.' So I don't have to explain why it's good."

Beth stared up at Jessica through narrowed eyes, her little brain racing as she took a sip of orange juice. "I didn't say you said it was good. I was just asking a simple question."

"That is so lame. Dad, tell Beth that's lame."

"Girls," Jessica's father murmured in an abstractly threatening way, not bothering to

37

look up from his newspaper.

"He can't help you, Jess. He's not actually hearing what we say," Beth explained. "He only reacts to our tone of voice. Sort of like a dog."

"I heard *that*," Don Day said, giving Beth an actually threatening look. She hid behind her orange juice again.

Mom breezed in dressed for work, which was usual for Sunday mornings these days. Her new job at Aerospace Oklahoma was what had brought them all to Bixby.

"Morning, Mom. Want anything to eat?" Jessica turned to pop the bread into the toaster.

"Hey, guys. No thanks, Jess. We're having breakfast at the meeting."

"So when does your new job become an old job, Mom? And you get to stay home on the weekends?" Beth asked.

Jessica turned around and saw that her father was also waiting for an answer.

Her mother looked at the three of them and sighed. "I don't know. Today's my fault, though. I volunteered to be on this committee about the new runway."

"Never volunteer," Dad said, his eyes dropping

back to his newspaper.

Jessica's mother glanced at him in that new way that had evolved over the last few weeks, a cold look that probably had something to do with the fact that he didn't have a job here yet. Waiting up late for the secret hour, Jessica had heard them arguing about him taking temporary noncomputer work to make some extra money and to get him out of the house.

Donald Day didn't see the look, though. He never did.

"I saw a dust devil last night," Jessica said, trying to break the tension.

"Last night?" Beth asked sweetly.

Jessica looked down, buttering her toast. "Night before last, I mean. On the way home from school. It was really big, like a hundred feet tall."

"This *is* tornado country," Dad said, his paper rustling as he looked up. "It's because of the Coriolis force. I saw this thing on the Weather Channel—"

Beth groaned. "Not the Weather Channel again."

Jessica stuffed toast into her mouth. Unemployment had caused her father to become addicted

39

to some strange activities.

"What's wrong with the Weather Channel?" he asked.

"Two words, Dad: *weather . . . channel.*"

He ignored her. "Anyway, the Coriolis force is caused by the earth rotating under us, leaving the air behind. It makes the wind blow harder in flat places like Oklahoma; there's nothing to stop it."

Jessica blinked. "Actually, that makes sense." Maybe that was why wind didn't blow in the secret hour: the earth had stopped spinning beneath Bixby.

Beth was staring at her, annoyed that Jessica was showing any interest. She just assumed her big sister was sucking up. "Yeah, Jess, like we never had any wind back in *Chicago.*"

The phone rang. Before Jessica could move an inch, Beth had spun around in her chair and reached up to answer it.

"Is that for me?" Mom looked at her watch and pulled a leather bag onto her shoulder, turning away from the fresh coffee she'd started.

"No, it's for Jessica." Beth held out the phone sweetly. "Someone called Hank?"

Jessica managed a thin smile. "Hank" was

Jonathan's code name when he called her house. Jessica was pretty sure Beth didn't know this yet, but her little sister always acted like she knew *something*, just on principle.

"I'll take it in the hall. Bye, Mom."

Jessica didn't say anything until she heard the reassuring click that meant Beth was off the line.

"Hello?"

Jonathan's voice was ragged, like he was coming down with a cold, but it was good to hear him. He told her what had happened the night before, about the man driving away right after the secret hour ended. Then the big news: he'd been taking pictures at the exact moment of midnight.

"So, he knows," she said softly. "He has to."

There was a pause. "I guess so."

"Okay, I'll go tell Rex about it today." Jessica sighed. She could let her father believe that she was going to Rex's to study, although it would probably count as her one event per week of ungroundedness. Of course, anything was better than being stuck in the house all day with Beth, who still seemed to have found no friends here yet and envied her older sister for the ones she had.

"I'll go with you," Jonathan said.

"Really?" she exclaimed, but her happiness faded quickly. The fact that Jonathan was willing to put up with Rex Greene's company just showed how serious the situation was.

Jessica Day had human enemies now.

"Believe me," Jonathan said, "you don't want to go to Rex's alone."

"That's comforting."

"You know where he lives?"

She didn't. Now that she thought of it, Jessica had never been to any of the other midnighters' houses, not even Jonathan's. Between the lethal dangers of the secret hour and the inconvenience of being grounded, there hadn't been time for just hanging out. Normal life was still on hold—frozen.

Jonathan gave her the address and they agreed to meet in an hour.

As Jessica put the phone down, she glanced down the hall at the front door window. The day looked bright and cold. She shivered, realizing that the man might be out there at this very moment. At least when darklings had been stalking her, she'd had twenty-four hours of safety every day. But now the daylight had been invaded.

She'd only felt secure here in Bixby for one week before everything had changed again. Now it was back to danger mode.

From the kitchen she heard her sister's voice. "Face it, Dad. There's no Coriolis force. Oklahoma just blows."

5 | 10:51 A.M.

ICE-CREAM SOCIAL

Jessica stopped her bike and stared at Rex Greene's house, which sat forlornly on the street, crowded by newer homes on either side, the front lawn reduced to dying patches of brown.

The place looked empty, as if it had been abandoned for years. But Rex's father had answered the phone an hour before. He'd said that Rex was there and then hung up, not bothering to get him. From the other midnighters Jessica had gotten the impression that something was wrong with the old man, but no one had ever said exactly what.

She looked at her watch, still an hour fast from keeping time during the secret hour, and wished that Jonathan would show up already. She didn't want to face the weirdness of Rex's father alone.

"Jessica!"

She jumped, whirling to face the sound before realizing who it was.

"Man, Jonathan. You scared me."

He emerged from behind the aging oak that cast an ominous shadow across most of the front yard. "Sorry." His voice was very scratchy. "I was kind of . . . hiding, in case your dad drove you. I didn't want him to see me."

Jessica rolled her eyes. "Not that he knows what you look like. Anyway, ever since he and Mom decided that I was only *mostly* grounded, he hasn't been as paranoid." Although as predicted, Dad had counted this visit as Jessica's weekly get-out-of-jail-free card. She hoped that her mother would overturn the ruling after work tonight if she wasn't too exhausted.

Jessica walked her bike up to the sagging front porch and began to lock it to the iron rail.

"You don't really have to do that here," Jonathan said.

Jessica threaded the chain through her spokes

and snapped it shut. "Humor me. Big-city habits die hard. Besides, I like to have Anfractuously around."

"'Anfractuously'? That's your bike lock's name?"

"Thirteen letters. And because you're about to ask, it means 'snakily.'"

Jonathan blinked. "'Snakily'? Did Dess come up with that?"

"Who else?" She clicked the lock into place. The way its metal links coiled through the frame of her bike did kind of remind her of a snake.

When she turned back to Jonathan, he stepped forward and gathered her into a long hug. She pressed against him, enjoying the warm solidity of his body. In the midnight hour Jonathan felt so slight, almost fragile in his weightlessness, as if he weren't really there. Midnight might allow them to fly, but in some ways it cheated her of Jonathan's substance.

"Are you okay?" he asked.

"Sure. Not much sleep. How about you? You sound like you're getting sick."

He shrugged. "Forgot to bring a jacket last night. It was a cold walk home."

"Oh my God." She looked up at him. "I for-got. . . ." She hadn't thought of Jonathan walking home—she never imagined him walking any-where. "But it was *freezing* last night."

He smiled and croaked, "Tell me about it."

Jessica stared at the ground. She'd been afraid, but at least she'd been warm and inside. It was *miles* back to his house. She looked up into his brown eyes and said quietly, "You know, you could have come—"

The front screen door was wrenched open with a shrieking of rusty springs.

"Where are they? You seen them anywhere?"

They both turned to face the clamor. Emerging from the dilapidated house was an old man, his face weather-lined and unshaven. Hands shaking wildly, he spread his fingers and stared down at the porch, grasping at something invisible.

"They got away!"

"I'm sorry," Jessica spoke up. "Um, who did?"

"My babies . . ."

His eyes swept up to her, squinting through a film of milky white. A look of confusion overtook his panicked expression, and a bright line of drool on his chin sparkled in the sunlight. Tufts of white beard poked out along his wrinkles, as if his razor couldn't reach into the crevasses of his ancient face.

"It's okay, Dad, I'll find them."

Through the screen door, Jessica saw Rex's pale bespectacled face come into focus. The rusty springs screeched again as he reached out to take his father's shoulder firmly.

"You just sit down in here and we'll look for them."

Rex pulled his father in through the door, the old man's words reduced to mutterings at his touch. The screen door swung closed behind them, bouncing to a stop in a series of claps against its frame.

Jessica reached out and squeezed Jonathan's hand. "Did I say thanks for coming, by the way?"

"Wouldn't miss it for the world," he croaked.

Footsteps returned, and Jonathan dropped her hand.

"Was it you guys who called earlier?" Rex opened the door and stepped out, squinting in the sunlight. He waved them over to a trio of lawn chairs at the far end of the porch. He was dressed in the same uniform he wore every day to school:

dark pants and a collared shirt so black that his pale face had seemed to hover in the air behind the screen door. His heavy boots clumped along the porch, the metal chains around the ankles jingling and flickering in the sun. He'd told Jessica the anklets' names a few days before—tridecalogisms like Conscientious and Dependability.

"Yeah, that was me." The wooden steps bowed slightly under Jessica's feet as she climbed up onto the porch. She noticed that Jonathan waited until she was all the way up before following, not wanting to test the old planks with their combined weight. He seemed to be limping. What *had* happened to him on the way home last night?

"Sorry about my secretary," Rex said dryly. "He's a bit distracted lately."

"Uh, sure. But he told me you were home. So we came over."

Rex took off his glasses, looking into Jessica's eyes with an intensity that made her look away. Without the glasses, she knew, the world was a blur to Rex in normal time. But the faces of other midnighters were different: he could see them perfectly, daylight or midnight.

"I thought you were still grounded," he said.

"Yeah, but I can see friends once a week."

Rex sat down and then glanced at Jonathan. "I'm honored."

Jessica eased herself carefully into a lawn chair, half expecting it to collapse. Its aluminum frame was cold even through her wool skirt, and the arms were sandpapery with brown rust.

"Something happened," Rex said simply. He knew they hadn't come by for a chat.

Jessica looked up at the window next to their heads. It was open, chill gusts sucking the loose mosquito screen in and out as though it were some living membrane.

"Don't worry about him," Rex said, smiling faintly. "I keep no secrets from Dad."

"We saw something last night," Jonathan said. He gave the word *night* the subtle emphasis they all used when they meant the secret hour.

Rex nodded sagely. "Animal, vegetable, or darkling?"

"Human," Jessica said. "Frozen across the street from my house, pointing a camera at my window."

Rex frowned, boots scraping along the porch as he drew himself up smaller in the lawn chair.

50

Suddenly he looked the way he did at school: nervous and indecisive. His swagger only appeared in the secret hour or when midnighter business was being discussed. The mention of an ordinary human had deflated him.

"Like a stalker?"

"Nothing that normal," Jonathan said.

Jessica glanced at him sidelong. Stalkers were *normal* now?

"I watched him after the hour ended," he continued. "The guy was taking pictures exactly at midnight. He had one of those cameras that . . ." He held up an invisible camera in his hands and sucked his teeth, making a series of hissing noises. "You know, takes a lot of pictures in a row. I think he was trying to see if anything . . . changed at midnight."

"You exposed the film, right?"

"Um . . ." Jonathan and Jessica looked at each other.

"No?" Rex smiled, put his glasses back on, and tipped back in his chair, as though on familiar ground again. "Well, it's no big deal. The pictures might reveal a shift at midnight. I mean, you probably moved your curtains during the secret hour." He shrugged. "People tried something called 'spirit photography' back in the early 1900s. Especially here in Bixby. But it doesn't really show anything."

"How can you act like this is no big deal?" Jessica cried. "The guy obviously knows about midnight!"

Rex nodded, rocking his chair slowly. "It's not unprecedented."

"What do you mean?"

He stood, clumping to the screen door and opening it with a screech.

"Let me show you something."

Even with all the windows open, the house had a smell. More than one, in fact. There was old-person smell, like the rest home outside Chicago where Jessica's grandmother was quietly growing senile. And there was also the distinctive scent of spent cigarettes marinating in water-filled ashtrays. "It's a safety thing," Rex said when she raised her eyebrows at a bowl of soggy, disintegrating stogies. "Dad isn't very good at putting his butts out. The water helps."

Under everything else was the insistent smell of cat piss. A big tom splayed across a well-clawed couch watched them pass, managing to look bored, annoyed, and regal at the same time.

Rex's father was stationed in a big wing-backed chair, his eyes locked on an empty aquarium with scratched glass sides.

"Where are they?" he asked feebly as Jessica tiptoed past.

"We'll find them," Rex called. "They must be around here somewhere."

"What?" she whispered as they turned into a dark hallway. "His fish?"

Without looking back at her, Rex shook his head. "No, his spiders."

She glanced at Jonathan, who shrugged.

Rex's room was at the end of the hall and had a different smell from the rest of the house. The mustiness here was of old books and museum exhibits. Piles of notebooks and unbound paper were arranged precariously in towers, and rows of books covered every wall. One bookshelf blocked the room's sole window—it certainly seemed as if Rex was more afraid of the light than the dark.

"Home sweet home," he said.

As Jessica's eyes adjusted to the dimness, a few titles came into focus. Pretty much what she would have expected, but more. There were histories of Oklahoma, settlers' diaries and accounts of the displacements and the Trail of Tears, when Native Americans had been crowded into the Oklahoma Territory more than a hundred years before. Stretching farther back, there were books on pre-historic peoples of the New World and on Stone Age tools and animals. She and Jonathan stepped over stacks of paper—handwritten documents bearing the Bixby town seal and old pages from the *Bixby Register*.

As far as Jessica could tell, Rex had photocopied about half the local library and piled the results in his room. Even his bed was covered with papers. On a few were inscribed the spindly figures that recorded midnighter lore. She recognized the torchlike rune for her own talent—flame-bringer. A few lunches ago Rex had tried to teach her the symbols for the other talents: polymath, acrobat, seer, and mindcaster. But she could hardly make anything out on the densely scrawled pages.

A backpack was slung on the only chair in the room. Rex took a seat and cleared his throat.

"Dess told you about Bixby, right?"

Jessica looked at the stacks and shelves around

her. "Maybe not *everything* about it. What exactly?"

"The signs of midnight. The staircases with thirteen steps, the symbols."

"Sure." Dess had hinted about Bixby's oddities the first time they'd met, before Jessica had realized that the secret hour was anything but a dream. Since then she'd seen the signs everywhere: the thirteen-pointed stars in the town seal, on the high school emblem, on the antique plaques that people hung on their houses. Even the words *Bixby, Oklahoma,* totaled thirteen letters.

"Did you ever wonder who put all those signs in place?"

Jess frowned. "Haven't there been midnighters here for a long time? You said they'd been fighting the darklings for ten thousand years. Since the blue time was created."

"True. But the struggle wasn't always as secret as it is now. In the old days it wasn't just us midnighters who knew what was going on."

Jessica nodded slowly. According to Dess, the whole town had been built to antidarkling specifications. It stood to reason that a handful of midnighters would need help pulling off something like that. Unless there was some sort of architect talent that no one had told her about yet.

Rex continued. "Every small town has its secrets, things that outsiders don't need to know. A long time ago Bixby was a much smaller town, with much bigger secrets than most."

"It's still a weird place, even if you don't ever see the secret hour," Jonathan said. "I could tell that the moment I moved here."

"All you have to do is taste the water," Jessica said.

Rex nodded and placed one hand on a pile of photocopies. "If you know what to look for in these old papers, it's easy to read between the lines. It wasn't just local superstitions that made this town the way it is. The building codes are designed to repel darklings, newspapers report strange animal sightings that could only have been made at midnight, and there are an awful lot of clubs and societies dedicated to 'the preservation of Bixby.' This one's my favorite."

He lifted a well-worn piece of paper from the top of the stack and handed it to Jessica. She read:

LADIES' ANTI-TENEBROSITY LEAGUE
ICE-CREAM SOCIAL AND PIE AUCTION

5 CENTS ADMISSION
LEAGUE MEETING TO FOLLOW
(MEMBERS ONLY)

Jessica lifted an eyebrow. "What's *tenebrosity*?"

"It's an old word for darkness."

"Okay. But an ice-cream social?"

Rex smiled. "It's one way to fight evil. They had bake sales too. Practically everybody must have known what was going on."

"There's always someone who doesn't know what's going on," Jonathan said.

Rex looked at him directly for the first time since they'd arrived, peeking over his glasses to gauge Jonathan's expression. Then he shrugged. "Yeah, you're right. For most it was probably just a social thing, like going to church is for a lot of people. But back then midnighters were supported by the community." He took the paper back from Jessica and muttered, "More than *we'll* ever be."

"But what changed?" she asked. "I mean, how could everyone just *forget*?"

"That's a good question." He waved his hand at the bookshelves, the stacks of paper. "One I've been working on. As near as I can figure, it all changed about sixty years ago. First there was the oil boom, a lot of new people coming in to work the fields. Folks who wouldn't understand."

"So the old-timers kept quiet about Bixby's little darkling problem," Jonathan said.

"Yeah. Wouldn't you?" Rex picked up a stack of papers from his bed. "The town went from a few hundred to twelve thousand in ten years. Boom time. Hang on, I've got the exact numbers somewhere in here."

Jessica and Jonathan waited silently while he leafed through the papers. She tried to imagine a town where a hundred or so people knew the truth about midnight while thousands more remained in the dark. Of course, even if someone leaked the secret, it seemed unlikely the newcomers would believe them, except for the few born at the stroke of midnight who could see it with their own eyes.

And sharing the secret with a hundred people would be a whole lot easier than being just one among five. . . .

The tomcat pushed its way into the room and rubbed itself along Jessica's ankles, slinking through the piles to disappear under Rex's bed.

She wondered where the old man's spiders had gone, and her bare legs tingled.

Finally Rex shrugged, placing the papers atop a stack on the floor. "Can't find it, but that's pretty much what happened. The obvious part."

Still tingling from imaginary spiders, Jessica asked, "What's the not-so-obvious part?"

He pulled off his glasses and looked up at her. "The midnighters disappeared."

"Disappeared?"

He nodded. "There's no lore after 1956. No marks or recordings of any kind that I've found. And when Melissa and I were kids, there were no midnighters older than us, no one to tell us what was going on. She had to find me on her own, back when we were eight years old. Before that night, I thought I was the only one."

He sighed and lowered one hand almost to the floor. The cat emerged to sniff it, then allowed itself to be scratched.

"In the old days it was different. There was always at least one mindcaster, someone to find the new midnighters. When they got old enough to understand the blue time, there were initiation

59

ceremonies, teachers. You knew you belonged to something." He put his glasses back on. "But that all disappeared around fifty years ago, as far as I can tell."

"So something happened to them?" Jonathan said.

Rex nodded. "Something bad, we can assume."

"But the guy last night . . . ," Jessica said. "Maybe he's left over from the old days or something. Like he moved out of town way back then and just got back?"

"He looked that old?" Rex asked.

"I don't think so." She looked at Jonathan, who nodded.

"Young." He shifted uneasily on one foot. "He jumped an eight-foot fence a lot easier than I did. Rich, too. His watch had jewels on it."

"So how does he know?" Rex said softly. "Melissa's never felt another midnighter besides us five, and she's never tasted a daylight mind that knew the truth. Of course, she hasn't been looking out for any lately. But when we were little kids . . ."

He fell into silence, and Jessica found herself gazing at the four walls of books surrounding them. The room was its own little world, an imaginary slice of the past. Suddenly she understood Rex a little better. No wonder he always seemed misplaced, unhappy with the world he found himself in. He wished he'd been born in the old days, when there were rules and meetings and initiations, even ice-cream socials. When a seer was probably the boss of the whole thing.

"I got the guy's license plate number," Jonathan said.

Rex smirked. "Maybe Sheriff St. Claire can help you with that."

Jonathan's face darkened, and he glared down at the cat, which was rubbing its head against his feet. "Well, it's something, anyway."

Jessica sighed. "So what are we going to do, Rex?"

"Melissa's coming by tonight, after I get my dad to bed. I'll tell her what you saw. Maybe she can do a little mindcasting and find out what's new in Bixby. We'll take a drive around your neighborhood tonight, see if we run into any stray thoughts. If your stalker's there late, when most everyone else has gone to sleep, he should be easy to find."

"What should we do?" Jessica asked.

"Be careful."

"That's it?" Jonathan said. "Be careful?"

Rex nodded. "Very careful. That's what history seems to recommend. When the old midnighters vanished, it happened all at once, so quickly that nothing was recorded in the lore. Something got rid of them in one fell swoop."

"Like darklings, right?" Jess felt the reassuring weight of Demonstration in her pocket.

Rex shrugged. "Maybe it was darklings . . . or maybe it happened in broad daylight."

6

TOUCH

"Are you sure you're ready for this?"

Melissa stared at him across the front seat of the old Ford, a wry look on her face. "Well, it *is* an awfully big step."

Rex felt himself flush. After eight years he was used to the idea that Melissa could sense his emotions and read him better than anybody had a right to, but none of that made it any easier when she used her power to embarrass him.

"I mean," she continued, "I only want to do this if you think *you're* ready."

"I thought that you . . ."

His jaw tightened. The whole thing had been her idea, and now he was getting mocked for his

63

trouble. This was just like Melissa: she took midnight and its lore seriously—more seriously than any of the rest of them—but sometimes she had to demonstrate that everything was still a big joke to her. A waste of the precious little energy she had left over from merely existing in the world.

Even when he'd repeated the news that Jessica had delivered this morning, Melissa hadn't seemed very alarmed, as if no mere human threat could unnerve the unflappable bitch goddess.

She nodded, pulling at the fingers of one glove. "Yeah, it was my idea. But maybe we're rushing things. I'd hate to ruin a beautiful friendship."

At those words Rex felt a clenched laugh escape him. He looked up from her hands and saw that her smile had softened. His anger faded, taking with it the anxiety that had gradually built all day.

He cleared his throat. "I'll still respect you in the morning."

She laughed, radiant for a moment. But then her face turned serious, and she stared out the front windshield. "We'll see about that."

Rex could see now that she was nervous too. Of course, if the lore was right, he was about to feel exactly how nervous. The touch of normal people disgusted Melissa, redoubling their usual intrusions into her mind—she could barely stand visits to the doctor. But with other midnighters the connection went both ways and was much more intense. He swallowed, some of his own apprehension returning, and reminded himself that he had wanted this for a long time. It was a test of the lore, a way to find out more about how the talents worked together. Maybe it was even a way to break through Melissa's shell and finally connect her with the rest of the group.

And perhaps, Rex allowed himself to hope, he might make his own connection to Melissa, as he'd always wanted to and never could. He quenched that thought.

"Let's just get it over with," she said.

"Okay. Any cops around?"

"Gee, not since I checked three minutes ago." But she sighed, dutifully closing her eyes. They were pretty far from the center of town, out where Melissa's casting was clearest. The blasting mind noise of Bixby was miles behind them, and at this hour most of the population had already succumbed to sleep. The beings out in the desert that filled her mind with their alien tastes and ancient fears—the midnight things—hadn't awoken yet.

After a moment she shook her head. "Still no cops."

"Okay. Let's do it, then." He took a deep breath.

Slowly Melissa pulled off her right glove. Her pale hand was luminous in the darkness; there were no streetlights this far out, and the moon was only a glowing smear on the high, fish-scale clouds.

Rex laid his own right hand on the car seat, palm up. He saw it trembling but didn't bother to hold still. With Melissa it was pointless to pretend.

"Remember the first time?"

Rex swallowed. "Sure, Cowgirl."

It had all happened long ago, but he recalled their early experiences in the secret hour with a marvelous clarity. They had taken a long walk through the blue and empty streets of Bixby. Melissa was showing him how her talent worked, pointing at a house to say, "An old woman died slowly in there; I can still taste it." Or, "A child drowned in their swimming pool; they dream about it every night." Once she stopped to stare at a normal-looking house for a solid minute, Rex conjuring horrible images as he waited. But finally Melissa said, "They're happy in there. I *think* that's what it is, anyway."

At some point when he was eight years old, Rex had reached out—unknowingly and innocently—to take her hand, that first and last time.

"I was real sorry about that, Cowgirl."

"I got over it. It's not your fault I'm like this."

"Yours either."

Melissa just smiled at him and reached out slowly, her hand trembling as much as his. In that moment Rex knew that she wanted this too. No mind reading required.

He didn't dare move, so he just closed his eyes.

Their fingers brushed, and it was fiercer, more intense than Rex remembered. He felt the wild hunger first, her animal need to consume his thoughts, and he almost pulled his hand back but fought to keep it still. Her mind came then, entering his in a bold, unstoppable surge of energy, rushing into corners and crannies and uprooting long-buried memories. The car spun around Rex, his hands clenching to take hold of anything real and solid, but his fingernails only sank into her flesh, making the contact stronger.

Melissa's own emotions followed the first onslaught, carried along like bitter backwash. Rex could sense her constant phobia of being touched, as well as her new misgivings about the sudden and overwhelming intimacy between them. Rex felt his throat tighten, his stomach lurching as he recognized her long-simmering fear of this moment, suddenly understanding how much greater her anxiety had been than his.

But still, she'd trusted him enough to reach out her hand. . . .

Pieces of dark knowledge came through then: the way a darkling's mind tasted when it was very old, as bitter as a rusty nail held under a dry tongue; the chaos of Bixby High just before the late bell rang, almost loud enough to break her mind; the terror that with one touch, one of the clamoring minds that harassed her every daylight moment would invade and trespass on hers; and finally the sweet onset of the blue hour, a silence so glorious, it was as if everyone in the world had been exterminated, their petty thoughts all finally extinguished.

Then, suddenly, it was over.

He looked down at his hand, empty and slick with sweat. Melissa had somehow managed to pull away. Rex stared dumbly at his palm, watching four red half-moons appear, the marks of his own fingernails digging in after she had slipped out of his grasp.

But at least it was silent now. He was alone again inside his head.

He turned away from her to look out the window, feeling as bleak as the charcoal desert stretched out before him. Strange. Rex had expected to feel full once it was over. This was new information, like the wisdom of his books or the surety of lore, things that always made some part of him feel larger. This was something he'd wanted from her as long as he could remember. But somehow the knowledge of Melissa, of what it was like to be her, had emptied him.

"Maybe next time," she said.

He blinked at her. "What?"

"Maybe it'll be better next time." She tore her eyes from his and turned over the engine, the car springing to life beneath them.

Rex tried to offer reassurances and say something hopeful. Perhaps she would build up resistance. Or they would gain more control, sharing thoughts and ideas instead of raw sensations and blind fears. Maybe one day they could do more than touch for a few moments—maybe anything was possible. But Melissa shook her head at every thought that crossed Rex's mind, never taking her gaze from the road. This wasn't just her usual sensitivity, he realized. Melissa had been inside him every moment of the maelstrom and felt the desolation she had left in him.

There was nothing he could say that she didn't already know.

He watched the signs of midnight pass. It was better than thinking about what had happened between him and his oldest friend.

The midnight invasion had stopped, that much was for sure. When Jessica Day had first appeared in town, the marks had been everywhere, swaths of sharp Focus across the blur of Rex's vision, revealing where darklings and their foot soldiers had disturbed the daylight world. They had pushed farther into town every night, despite the clean metal and thirteen-pointed stars that protected Bixby, emboldened by their hatred of Jessica.

But now the marks were fading. Since she had discovered her talent, the darklings were powerless to attack Jessica directly. The town was softening again, losing the Focus. The darklings were in retreat.

Melissa made a turn. Rex frowned, unsure of where they were headed but unwilling to disturb the silence that had fallen between them since they'd touched. The plan had been to drive around Jessica's neighborhood and try to catch the thoughts of her human stalker. But they weren't headed into town. The desert was still in view, a black horizon stretching away toward Rustle's Bottom and the snake pit.

"Didn't you get my message?" Melissa said.

"What message?"

"About where we're going."

Rex chewed his lip. For a moment he wondered why he should bother to speak since she could evidently read every thought in his mind now. "Message? You know my father—"

"Not a telephone call. From my mind, moron." She turned to glare at him. "All you got was crap?"

"I wouldn't call it crap." The majesty of midnight's tastes, her profound loneliness, her long-tended hatred of humanity—none of it was crap. All of it was . . .

"Don't get all depressing on me, Rex. I tried to

send you a message, that's all. I thought that was the way you wanted it to work. So quit feeling sorry for me and *think* for a second."

Rex took a deep breath, turned to stare out the window, and began to examine the mental fragments she had left inside him. He had to ignore what he'd learned, the awesome sadness of it. He had to forget for a moment that he had never managed to understand what his best friend—

"Rex . . . ," she growled.

"Oops, sorry. Thinking about the message now."

And suddenly there it was against the bleak backdrop. A kind of undigested thought in his head, like a dream not quite remembered in the morning. He closed his eyes, but strangely that made the thought disappear, so he opened them again and stared out at the passing oil fields. Gradually his attention was caught by the rhythm of derricks rising and falling under the bright orange suns of mercury lamps. And then it became clear, like looking just to one side of a faint star and discovering that the periphery of vision is stronger than the center.

"We must have Jessica Day," he murmured.

"Bingo," Melissa said.

"You heard that . . . ? In *normal* time?"

"Give the man a cigar."

Rex blinked, hearing the voice, distant but clear, exactly as Melissa had when they'd driven back from Rustle's Bottom that night. "It was a human. You've known for a whole week that something *human* wanted Jessica."

"The Eagle has landed. Houston, we have a winner."

He stared dumbly out the window, unable to believe what he had heard in his mind or to comprehend the hysteria in her voice. Why would she hide this from him?

Then suddenly he blinked. Melissa's old Ford was passing a house he recognized, the two-story colonial fitting neatly over a vision she had left inside him. They were at the exact point on Kerr Street where she'd heard the voice.

"Why didn't you tell me?" Rex asked in amazement.

"Because . . ." Melissa's voice choked off, and she breathed deeply, getting herself under control. Finally she sighed. "Well, Loverboy, why don't you figure that one out on your own?"

DARKLING MANOR

Rex was pissed. You didn't have to be a mind-caster to know that.

He stared glumly out the window, watching the houses flash by, his mind tasting of stomach acid and day-old Mountain Dew, the flavor of betrayal with a topping of wounded authority.

As for Melissa, she didn't much care that Rex was angry. It was far better than having to feel his pity.

She still felt the tingle in her right hand, as if the flaking plastic of the Ford's steering wheel were buzzing under it. The touch hadn't been so bad, really. A little mindless maelstrom never hurt anybody, and just before the end she'd felt some kind of release, something shared between them that wasn't just night terrors and cosmic angst. Something she wanted to try for again.

But then Loverboy had to freak out. Like there was any reason to get all upset about the psychodrama that was her existence. Melissa figured that was just the way things were. And she had managed to give him the memory, one little token of communication amidst the crap-storm. That was something, at least.

"I still don't get it," he said.

She sighed. He never would.

Why hadn't she told him? The reasons all seemed to splinter as she thought of them, dividing into more and more . . . because she hadn't been really sure she'd heard it. Because you couldn't get upset about every stray thought. Because Jessica Day wasn't her problem anyway.

Nevertheless, he knew now. And she'd given the knowledge to him in a way that was more . . . interesting than just telling him. Funny—she hated seeing other people hold hands in school, their thoughts all syrupy and self-involved. But with Rex it hadn't seemed so bad.

Maybe next time he wouldn't freak out.

Melissa's mind wandered again, opening itself wide to catch the dreams and nightmares of sleeping Bixby. Hardly anyone awake, even before midnight. (What a loser-magnet this town was.) Most of the conscious minds were locked into TV shows. Hundreds of psyches spread across town were all laughing at the same jokes at the same time like goose-stepping circus clowns. Sometimes on Thursday nights Melissa had to suffer through all of Bixby yucking in tandem to the latest hit sit-com or mindlessly sweating out the million-dollar finale of some so-called reality show. She shud-dered. Only four months until the dreaded Super Bowl.

Didn't any of these brainless wonders ever notice that TV shows were called *programs*? The same word that meant a bunch of numbers stuck into a computer to make it dance for its masters?

Melissa snorted, realizing she'd borrowed that last image from Dess's brain. The girl was work-ing on some secret project, her little hamster wheels spinning so fast that Melissa could smell the smoke at midnight. Soon she and Rex were going to have to sit Miss Polymath down and ask her exactly what she was up to.

She glanced at Rex. Because keeping secrets was *wrong*, wasn't it?

A fragment of a thought struck her, and Melissa slowed the car.

Nothing in the content, but something about the flavor made her replay the words in her head. . . .

We can't be late.

Probably just someone racing to get home, trying to catch some movie on cable for the dozenth time. But there was something about the mind, as familiar as the smell of last year's homeroom.

"Catch something?" Rex asked.

"Maybe."

She took the next left, through a stone gate and into a plantation of McMansions, giant new cookie-cutter houses stamped onto tiny lots just out of the reach of Tulsa property taxes. The thought had come from in here, she was positive.

No one seemed to be awake; half the houses still hadn't been moved into. She could see the curtainless windows and feel the empty rooms behind them. Ugly as they were, Melissa dreamed of living in a house like these one day—unstained by years of human habitation, no sleepless worries seeping out of the walls, no residue of ancient petty arguments.

Most of the people who'd already moved into the complex were fast asleep, their dreams as smooth and interchangeable as the manicured front lawns.

Then she felt it again and gripped the wheel hard. Melissa knew it was the one, the same mind that had thought so intensely a week ago, *We must have Jessica Day.*

"What're you—?"

"Shush!"

It was already slipping away, moving fast across the empty psychic terrain.

"Crap!" It was in a car. (*He* was in a car—a male, she could tell suddenly.) The tendrils of his mind trailed away like a condensation cloud behind a jet plane. "I tasted him, Rex. But he's driving."

"Which way?"

"I . . . don't know." She shook her head; the last traces were fading. She brought the car to a halt. "He was around here somewhere."

"Same guy?"

Melissa nodded. "And we're only about a mile from where I heard him the first time. But we just

78

missed him, running off to something he was late for. Want to look around some more?"

"Sure." Rex's glasses were off, and he was staring at the overgrown houses. "There are signs here. Focus."

She took her foot off the brake, eased back onto the road.

"Really? In *this* place?" Sure, they were close to the desert, but Melissa couldn't imagine darklings taking an interest in this development, full of shiny new fixtures and stainless steel sprinkler systems. But the marks that Rex could see lingered longer than darkling mind traces, so there was no point arguing. She drove the car slowly along the meandering streets, keeping her mind watchful for cops or private security guards. Her old Ford stuck out here like a helping of dog turd on angel food cake.

It was good to feel Rex's mind at work, clear and pure as he looked for signs of Focus. In his excitement he had forgiven her slight against his authority, too intoxicated by his seer's powers to hold a grudge. In some ways he was still the kid she'd rescued from solitude eight years before, enthralled by the mysteries of midnight, driven by his need to know more. Melissa was sure they would hold hands again soon.

"Stop," he whispered. Melissa halted the car, feeling the buzz of his excitement.

The house he was staring at looked like all the others, two-storied and big-windowed, an overpowering double garage presented proudly to the world.

"I wish you could see this, Cowgirl. It's so Focused. They've been crawling all over it."

She let her mind drift in through its big front door. The place had hardly any human taste at all. "No one home. And if anyone lives there, they haven't for very long."

"Darkling Manor," Rex said quietly. "Not a clean brick on the joint."

She looked at her watch. Twenty to midnight. "Well, shall we take a look before the witching hour?"

"What about your friend?"

"He was headed somewhere in a hurry." She tasted the air. "Long gone."

"Okay. But ten minutes max. We should be back in the car and a couple of miles from here before midnight comes." He shook his head. "Don't want to be crashers at a darkling house party."

* * *

The door was unlocked.

"That's interesting." Melissa pushed it open, its new hinges utterly silent. The entrance hallway was grand and echoey, no rugs to muffle the sound of their boots across the polished wooden floor. No *anything,* she realized. The walls were bare of pictures, and no shoes or hanging coats cluttered the foyer. The two large front rooms were empty except for a portable phone. It sat lonely on a windowsill, its cord winding across the blank expanse of carpet, a demonic red eye showing that it was recharging.

And the place tasted completely dead. Not a leftover thought anywhere. Even the dull roar of central Bixby miles away seemed muted by its walls.

"Nothing to steal, I guess," she said.

"But lots of darkling action." Rex was looking up the stairs, into corners. "Just like outside, it's all in Focus."

"Maybe it's some kind of darkling frat house."

"I've never seen them set up shop in a human dwelling before. Maybe a tire yard or a vacant lot, but not a house. Of course, nobody lives here."

81

"No," Melissa said, "but the darklings aren't paying the phone bill. . . ."

Rex chewed his lip. "Good point."

In the kitchen they found signs of habitation. Or maybe vandalism. The faucet had been yanked out from the sink, the handles of the cupboards torn off, every piece of metal removed. There were no appliances, and the lightbulb hung bare from the ceiling.

"A darkling-friendly kitchen. What do they eat, anyway?"

Rex just looked at her, sending out a stab of annoyance.

"Oh, right. Us." Melissa didn't think about it in those terms much, but that was and always had been the prime source of conflict between the two races: the whole food-chain thing. Funny how that could mess up a relationship.

"Let's check upstairs," Rex said, having gone through the drawers and cupboards and found them empty.

She checked her watch. "Okay. But five minutes and we leave."

He turned his head slowly from left to right as they climbed the stairs, his eyes wide with the

Focus. "Absolutely."

Upstairs was divided into three empty bedrooms, the largest with a big balcony that looked out into the dark Oklahoma night. Melissa stared through the sliding door and realized something. She pulled off a glove and put her hand to the cold glass.

"You know, Rex, it's warm in here." Outside it was almost freezing, but someone had left the heating on, though they hadn't bothered to lock the door. . . .

"Look at this!" he cried, his mind flooding the room with delight.

He had pulled something from a closet, a box of small rectangular tiles that glowed white in the darkness. He squatted on the floor and dumped them out with a clatter. As his hands swept through the tiles to spread them out, she recognized the wooden sound.

"Didn't know you liked dominoes so much," she said dryly.

"Not dominoes." Rex was flipping them all faceup. He hadn't put on his glasses, so they must have been marked with Focus.

She knelt beside him and squinted at the

symbols on the tiles. They were the spindly figures of lore, the secret alphabet used to record midnighter history for ten thousand years.

"Oh." The thought that anyone besides Rex would use the ancient signs left her speechless for a moment.

"But they're not quite the same," he muttered. "It's like a slightly different alphabet. . . ."

Melissa didn't respond. She steadied herself with one hand on the floor. The feel of him parsing the symbols was dizzying; his mind battered hers with a frenzy of calculation.

"Or maybe some of them are signs I don't know," he said, picking through them, lifting one for closer inspection. "Symbols for concepts that don't exist in the lore."

Melissa forced her mind to shut out his mental pyrotechnics. "But what are those things *for*, Rex?"

The question brought his brain to a spinning halt. "I don't know."

She thought of the stiffs they often found at the snake pit, frozen while staring at the piles of rocks that Bixby legend held would move at midnight. (Of course, sometimes Melissa moved them herself, just for fun—and to terrify the little

84

trespassing morons.)

"Could someone use them to communicate with the darklings?" she asked.

"That doesn't make any sense. Darklings hate symbols and signs, any written language. That's one of the new ideas that scared them off ten thousand years ago, along with math and fire and metal."

"But Rex, you've got your glasses off."

"I what?" He put one hand to his face. Melissa realized that Rex had momentarily forgotten he wasn't wearing the thick lenses. The house was so marked with Focus that he could see everything clearly anyway.

"So darklings *have* touched these," he murmured, a few of the dominoes slipping through his fingers. "But how?"

"Rex . . ." A familiar taste was penetrating the overwhelming clamor of Rex's excitement. "What time is it?"

He checked his watch. "You're right. We should go soon. Just let me grab a few of these—"

"Rex!" It wasn't impending midnight that had her worried; it was something she'd felt before, and it was rushing back toward them. The voice seemed to suddenly crack through the psychic silence of the house.

We're just going to make it, no thanks to you, Angie.

Her head spun, trying to sort Rex's mental turmoil from the approaching thoughts. They came through grim and determined, angry at some inconvenience, and, most of all, anxious.

"It's him . . . ," she whispered.

"Who?"

Keep it on the road, idiot. We're almost there.

She recognized the exact kind of fear now; it was of a type familiar from a thousand school mornings. There was always at least one mind trailing in after everyone else had settled into their desks, rushing along panicked at the thought of punishment. That was what she tasted: fear of being late.

"He was in a hurry when he left," she muttered, "but he was in a hurry *to get back by midnight!*"

"The guy you heard?"

"Yes! We have to get out of here *now.*" She stood, still dizzy. For some reason, mindcasting in this house was like walking through syrup.

Rex was scraping at the tiles, trying to return them all to the box.

"There isn't time!" She tasted the man's bitter curses as he twisted at the steering wheel, felt his body sway on the quick turns, heard the skidding of tires. . . .

Rex looked up. He'd heard the tires too.

Headlights crawled across the ceiling, and a screech came from the driveway.

"He's here," she said, too late.

"Don't worry about him," Rex said, taking her gloved hand softly as he checked his watch. "We only have to stay hidden for four minutes. It's what's coming after midnight that worries me."

They shoved the darkling dominoes back into the closet and crept to one of the smaller bedrooms. Hopefully the man wouldn't poke around the empty house with so little time remaining before midnight. Rex pointed to a wide, shallow wardrobe with sliding doors.

The sound of the front door opening carried up the stairs just as they made it into the darkness of the wardrobe. Melissa felt Rex breathing hard next to her, off balance as he tried to avoid touching her accidentally. She slipped her other glove back on and steadied him with that hand, whispering,

"Relax. Let me concentrate."

Rex's mind calmed, and she could feel now that there were two of them downstairs, the man and . . . Angie. The woman radiated only calm; no wonder she'd been invisible to Melissa before now.

"You're lucky we made it," came the man's muffled voice, his footsteps audible on the stairs.

Melissa controlled her breathing. The way sound echoed through the empty house, one bump against the wardrobe door and they'd be discovered.

"I didn't ask to break down. Next time I won't bother to call you." Her voice was low and controlled, not out of breath like his. Her mind held none of his fear of being late. Melissa felt the woman check her watch—a burst of satisfaction as she confirmed that everything was on schedule. Now that they were inside the house, Melissa could taste them clearly.

"Promises, promises," the guy shouted from the master bathroom. A rush of release filled his brain just as the trickling sound of piss reached Melissa's ears. She shuddered at the intimacy.

"Like you could handle this on your own," the woman said in a voice so soft that it mostly reached Melissa as thought. She had a lock on Angie's mind now: it was saturated with a sickly sweet contempt for the man. Angie didn't need him here in the first place—he could barely interpret lore symbols, couldn't see the big picture, was always lugging around his stupid camera, which of course never captured the spooks anyway. *If he wasn't related to the patriarch . . .*

The woman's mind grew closer, her slow footsteps carrying her through the upstairs hall. She came to a halt just outside the room they'd hidden in.

"Did we really need this big a house?"

Rex's shoulder muscles tightened under Melissa's grip, his mind clouding hers with a wave of fear. *Relax,* she willed him.

"Location, location, location," the man said. "That's all the spooks care about. Anyway, if this field is as big as they say, we should make about a hundred times what this cracker box cost."

The woman took one more step into the room and flicked on a light. A blinding wedge of illumination forced its way through the crack between the wardrobe's double doors. Melissa squinted, feeling as if the light was slicing her in half from top to bottom. Rex had stopped breathing.

Melissa closed her eyes, trying to tease from the woman's mind what she was thinking, why she was staring at the closet door. But Rex's terror drowned out those smooth, collected thoughts.

"Come *on*, Angie! Thirty seconds."

The woman didn't move. Melissa made a fist with her free hand. One solid punch to the gut would put anyone down for half a minute. Long enough.

"Angie!"

Finally the footsteps retreated, quick and determined now. Melissa heard the clatter of dominoes being spilled in the other room, felt anticipation growing in the two intruders as relief flooded through Rex.

And then, seconds later, always glorious . . . *Silence.*

8

12:00 A.M.

HALFLING

"Come *on*! We've got to run!"

Melissa shook her head and tore away from him. Her eyes shone with the terrible clarity they always had in the blue time; freed from the tumultuous mind noise of humanity, she could be fearless, imperiously bold.

Rex sighed. She could also be a pain in the ass.

"I am so going to rip this woman," she said, pushing past him and into the master bedroom.

He followed, coming to a halt at the door. The two normals were frozen on either side of the clutter of tiles, the man kneeling, the woman standing. The man's face was obscured by a camera pointed at the floor. Rex noticed that his

91

watch was set exactly to Bixby midnight and that its face was marked with the tiny glittering eyes of jewels.

"Well, what do you know?" Rex said. "He stalks darklings as well as Jessica."

"She's the one that matters," Melissa said.

The motionless woman was tall and fair, dressed in business clothes. Midnight had caught her expression: awe and fear mixed with expectation. All the tiles were facedown on the floor, ready to be turned over and arranged into messages.

Rex shook his head, still unable to wrap his mind around it. How could a darkling communicate using hated midnighter symbols? And where had these people hidden themselves for fifty years?

Melissa stood before the woman, reaching out her hands.

"There's no time!" Rex shouted. "The desert's only half a mile away. Whatever's coming will be here soon!"

"She's the smart one, Rex. You should have felt her mind. She knows what's going on."

"What's going on is we're about to get overrun by darklings!"

"Get ready, then. I'll be downstairs in five."

Rex flinched. Why didn't anyone ever listen to him? Especially at times like this, when it really mattered. However expensive it looked, this house was a darkling place. Not for humans. He could *see* that; Melissa couldn't.

He noticed that the sliding glass door of the balcony was now open.

"Make it three," Rex said coldly, and ran downstairs.

He burst through the front door and ran to the car, not bothering to check the skies. They had a few minutes, anyway. Even Jonathan Martinez couldn't have gotten here this fast.

Perversely, he hoped that something big was coming. The oldest ones lived in the deep desert and would take longer to get here. And having to face something really scary might convince Melissa to *listen* to him next time.

Of course, if it did turn out to be just some second-string darkling and a few slithers, Rex wasn't going to complain.

He reached into the backseat and pulled out his duffel bag. It was depressingly light; they hadn't brought any serious metal tonight, thinking they'd be facing a human threat and not some darkling house party.

Rex cursed. The awesome power of the flame-bringer had made him overconfident.

The duffel bag's zipper caught in his nervous fingers, but he managed to yank it open. A big plastic flashlight, useless without Jessica to spark it up. A ball-peen hammer called Arachnophobia. A bag of assorted screws and nails for throwing. And a tire iron with the name Stratocumulus that Rex only now remembered had been used to ward off slithers before. Its power had probably sizzled down to nothing. Melissa only kept it in the trunk to change tires.

That was it.

Time to break out the big guns.

"Back left, back left," Rex muttered to himself, slamming the door and running around the car. He pried at the Ford's left-rear hubcap with Stratocumulus, useful for something at least. As he pulled, Rex allowed himself a satisfied grin. He and Dess had worked hard on this one, agreeing to use it only when absolutely necessary.

Which would be now.

The hubcap sprang off, clattering to the street.

Around its inside edge were a host of tiny symbols, Stone Age pictograms, thirty-nine of them, etched by Dess as per Rex's instructions. She had used a drill bit stolen from shop class, made from a tungsten alloy so high tech, it could bore through steel like wet plaster.

Rex shoved the hubcap into the bag, hoping it would be enough.

He ran back to the open front door and shouted up the stairs.

"Melissa!" She didn't answer. "Come on!"

Then he heard a sound from above.

She was whimpering.

Rex found her on her knees before the woman, her fingers still splayed in their mindcasting grip, shaking her head and moaning.

"Something's coming. . . ."

He sighed. "Like I said."

"It's so sick, Rex. . . ."

He swallowed. It wasn't like Melissa to freak out at darkling thoughts. She always said their ancient, arid minds were a hundred times easier to tolerate than those of humanity.

"Come on." He hauled Melissa to her feet and

pulled her toward the stairs. She didn't fight him, just trailed along, making hiccuping noises, like a kid trying to keep from crying.

Rex tried not to think about what she'd seen.

The front door was still ajar, and he kicked his way through. The house across the street looked occupied, hopefully full of shiny metal and modern machines. Rex had one more trick up his sleeve—or stuffed into the buckle of his right boot, actually.

Melissa ran with him across the asphalt, finally shaken out of her panic. But when he looked back at her, the cold light of the rising blue moon glimmered from a single tear on her cheek.

She was crying. *Melissa* was crying.

Rex swallowed hard. *We're dead.*

The front door was locked, so he swung Stratocumulus through the little stained-glass window at its center, stuck his arm in, and searched for the knob on the other side. Broken glass stabbed at the crook of his elbow, but his fingers found the dead bolt and spun it. As the door swung inward, Rex heard the sound of tearing cloth coming from his sleeve.

"Kitchen," he said. Always the best tools there.

Melissa ran ahead as Rex paused to check his

arm, spreading the ripped cloth to reveal torn flesh. As the blood welled up from the wound, the red color leeched away, turning to a steely blue-gray before his eyes.

"In here!" Melissa shouted from the back of the house.

He tore his gaze from the cut and ran, wondering for a moment if darklings were anything like sharks. Could they be driven into a frenzy by the smell of blood?

The kitchen was huge, bigger than Rex's living room, with long stretches of counter space and two full range tops. The ambient blue light of the secret hour glowed from metal appliances and a block of knives.

Rex smiled. They weren't dead yet.

He pulled open drawers until he found the silverware and brought a spoon up to his sharp eyes.

"Stainless Korean," he read happily, and thrust the whole drawer into Melissa's arms. "Find a room upstairs with no stiffs."

She nodded mutely, her face still blank with shock.

Rex ransacked the kitchen, filling his duffel bag with nonstick ceramics, high-temperature alloys, all the space-age materials that always started out in jet fighters and wound up in frying pans. After thirty frantic seconds he hoisted the heavy, clanking bag over one shoulder and grabbed the knife block with his free hand—the knives looked fearsome if nothing else. He headed for the stairs.

Melissa had found the perfect room. It was a study, with only one small window that looked out across the street at Darkling Manor. A computer dominated a small desk, and a pegboard full of cables filled one wall. More clean metal for the taking.

She was staring out the window, shuddering again.

"They're almost here."

Rex dropped the bag and slammed the door shut. Drawing a knife from the block and peering closely, he smiled.

"Somebody likes to cook."

The knives were Japanese and gorgeous, bearing the magic words, *Never needs sharpening*. That meant high titanium content and laser shaping, the modern-day equivalent of a late-Solutrean spear point—the Stone Age technology that had finally driven the darklings into the secret hour.

He pulled the slip of paper from his boot strap and unfolded it, then turned to the door and thrust the knife hard against it. The wood split with a satisfying *thunk*.

"Abnormalities." Rex pulled another knife from the block. "Aboriginality," he read from the piece of paper. *Thunk*. Pulled another knife . . .

He smiled grimly. This was one little resource Dess had never thought of (not that she needed help finding tridecalogisms).

"Acceptability." *Thunk*.

The piece of paper was the second-to-last page of a Scrabble dictionary, the only kind of lexicon Rex had ever found that listed words by length.

"Accidentalism." Whatever that was. *Thunk*. The door would be rock solid once he got to thirteen. . . .

The knives ran out at twelve.

Rex squeezed his eyes shut tight. Why hadn't he counted before starting? Nine would have been good enough. And *anything* would have been better than twelve.

He whirled around and grabbed a butter knife from the silverware drawer, turned back, and propelled it against the door with all his strength. The blunt tip skated off, taking his wrist a few inches from the serrated edge of a beautiful Japanese carving knife.

"Damn," he said. Still twelve knives. He'd turned the door into a darkling magnet! How could he have been so—?

Thunk.

Rex blinked, staring at the knife trembling in the wood beside his head. Its blade was etched with snakes and frogs, its hilt cast like two scaly lizard tails, and its pommel, a tiny metal skull with glass eyes, seemed to be smiling at Rex. He'd never seen the knife before and found himself realizing that he wasn't the only midnighter who had a few weapons put aside for a rainy day.

"Magnificently Instantaneous Gratification," Melissa said.

He turned to face her. She was still on the other side of the room—she'd *thrown* it past Rex's head.

Melissa had wiped the tears away, and her expression had returned to its usual midnight sneer. "I'm okay now."

He let out his breath and started to nod, but

movement out the window caught his eye. He crossed the room.

"Don't look, Rex. You don't want to—"

But he'd already seen it.

The thing came down on undulating wings, two leathery sails that billowed from long, multijointed arms. Its hands, long-taloned and grasping the air with compulsive little twitches, must have been thirty feet apart. Its spiked tail whipped through the wind with every beat of the wings, as if to counterbalance the beast's grotesque cargo.

Its body was thin, the darkling part of it anyway, ribs showing through its leathery flesh. The thing's spindly hind legs stumbled, trembling feebly as it landed on the rooftop across the street, and its wings took one steadying stroke as it gained its footing.

Melissa, still facing away from the window, made a choking noise.

It had no head. Not a darkling head, anyway. A human torso seemed to be submerged into the creature's flesh, and a half-visible human face stared glassily from its emaciated chest. Two secondary arms thrust from the sunken torso, ending in the hands and fingers of a person—a *child,* Rex now saw—which were clenched as if in pain.

"It thinks . . . ," Melissa rasped, ". . . like us."

Something burst through the window, an explosion of broken glass, fluttering wings, and ratlike squeaks. Needles of ice shot through Rex's chest as the winged slither struck, and a sudden tangle of black filaments seemed to clutch his heart.

Blue sparks blinded him, the metal chains swinging from Melissa's fist knocking the slither to the ground. Rex gasped for breath through frozen lungs, watching as she casually tipped the silverware drawer over onto the still-fluttering beast. The metal spat more sparks as the thing sizzled underneath the pile.

"You do the window," she ordered, kicking the glowing forks, spoons, and knives around on the floor to prevent any crawling slithers from sneaking up on them.

Rex nodded and reached into the duffel bag. He tossed two handfuls of Dess's nails and screws out the window, bringing screams and blue fire from the things that hovered or slithered just outside. A swing with Arachnophobia, the ball-peen hammer, dislodged something large that had taken hold of the sill.

"Help me with this," he shouted, ice from the slither strike still grating in his lungs.

The pegboard full of computer cables came down easily from the wall. Some of the cables were filled with useless copper and gold, Rex knew, but some would also contain advanced alloys, insulating plastics, and hopefully some fiber optics, all of which would bedevil their attackers. They leaned it against the window, and Rex began to empty the duffel bag, naming the pots and pans with the last tridecalogisms from his tattered Scrabble dictionary page.

"I got it," Melissa said, pushing him away when his list ran out. She named the last few bits of metal, calling on the memorized emergency words they all kept in their heads.

"Unintelligent," she murmured.

Rex leaned against the wall and shuddered. Every breath was icy from the slither strike. His shoulders were numb and his fingers moved slowly, like after a snowball fight without gloves. A few inches higher and the slither would have gotten him on the neck. The lore said that a few midnighters had actually died that way—suffocating, their windpipes choked with ice.

He'd been so awestruck by the . . . *thing* they'd seen, he'd almost been killed by a mere slither.

"Irresponsible," Melissa named a frying pan.

"What was it?" he croaked.

She turned to him, shook her head. "It thinks like us."

"A human, you mean?"

"A midnighter. I think she's . . . she *was* one of us."

"Mixed with one of them."

Melissa stared at the meat thermometer in her hand and whispered, "Indescribable."

Something big hurled itself against the pegboard. The coiled computer cables turned into flickering circles, like Christmas lights still in their boxes. A long tendril snaked from behind the flimsy board, wrapping itself around Melissa's waist. She thrust the point of the meat thermometer into it, and the tendril retreated with a shriek.

"Just a lower darkling," she said.

Rex sank to the floor. Melissa shoved the last of their defenses into place and crouched next to him, holding his hand, protected by her thick woolen glove.

"I'll show you what I felt," she said. "From the thing and that woman. After we get out of here. Tomorrow we'll touch again."

"*After* we get out of here?" He looked at the door with its thirteen knives, the pegboard full of glowing metal. Maybe it would hold, maybe not. Of course, after what he'd seen, death was relative.

Better eaten than . . . changed.

"Yes, Rex. After we get out of here."

A fluttering and shrieking came from the blocked window, a slither beating its wings as it died, the pegboard trembling.

"They're unhappy about us seeing that thing, aren't they?"

Melissa nodded thoughtfully. "You said it. They aren't going to give up easily."

Another slither launched itself through the window, the smell of its burning flesh making Rex gag. The darklings' mindless peons were sacrificing themselves to deplete the room's defenses. Rex smiled grimly; it would take more than slithers to get through that pile of space-age metal and tridecalogisms.

Noises came from inside the house now, the beating of frantic wings filling the hallway outside. The thirteen knives began to glow.

A black snake head squeezed under the door, then another—crawling slithers testing them. The first few burned up in the clutter of silverware and fallen nails, but more came. Melissa stomped on their writhing forms, the anklets around her boots glowing blue, then white. Rex wielded Arachnophobia, crushing slithers with the hammer until his arm ached.

After long minutes the slither attacks subsided. The fluttering of wings died away, the metal scattered around the room, losing its wild glow.

Rex sank to the floor, wiping sweat from his eyes. His lungs were full of the reek of burned slither flesh, his muscles completely exhausted.

"They're giving up?" he croaked.

Melissa stood unmoving, eyes shut.

Then Rex heard it. Something coming up the stairs.

He couldn't imagine the half-human thing moving through the house, so it was probably a normal darkling, a brash young one to invade this modern place. Melissa didn't say what she tasted, just stared at the door with blank-faced fatigue. The stairs creaked under its weight, and the thirteen knives began to glow again.

Terror threatened to paralyze him, but then Rex's mind went back to what she'd said: *Tomorrow we'll touch again.* His head swam at the thought. Finally there was some promise of something more between him and Melissa. They were not going to die tonight.

He pulled the hubcap from the duffel bag.

"Come and get it," he said softly.

The knives shivered in the wood, lances of tremulous blue fire jumping between them. The scratching sound of claws traveled slowly down the door, and Rex could hear the harsh panting of a big cat. It had taken a hunting shape.

A carving knife began to wobble, almost slipping from the door, but Rex thrust it back into the wood. Brief contact with the glowing metal scalded his palm.

He brought the hubcap to his lips.

"Categorically Unjustifiable Appropriation."

The metal ignited, coursing with blue fire along its rim, the tiny pictures seeming to dance. The hubcap vibrated in his hand, giving off a buzzing heat that crawled up his arm and into his shoulder. Rex smiled grimly. He had seen what Dess's really good work could do. So had the darklings.

The panting outside stopped for a moment, a catch in the creature's breath.

A chuckle escaped Melissa's lips. "Scaredy-cat."

A roar answered from outside, a huge howl of pain and anger that made the whole room shudder. But Rex knew from the defeated sound that the darkling had sensed the pulsing weapon in his hand and had decided not to throw away its cold, lingering life.

The stairs creaked again as the darkling descended, the knives fading to a dull, spent gray, and the dread that had hung over the room slowly diminished.

Before the hour ended, Rex took one last look through one of the rips in the clawed and battered pegboard. He saw the halfling leave, making its ungainly way from the balcony of the master bedroom to the roof, then taking to its overburdened wings.

"Ready to run?" Melissa said.

"What?" he asked.

"They're all leaving. The entourage too." Melissa smiled. "We'll have a couple of minutes, but I don't think our motionless friends are going to like what we did to their house."

He looked around the room. "Could be you're right."

"Damn kids with their senseless vandalism," she said.

Rex sighed, thinking of the broken window downstairs. "They might have an alarm system, come to think of it."

Melissa pulled Magnificently Instantaneous Gratification from the door.

"It won't work any—" he started, but her expression silenced him.

"I also use it for the regular kind of protection, Rex. In case anyone tries to touch me."

"Oh." He looked at his watch. Two minutes.

They ran down the stairs. At the front door Melissa gathered herself for one last mindcast, then nodded. "All clear."

They reached the old Ford as the blue hour ended. Rex had never been so glad to see blackness sweeping across the sky. At the moment normal time reached them, carried on a cold Oklahoma wind, a high-pitched ringing filled the night.

"Damn," he said. "They did have an alarm."

Melissa jumped in and started the car, and they pulled away with a screech. Rex stayed quiet as she drove, letting her mindcast for police. A few minutes later she pulled over and turned off the Ford's headlights, huddling down out of sight.

Rex also slunk down in his seat, catching a glimpse of two private security cars as they zoomed past.

Melissa took his hand, her wool glove warm against his skin. "Get some poison, Rex."

"Do what?"

"Something that kills fast. Like one of those snakes that stops your heart in twenty seconds."

Had what she'd seen tonight finally pushed Melissa over the edge? "Melissa, you can't—"

"Not for me, moron." She shook her head. "You know the midnighter inside that monster?"

"Yeah?"

"She's still alive in there, somewhere. I could feel her. They keep her mind alive so they can use the human part of her to think in signs and

110

symbols. But she knows what's happened to her."

Rex put his face in his hands. After a few moments he said, "But how would we get the poison to her?"

"Not for her. *You.*" Melissa turned on the headlights, stared out the front windshield. "She's sick, probably dying, and soon they'll decide they need another one and come looking for you."

He blinked, shook his head. "What . . . ?"

"*Think,* Rex. They can already fly, they can already mindcast, and they hate math." Melissa pulled onto the road. "She's a seer."

9

MONDAY BLUES

"Have you heard the excellent rumors?"

Jessica sighed. "Only the one that I crashed and burned on my physics test this morning. Of course, that's more in the fact than the rumor category."

Constanza Grayfoot frowned and pressed closer to Jessica's locker, letting a pack of freshmen past. "Oh, Jess, that's too bad. Maybe your mom will finally let you bail on some of those advanced classes."

Jessica lifted the weighty tome that was her trig textbook. "Fat chance."

"Weren't you studying with you-know-who?"

"Yeah, I was. Except we kept . . . getting distracted."

112

A radiant smile lit Constanza's face. "Jess, you wicked girl! That kind of distraction doesn't sound too bad."

Jessica returned the smile, but the expression felt shaky. If the interruptions had been what Constanza was thinking, it might have been worth failing a physics test. But spending all last midnight looking for frozen stalkers around her house hadn't left any time for the good kind of distractions or much studying. Rex and Melissa hadn't even bothered to show up and help. Maybe Melissa figured a threat from a mere human being wasn't worth her time.

"Well," Constanza continued, "perhaps this morning's rumors will distract you from your physics tragedy. So it turns out that someone's mother works for the sheriff's department. She's like a forensic expert, or a police psychic, or something like that. Anyway, there was some kind of demonic vandalism last night out in Las Colonias."

Jessica shoved her trig book into her backpack, wondering what else she should bring to study period. "Demonic what?"

"Vandalism," Constanza repeated, then added in a whisper, "but with weirdo rituals. What happened was, this family's all asleep, and suddenly their burglar alarm goes off—right at the stroke of midnight."

Jessica's hand froze, the zipper on her backpack halfway closed. "Midnight?"

"Yeah. Someone broke into their house—while they were *sleeping*—and did all this psycho stuff without waking them up."

Jessica took a slow, even breath. "And this was last night?"

"Yes, last night," Constanza insisted. "Pay attention, Jess. I'm getting to the spooky part. So when the burglar alarm goes off, the family wakes up and looks around, but the burglars, or demon worshipers, or whatever are already gone. It's like they just disappeared."

Jessica nodded slowly, getting the head-rush feeling she always did when midnight intruded on the daylight world. Constanza was the only real non-midnighter friend she had here in Bixby. Hearing her talk about events that could only have happened in the secret hour made Jessica dizzy.

"So what kind of stuff did they do?" she said.

Constanza looped her arm through Jessica's and pulled her toward the library. "The weird thing is they didn't steal anything. Just trashed the house and left all these psycho symbols. Like for one thing, there was this door with twelve knives stuck into it. And *blood* on one of them."

"Twelve? Not thirteen?"

Constanza blinked. "Well, that's what everyone's saying. Why?"

"Just . . . you know." Jessica shrugged, trying to sound nonchalant. "Thirteen sounds much more demonic than twelve."

"Uh, I guess." Constanza giggled. "Maybe they were demon worshipers who couldn't count."

"I hope not," Jessica said softly to herself. It seemed pretty obvious where Melissa and Rex had been last night. The scary thing was, she hadn't seen them at school all morning.

In the library Constanza's table was already in full swing. Details of the previous night's demonic vandalism were being traded and analyzed—silverware, pots, and pans arranged mysteriously in a computer room; spots of blood found on the carpet and on one of the knives; an upstairs window smashed from the outside or, alternatively, the front door broken down. But there was one thing everyone agreed on: there had been exactly twelve knives in the door.

As Jessica listened to the gossip, she glanced at Dess seated in her usual spot in the corner. Jessica wondered if she knew what had really happened last night.

"Just the thought that they were sleeping while it was all happening," Jen kept saying. "How creepy is that?"

"Maybe they were drugged," Liz said.

"Maybe they did it themselves!" Maria suggested.

"What? The family?" Constanza looked dubious. "In Las Colonias? Those are some *very* nice houses out there. I think my cousin owns one. Not really a demon-worshiping neighborhood."

Maria shrugged. "Sure, but it doesn't make any sense if someone else did it. How could you do all that stuff in total silence?"

A voice carried from the librarian's desk. "Speaking of total silence—don't you girls have *any* studying to do?"

"Yes, Ms. Thomas," Constanza answered, then rolled her eyes and whispered, "Speaking of demons."

Jessica looked over at Dess. She was probably listening, her expression unreadable behind sunglasses. Come to think of it, Jessica had no idea what Dess had been up to all weekend. Did she even know about the stalker situation?

"Actually, I better get to work. Trig is my next big midterm."

Constanza nodded slowly and glanced over at the corner. Jessica smiled faintly. Constanza had begun to notice how much time Jessica spent with Dess and the others, lunches as well as study periods, and was probably wondering what the appeal was. Except for Jonathan, the other midnighters were into the wearing-all-black thing, and their sensitive midnight eyes forced them to wear sunglasses whenever they could. They weren't really the kind of people Jessica had hung around with back in Chicago.

She wished she could get to know Constanza better, but between being grounded and surviving the secret hour, Jessica hadn't spent nearly as much time as she wanted with her. Like with Jonathan, midnight seemed to keep anything *normal* from happening.

"Dess isn't really that bad," Jessica said quietly,

and immediately hated herself for putting it like that.

Constanza giggled. "Well, Jess, at least with her there's not much chance of getting distracted."

"You look like you're in a good mood."

Dess removed her sunglasses, revealing a serene expression instead of her usual Monday glower. "Had a really good weekend. Playing with a new toy, which is top secret, by the way—can't tell you anything about it. And this morning is proving . . . interesting."

Jessica looked back at Constanza's table and lowered her voice. "You heard about the thing last night?"

Dess snorted. "Sure, but that's nothing. Happens a lot in Bixby—rumors about kids doing random stuff, mostly based on the last bunch of rumors."

"I wouldn't be so sure. What about the knives?"

"*Twelve* of them? Obviously a misprint. Anyway, who could it have been? I was busy. And Las Colonias is way out near the badlands. Weren't Rex and Melissa in town, helping you guys look for your stalker?"

Jessica wrinkled her nose. "So you know about him?"

"Rex called me yesterday. Warned me to be on the lookout." She shrugged. "Kind of weird, I guess."

"Yeah." Jessica leaned forward. "But here's what's weirder: Rex and Melissa didn't show last night. And I haven't seen them today either."

"They didn't? But Rex said . . ." Dess went silent, a faraway look in her eye that Jessica knew from doing trig homework together. It was Dess's look of figuring all the angles.

"Well," Dess said finally, "that means one of two things. Most likely, some moron along the rumor chain didn't get the number right because most people don't ever get the numbers right. So Rex and Melissa got into a rumble last night, got cornered, stuck thirteen knives in a door, and slept late this morning."

Jessica swallowed. "What's the other possibility?"

"They got into a rumble last night, stuck thirteen knives in a door, and one fell out."

"Fell out? What do you mean?"

"Well, that would mean"—Dess chewed her lip—"that they won't be coming to school today."

When the noon bell rang, Dess and Jessica headed for the cafeteria, making record time. Jonathan was waiting for them at Rex's usual table. Alone.

"Martinez?" Dess said, obviously surprised to see him there. Jonathan hardly ever ate with the other midnighters. He must have heard the rumors too.

"Hi, Dess," Jonathan said through a mouthful of peanut butter sandwich on banana bread. He pulled out a chair for Jessica but didn't say hi, just smiled tiredly and kept on eating. His concern for Rex and Melissa evidently hadn't affected his acrobat's appetite.

Jonathan's voice was still scratchy from walking home two nights before. Jessica had begun to realize that he never wore a coat, no matter how cold it got. He didn't like anything (or anyone) that restricted his movement.

"You guys heard?" he said between bites.

"Yeah." Dess's eyes swept the cafeteria, which was beginning to fill with jostling bodies and the

120

smells of cafeteria food. "And they definitely aren't here." She sighed, looking at the two of them. "Okay, I guess *I* have to go make the phone call. Got any change?"

Jessica fished in her pocket and found a single coin, the quarter she'd flipped two nights before. She'd been carrying it around, hoping its luck would change. So far, it had brought only trouble.

Dess swept it from her hand and stomped off, not bothering to say thanks.

Jessica watched the angry sway of her long black dress until it was swallowed by the crowd. "What's she so grumpy about?"

Jonathan shrugged, as if it were obvious. "Me and you. Rex and Melissa. And then there's Dess." He bit into an apple.

"Yeah, I guess." Jessica couldn't disagree, although at the moment she was wondering whether Jonathan and she were worth being jealous over. She'd bombed her physics test, a stalker was trailing her, and Rex and Melissa were missing amid rumors of midnight blood and destruction. Yet Jonathan was sitting there, eating like a demon and, as always in normal time, not touching her.

In the secret hour it was always automatic—

fingers brushing, the light pressure of shoulder against shoulder, or arms intertwined. But in daylight Jonathan didn't seem to see the point of physical contact. As if he didn't realize there was more to life than flying.

Still, Jessica told herself, it wasn't like she couldn't hold *his* hand, right now. Just reach over and take it. How lame was this? Waiting for him to do everything and hating him for not reading her mind?

Of course, if she did reach out and he pulled away, no matter how slightly, it would really, really suck.

She sighed, feeling selfish to be worrying about this with Rex and Melissa missing. Something awful had happened last night, and not too far from the badlands. She couldn't get the image out of her head of twelve bloody knives stuck into a door. According to the rumors, no bodies had been found, but did darklings leave bodies behind when they . . . did whatever they did?

"So, you still think you blew it?"

"What? Oh." Jessica groaned, remembering now what the demonic rumors had allowed her to forget. "Physics. I *know* I blew it. I drew a total blank on the formulas part. And the laws part. On the physics part, basically."

Jonathan was still smiling; he was breezing through the class, as confident with the laws of motion as Dess was with numbers.

"Still, you must have gotten the extra credit."

"No. Didn't get that far."

Jonathan laughed. "About what happens when you flip a coin? Give three reasons why it never stops, even right at the top?"

Jessica just looked at him and sighed.

"No answer at Melissa's. And Rex's dad picked up. Couldn't get anything out of him; Rex must have doubled his meds." Dess didn't sit down, just folded her arms and stared down at them. "Waste of a good quarter."

"What's the deal with Rex's dad, anyway?" Jessica said. "It's so sad, the way he is."

Jonathan cleared his throat.

"Him, sad?" Dess snorted. "It was sadder before the accident."

"What do you mean?"

An unpleasant look crossed Dess's face. "Well, all of it happened before I met Rex, but I know he wasn't the world's greatest dad."

"Oh. *Still.*" Jessica remembered the drool on the old man's chin, the lost expression in his eyes.

Dess shook her head. "No, really. Save your pity. Ask Rex about the spiders under the house sometime." She turned to Jonathan. "You got your father's car today?"

"Yeah."

"Anything important happening this afternoon?"

Jonathan paused for a moment, then shook his head.

"Let's go, then."

Jonathan sighed, shoved his remaining sandwich into his lunch bag, and pushed his chair back.

"What? Now?" Jessica asked, wrenching her mind away from thoughts of Rex's dad. "But there's no way we'll get back before fifth period."

"Deeply tragic," Dess said. "But if you don't want to come, give Mr. Sanchez my heartfelt apologies. His little eyes get so sad when I skip trig."

Jonathan rested his hand on Jessica's shoulder, finally touching her. "You don't want to come?"

"Um . . ." She did, but Jessica couldn't ignore

124

the trickle of fear in her stomach. Trumping the image of bloodstained knives was a vision of her parents' faces, grim and in a grounding mood. "I *can't*."

"It's okay, Jess. We'll let you know." He squeezed her shoulder softly. "See you tonight."

They turned and walked away, leaving her alone.

10

12:14 P.M.

DESSOMETRICS

Dess stole glances at her new toy as they drove. The shifting numbers soothed her nerves, reminding her that every problem had a solution, every missing person a location, and every spot on earth a set of delicious coordinates.

Her mind was still buzzing from the weekend. Whatever the others had managed to get mixed up in, Dess had enjoyed herself. She'd spent all Sunday biking around town, watching Geostationary effortlessly reeling off coordinates, turning Bixby into *numbers*. What could be better?

She'd lived here all her life, but for the first time, Dess felt that she really *knew* the town, could see its patterns, could map its streets and

126

buildings in her mind. The world she'd grown up in was finally inventoried and enumerated; Dess had done the math at last.

Meanwhile the rest of them had spent the weekend being stalked, trying to stalk the stalkers, and getting themselves cornered by darklings. That was what always seemed to happen when she let them out of her sight.

"What's that thing?" Jonathan said, glancing down at the GPS receiver in her hands.

She jerked it out of his sight. "Nothing."

He just chuckled, biting into his third sandwich. "Okay."

They turned onto Rex's street, which ran almost due east, and Dess snuck a peek at the north-south numbers stabilizing, the east-west value dropping slowly. After this visit she'd have exact coordinates for both her own house and Rex's. Maybe there was some pattern in the location of midnighters' homes.

The car halted, and Dess forced herself to shove the receiver into her coat pocket. She would let Rex in on her discoveries soon enough, but she wanted the math firmly in her head before he cluttered it with his messy lore. Math was pure, but history was always full of weird little gaps and contradictions.

The sagging porch was empty, the creepy old dad nowhere in sight. Maybe Rex was keeping him inside these days.

Halfway across the threadbare lawn, a croaking voice erupted from the house. "Don't you damn kids know it's a school day?"

She flinched, then spotted Rex's face through the front screen door. Not a bad imitation of his father, she had to admit. It was good enough to have sent chills down her spine.

He came through the door, laughing at the scare he'd given them. Melissa followed, and Dess peeled her hand off the GPS receiver in her pocket, resolving not to think about it. Amid the clamor of Bixby High, Melissa's mind reading was almost as useless as a cell phone at the bottom of the Grand Canyon. But here in thinly populated suburbia, Dess would have to watch her thoughts.

"So what brings you two to my humble abode?"

Dess frowned. Rex seemed weirdly upbeat, especially if they'd had a messy rumble last night. And Melissa's hair was wet, as if she'd just showered. She wasn't in headphones and was even managing to smile behind her sunglasses. If it were any other two people . . . Dess shivered and reminded herself that Melissa might be listening. Plus there was no way—as in literally No Possible Way anything like *that* had happened.

Jonathan wasn't saying much, of course, so she answered, "We heard you had some trouble last night."

Rex chuckled and nodded. "It's already in the rumor mill? Man, I love this town."

Dess allowed herself to smile back at him. They really were okay. The worry she'd been fighting not to feel, that two of her friends might at last have run out of luck in the secret hour, finally evaporated into relief.

"What the hell were you doing out there, anyway? Dumbasses. Weren't you supposed to be in town?"

"Yeah," Jonathan added bravely. "We looked for you all hour."

Rex smiled and waved them over to a quartet of rusting lawn chairs. They sat there together, like a bunch of old farts on a porch.

"I tasted something on the way," Melissa said, "and we wound up chasing it."

"Sounds like it wound up chasing you," Dess observed.

Melissa nodded, drawing her jacket around her, though it wasn't that cold out here in the sun. "Yeah, I guess it did."

"I hope you had some decent metal with you," Dess said.

Rex shrugged. "Well, they kind of caught us by surprise. But we improvised. And Categorically Unjustifiable Appropriation scared off the last of the bad guys."

Dess smiled, delighted to hear it. She'd always thought the old hubcap was one of her best. It had fallen off a 1989 (which was 153 x 13) Mercedes-Benz (which was a tridecalogism, if you counted the hyphen) on 1264 Farm Road (1 + 2 + 6 + 4 = duh, 13). Obviously destined to kick ass.

"Hang on, Las Colonias aren't on the way to Jessica's," Jonathan said, like he'd *just* realized that Rex and Melissa weren't telling them everything. Dess could see that much from their faces. The two were grinning like shoplifters who'd made it out the door and around the corner, pockets bulging.

"No. But I smelled this guy from miles away," Melissa said. "Turned out to be your stalker, Jonathan."

"Not only that," Rex added, "but he apparently works for the darklings."

Dess's relief beginning to unravel. "He works for *them*? How?"

Rex took a deep breath, then launched into the whole story—the thoughts about Jessica that Melissa had overheard, Darkling Manor and the dominoes, the stalker and his girlfriend, the retreat across the street (Rex showing off the dinky cut that had produced the famous blood), then the appearance of the gruesome half-thing, and finally the rumble. Melissa added her own commentary and contradictions for the first half, then mostly just sat and shivered, eyeballs twitching beneath closed lids.

As Dess listened, fascinated and faintly sickened, she began to realize why the two of them seemed so giggly today. They were actually still scared, piss-in-your-pants scared, right down to their bones. What they'd seen out in Las Colonias must have kept them up all night—basically too terrified to go to sleep—and finally, after a few fitful hours of unconsciousness, they were as she saw them now: dog tired and still pretty much hysterical.

No wonder they hadn't showed up at school. Rex was in no shape for the real world, and *Melissa* . . . At Bixby High her brain would have melted like the wicked witch in a car wash.

When the story was over, Dess sat back and let her mind wander, stroking Geostationary. Horrifying as it all was, this little tale promised new data for her coordinates project. Maybe these darkling groupies, whoever they were, already knew the shape of the secret hour. They'd been hiding themselves *somewhere* for the last fifty years. . . .

"We've got to tell Jessica," Jonathan said, car keys already in his hand. "Those two could have orders to go after her *today*."

"Relax. It's not very likely." Rex had his smug smile on. After a dramatic pause he reached into his pocket, pulled out something, and opened his hand. Resting on his palm was a small rectangle of yellow ivory—it looked like an old domino, just as he'd said, except instead of the dots . . .

"Huh," said Dess. It was Jessica's tag, the lore symbol for flame-bringer.

"I took the liberty of stealing this and a few others. Like a set of dominoes for spelling out human names, which must have been used to tell the groupies who Jessica was." Rex's smile got even smugger. "There are hundreds of symbols. It should take the groupies a while to notice that a few are missing. In the meantime the darklings are going to be mighty frustrated if they try to communicate anything about Jessica."

Melissa rubbed one finger across the domino (perilously close to touching Rex's bare skin, Dess noticed). "Tastes like darklings and feels old. Maybe fifty years. There's probably only one set of these, passed down through the generations."

"Wait a second. If the halfling's a human, like you said, why doesn't she just write down what the darklings want to say?" Dess said, the image of the creature that passed through her mind giving her a shudder.

Rex shook his head. "Even through her, the darklings couldn't think in anything as new as English. The lore symbols are ten thousand years old, older than any language spoken today." His voice grew soft. "That's why they had to use a seer."

Jonathan spoke up, still clutching the rusty arms of his chair. "But who *are* these guys? Where did they come from?"

Rex shrugged. "That's what we have to find out. But I think we can assume they're the same people who did away with our predecessors. I didn't find any of our symbols besides Jessica's, so the rest of us should be careful too."

"But where have they been hiding?" Dess asked. She turned to Melissa. "Why haven't you tasted this half-thingie before?"

Melissa answered slowly. "There's something weird about that house. I can't mindcast in there for crap. The only times I could hear the guy were after he'd left and just before he got back. It's some kind of psychic dead zone. It's like the walls eat thought."

"Location, location, location," Rex murmured.

At those magic words another shudder passed through Dess, one of excitement. "Take me there."

Together all three of them said, *"What?"*

"Take me there, right now." She pulled the

134

GPS receiver from her pocket, waved it in front of them. "I *knew* there had to be places like that in Bixby—hiding places. I've been having these dreams. . . ."

She came to a halt. They were all staring at her as if her mouth had started to foam.

Dess groaned. "Listen, this little gadget turns places into numbers, coordinates. I've been trying to crack the patterns—the way the secret hour is shaped. It's like topology. . . ." Okay, blank faces on that one. "But *better*. Oh, screw it. Just take me there and I can figure out how it all works." She hissed through her teeth at their empty expressions. "I just need a paradigm!"

Rex was the first to utter a sound, a low, soft sigh. "Well, you've been busy."

She rolled her eyes. Time for a seer-knows-best lecture.

"But you may not have to go there, Dess."

"I managed to cast around a little bit in the woman's mind before the"—Melissa's lower lip trembled—"thing got too close."

"She's shared some of what she saw with me," Rex said. "We may have the numbers you need."

135

"Eh?" Dess felt her throat constrict at the expressions on Rex and Melissa's faces. *Shared?* Something was weirder about the two than just a little postrumble hysteria.

No possible way, Dess reminded herself.

"We'll try to write some of it down for you." Rex shrugged. "It looks like plans for something being built, something that has to do with the halfling. But it's mostly a bunch of numbers, so it's all Greek to me."

"Arabic," Dess said absently. Melissa was giving her this *look*.

"What?" Rex asked.

"Numbers are Arabic, moron." She tore her gaze away from Melissa. "All the old math is. Al Gebra—as in algebra—was this Arab guy a thousand years ago." Trying not to think any more about what had passed between the two of them, Dess imagined having a whole branch of mathematics named after her. Dessology? Desstochastics?

"Dessometrics?" Melissa said aloud, a smile playing on her lips.

Dess shivered. *Busted.*

She waved Geostationary. "I don't care what

you got from her." *Or how you* shared *it.* "This will give me everything I need. Just take me there."

Rex and Melissa looked at each other, and Dess allowed herself to feel a little burst of triumph as their expressions revealed absolute horror. They really were still terrified, all the way down to the marrow.

Rex shook his head. "Someone might have noticed the Ford. It kind of sticks out in that neighborhood. And we might have left finger-prints. . . ."

Dess snickered at the feeble excuses and gave Jonathan's thigh a slap. "Come on, Flyboy. We're going to Darkling Manor."

He stood, ready to leave, and gave her and Melissa a clueless look. "What's Dessometrics?"

She smiled. "I'll tell you on the way."

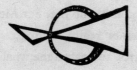

11 | 1:45 P.M.

MORE FLATLAND

"The art of reading Melissa's mind," Dess said out of the blue.

"Huh?" Jonathan was passing an eighteen-wheeler, trying to coax his father's car into doing more than sixty-five on level ground. He was also watching for the turnoff, fairly certain that the directions suffered from mindcaster vagueness. Not that he could blame her, but Melissa had a pretty thin grasp on reality at times.

"Dessometrics. You asked me what it was."

Jonathan looked at her biting her thumbnail as she stared out the front windshield. She and Melissa had gotten into *something* back there—a staring contest, it had looked like. "Yeah, right.

And you can do that? Read her mind?"

"Well, it helps if Rex is around. He's the one who gave it away."

The semi finally gave up drag racing him and slipped behind with an amicable wave from the driver. Jonathan relaxed. "Gave what away?"

Dess squirmed in the seat next to him. "You didn't notice a certain . . . *smarminess* between those two?"

"Hmm." He decided against passing the next truck up ahead. At this hour the north-south interstate was crowded with Mexican goods coming up through Texas. Even the smallest eighteen-wheeler could crush his father's car like a cockroach.

Despite how automobile ads tried to make it look, Jonathan had learned this year that driving was not like flying. In fact, driving pretty much sucked compared to flying. Flatland at sixty miles an hour was still Flatland.

And his sore throat from the other night hadn't gone away entirely. He swallowed gingerly before he spoke. "Actually, those two pretty much set off my smarmy meter twenty-four, seven. I tend not to notice the minor fluctuations."

Dess chuckled beside him, the low rumble of it bringing a smile to his face. Jonathan hadn't hung out much with Dess lately, he realized. At least not since Jessica had arrived in town.

"Weren't they kind of . . . chummy?" she continued. "And *chipper.*"

He glanced at Dess. Her expectant expression annoyed him. Who was supposed to be the mind reader here? He shrugged. "I think they were just freaked out by what they saw last night. Hell, I'd be."

The thought that he was driving straight back to where it had all happened wasn't thrilling Jonathan either. He wondered why he was here instead of getting back to school to tell Jessica what had happened and make sure she was okay.

Maybe because of all of them, he most trusted Dess to help Jessica when she really needed it. Ten days ago he'd seen who had led the other two across darkling-infested desert when he and Jessica had been trapped in the snake pit.

"Sure. The trauma thing was part of it." Dess was nodding to herself. "But there was more."

"Like what? What more *could* there be?"

"So you know what I mean."

140

A trucker blasted his horn just behind them, looking to keep up the speed his rig had gathered down the slope of an overpass. Jonathan wrenched the car out of his way, earning a respectful middle finger as the truck roared by. This conversation had become dangerously distracting.

"You're nuts," Jonathan said. "No way."

"True. No possible way. It's more complicated than that."

He snorted. "I can't imagine anything more complicated than *that.*"

She snickered, then said, "You know they did . . . once."

Jonathan looked at her with alarm. "Did what?"

"Not *that.*" She laughed. "But back when they were kids, Rex touched Melissa by accident."

"Oh." Jonathan's left hand trembled for a moment, a sense memory moving through his body in a wave of dizziness. He gripped the wheel hard, concentrating on the dotted white lines pulsing in front of the car, and managed to keep the vehicle in a straight line until the spell passed.

"Rex told me all about it," Dess was saying. "Said it was a total head bang, like she was crowding into his mind and he was getting into hers."

Jonathan nodded. "Yeah. That's what it's like."

"What? How would you know?"

He paused. He wondered why he'd never told anyone about this, not even Jessica. (*Especially* not Jessica, come to think of it.) Rex must have realized what was going on as it happened, but neither he nor Jonathan had ever brought it up. And of course, Melissa hadn't said a thing after that one *thank-you* in the desert.

"Well, it was the weekend before last, when we found out Jessica was the flame-bringer. When you guys were trying to get to the snake pit and you did your amazon thing."

"That was so cool. Resplendently Scintillating Illustrations kicked that darkling's ass."

"Yeah, well. But you may recall that you left Rex and Melissa surrounded by a zillion spiders. And *I* had to fly back out and save them."

Dess was silent for a moment, then she let out a long breath. "That's right! You *flew* Melissa back to the snake pit. So you must have . . ."

"Touched her." Jonathan felt a faint shadow of the dizziness come over him again—the nauseating rush of thoughts and emotions, the despair that permeated Melissa, her revulsion at those few seconds of human contact. Since that night he hadn't seen her the same way. He could detect something behind her scowl other than her hatred for humanity—something fragile.

Jonathan shuddered. Silent treatment or not, he somehow felt closer to her now. It had been much easier when she'd just been a royal bitch.

"Damn," Dess said softly. "Rex must *hate* you for that."

"What? For saving both their lives?" He shook his head, suddenly hoping Dess wouldn't answer. He wished this whole conversation hadn't started. Fortunately the turnoff was just ahead. "Forget I mentioned it."

But Dess didn't shut up. "Rex says in the old days, mindcasters could control their ability. They could tolerate crowds, even transmit information through a handshake. They were the ones who passed on the news, who bound everyone together."

"Really?" Jonathan knew there'd been mindcasters back in Bixby's history, but he'd never imagined *sane* ones. "So why's Melissa such a basket case?"

"Rex doesn't know. Maybe she's just a freak.

But he's always wanted to find out if she can learn to tolerate it. Maybe last night was some kind of bonding experience or something. And now they're trying to hook up."

Jonathan looked at his left hand; it had always seemed as if Melissa's searing touch should have left a mark. But his palm bore nothing but a thin layer of sweat.

He swallowed again, his throat still sore.

They exited the main highway, heading toward Las Colonias. Melissa's directions had turned out to make sense after all. The badlands were ahead of them now, a single tear of sun-leeched white across the horizon.

Jonathan remembered the two of them on the porch, Rex all smiley, Melissa as relaxed as he'd ever seen her in normal time. But then he felt another touching-Melissa flashback trembling at the edge of his mind and shook his head.

"I just hope they know what they're doing."

Dess laughed. "Haven't you figured it out, Flyboy? None of us knows what we're doing."

The arched entrance to Las Colonias was guarded by a private security car. Two rent-a-cops slouched against its hood, drinking coffee and turning redder in the sun. One held up his hand, his eyes sweeping across the old car with obvious contempt. Jonathan rolled down his window, the presence of an authority figure bleeding into his stomach like a drink of acid.

"What's your business here?"

"Just taking a drive, Officer." Rent-a-cops loved it when you called them *Officer*.

"Here to see the demon house, huh? Well, I'm afraid it's residents only today. So why don't you just turn your vehicle around and head back where you come from."

Jonathan thought of a few things to say but realized that if he mouthed off, one of the two might figure out it was a school day. So he tipped an imaginary cowboy hat and started to turn the car around.

"Smooth, Jonathan," Dess started in. "'Just taking a drive, *Officer*.'"

"What would you have said? 'Just here to investigate the paranormal'?"

Dess snickered and put on her good-old-boy drawl. "How about, 'Just taking my new girlfriend to meet my daddy? We're fixin' to get us married.'"

He laughed. "Next time you do the talking."

"So now what?"

"Now we look for the back door." Jonathan turned down the dusty service road that skirted the community, his eyes following the ten-foot-high metal fence surrounding it. Even in normal time his acrobat's brain still worked. He could see the angles—where a foot would go to get a boost up, then a handhold, another within reach of that one. . . .

Finally he spotted a place. A termite mound rose up close to the fence, cutting a couple of feet from its height. Jonathan slowed the car.

"We can't climb that," Dess said.

"I can. Just show me how that thing works."

Dess's eyes widened, and she pulled away.

He sighed. "Do you want your numbers or not?"

Her face twitched for a moment, but finally she scowled and said, "Okay. But if you lose it, break it, or get arrested and they take it, you're dead."

Jonathan just rolled his eyes and listened as she explained how to capture coordinates. As he walked away from the car, he whispered to himself, "You're welcome."

★ ★ ★

On the other side Jonathan dropped to the ground at the edge of an unfinished lot, then paused to shake the termites from his sneakers and the pain from his still-sprained ankle. Construction materials were strewn across the dry, bare soil. There was no frame yet, just a wide driveway leading to a gaping foundation. He moved quickly through the site, figuring he'd be less conspicuous walking down the street than creeping through an empty lot.

At this time on a weekday few cars passed him, and no one seemed to pay him any mind. Half the houses looked unoccupied. He could smell the fresh paint jobs and see the seams in the newly rolled-down lawns.

Spotting Darkling Manor was easy. It was across the street from the demon house, which had a broken window up on the second floor. The front door was sealed with yellow police tape. Jonathan wondered what the family was doing today. Sitting around watching TV and trying not to wonder what had happened last night? Or had they gone to a motel for a while?

Of course, the truly haunted house was on the other side of the street. Darkling Manor looked like every other home in the development.

Everything about it—the garage, windows, lawn—was unnecessarily huge. The driveway was empty, and Rex and Melissa said they hadn't seen a stick of furniture, so it seemed unlikely anyone was home. He walked around it, trying to look interested rather than criminal.

In the back he found the balcony with the sliding glass doors that Rex had described. Standing beneath it, as close as he could get to the house, Jonathan held up the GPS receiver and pressed capture. The shifting numbers froze.

According to Dess, that was it.

Jonathan paused. In daylight the house didn't give him the chills he'd expected. It was so new, unlike any other darkling place he'd ever seen. He wondered if there were some clue inside, something that would tell him who owned it and who was behind the new threat to Jessica.

Around front again, he spotted the mailbox. Its little red flag was standing up. He crossed the lawn, glancing up and down the still-empty street.

His gait slowed when he saw her. Peering at him out of the window of the demon house was a woman. She looked like someone who'd had a sleepless night, her face dark with suspicion.

Jonathan smiled and waved. She didn't wave back. He opened the mailbox and reached in to find a single letter. Pulling it out, he waved again and turned back toward the house.

"Crap," he whispered. The front door was probably locked, and the hairs on the back of Jonathan's neck told him that he was still being watched. He headed around the back of the house the way he'd come, taking one last glance over his shoulder.

The woman's face was still in the window, but she wasn't looking at him anymore. She was watching the private security car that was coming up the winding street.

Jonathan crammed the envelope into his pocket and ran, dashing across the backyard, rolling across a low fence and stumbling into another backyard. He passed yet another giant, empty house and crossed the next street over.

He kept going until he was breathless, moving across the streets instead of down them. The overweight rent-a-cops would never catch him on foot, even with his ankle screaming with every step. The screech of tires came from his right as they tried to parallel him in their car.

At the edge of the development, where Jonathan had come in, the houses were still under construction and the ground grew rough. A few workers silently watched him pass, not taking much interest. He dodged piles of dirt and broken bricks, wishing for a ten-second burst of midnight gravity to get him out of here. One hard jump in *that* direction would carry him all the way back to Dess.

Finally he reached the fence. He could see his father's car through the bars. But there wasn't any termite mound on this side, no footholds, no way to climb it.

He spun around. The security car crawled into sight a hundred yards away, leaving the road and growling onto the dirt strip of unsodded backyards, its tires spitting gravel and spinning up a cloud of dust.

Jonathan looked around frantically for something to get a boost from—a pile of bricks, a tree stump, *anything*. But the fence stretched along flat red soil as far as he could see.

Then his eyes fell on an old tire lying in the sun, its treads choked with dirt, its rubber cracked. He ran to it, lifted it upright, and sent it rolling ahead of him with a solid kick. Mosquito-breeding water sloshed from its innards as it wobbled along. Bracing it sideways against the fence, Jonathan planted a foot on it and pushed himself up.

The tire sagged as he jumped, but his hands managed to grasp the top spikes of the fence. The spitting tires of the car sounded as if they were right under him. Jonathan pulled himself up and over and dropped to the other side, every ounce of his normal-gravity weight landing on his bad ankle.

"Finally," Dess said as he limped up. "I was getting bored."

Jonathan started the car, looking back at the security guards. They slewed to a halt on the other side of the fence, their car immediately swallowed by its own dust cloud. The two rent-a-cops emerged, coughing in the dirt storm, and looked at him forlornly through the fence. One tested the tire with his foot, but it sagged almost flat under his weight.

Jonathan took a deep breath. *No reason to rush.*

"Hey, it's those buttheads again," Dess said. "Were they chasing you?"

"Yeah."

"Cool. You're not really a total loser in normal time, you know."

"Right." His heart was pounding, his throat was scraped raw from inhaling dust, and his ankle was throbbing. He never felt this way at midnight, half dead from running a paltry mile. He pulled the GPS receiver from his belt. "Hope this thing still works."

"It better," she said, flicking it on. She stared at the numbers recorded on the little readout. A moment later a grin of satisfaction spread across her face. "Oh, this is so good!"

Jonathan felt himself smiling too. Maybe it wasn't so bad, getting his heart beating. Not as good as flying, of course. "That's from right under the balcony, just like you said."

"I can see it. . . ." Her eyes were open wide like those of a four-year-old girl entranced by her first butterfly. "I've got the pattern now. This is *so* freaky."

She turned and leapt across the front seat, kissing him on the right cheek, hard and wet.

Jonathan laughed, then glanced at the cops again. They were getting slowly back into their car. It was miles back to the gate and then back here. He was enjoying just sitting here, ignoring them.

Then Jonathan remembered the letter in his

pocket. He pulled it out, and the smile dropped from his face.

It wasn't good news. Not at all.

"You think that's freaky, check this out." He tossed it to Dess.

She lifted it to her eyes as he pulled the car back onto the road, heading for the highway fast. They had to get back to school.

"What the hell . . . ?" she murmured.

"It was in the mailbox at Darkling Manor. That must be the owner's name, courtesy of Oklahoma Power and Light."

"Oh, man, Jonathan," Dess exclaimed. "With a name like that, they've got to be related." She started to shake her head. "Jessica isn't going to like this."

"No. And I don't either."

He drove fast and hard toward school.

153

12 | 2:58 P.M.

PATIENCE

They hadn't come back.

Jessica's eyes swept the student parking lot, trying to find Jonathan's car among the throngs escaping Bixby High. Everyone was full of last-bell energy, jumping up on hoods and playing catch across the lot, angling for rides home. On the street a line of school buses sat spewing gray smoke, their windows filling with impatient faces.

But nowhere did she see Jonathan or Dess.

"Hey, Jess. What's up?"

She turned to find Constanza Grayfoot beside her.

"Oh, just looking for someone."

Constanza smiled. "Mr. Gorgeous?"

"Yeah." She turned back toward the parking lot. "He left school earlier, but I thought he was coming back."

"Skipping, huh?" Constanza shook her head. "I thought you two were going to keep a low profile after getting arrested."

"Not arrested. Detained and transported to parental custody," Jessica said. "But yeah, we were." She would've explained that Jonathan was making sure that two of her friends hadn't been eaten alive, but somehow she couldn't find the appropriate words. "He kind of had to do something."

"Sure, I know the feeling." Constanza waved to a cluster of cheerleaders headed across the parking lot.

As more and more cars departed, Jessica became even more certain that Jonathan's was nowhere to be found. What did it mean that he and Dess hadn't come back? That everything was fine? That their worst fears had been true? It seemed like they could have bothered to tell her if Rex and Melissa were okay. Unless by not going along to Rex's she had proven herself irredeemably lame and the four of them had decided to ditch her permanently.

155

"What's wrong, Jess?"

Jessica turned and gave Constanza a tired smile. She wished she could share her anxiety with someone, but as the only midnighter who hadn't skipped school today, she was on her own.

"It's just . . ." What could she say?

"Trouble in Coupleville?"

Jessica nodded. "I guess."

"So tell me what's wrong." Constanza smiled. "You know you want to."

Jessica realized that she did want to, and she wasn't sworn to secrecy about *everything* in her life. "Well, Jonathan's really great, some of the time. Like, at night."

"But not so great the morning after?"

Jessica rolled her eyes. "It's not about morning afters, of which there have been none, by the way. I'm just talking about here at school. We never seem all that connected when we're together here."

"Oh, got you. He's afraid of PDA."

"Yeah. Not too much into public *or* private displays of affection, actually. Except at night. It's kind of hard to explain."

Constanza snorted. "Not that hard."

"I mean, it's not what you think."

"What do you think I think?"

Jessica felt a smile on her face. "What do you think I think you think?"

Constanza raised an eyebrow. "I think you *know* what I think."

The release of hydraulic brakes squealed across the parking lot, and Jessica looked up to see the first bus in line begin to roll.

"Oh, crap. I need to run."

"Hang on, Jess." Constanza took her arm. "That was just getting interesting. Let me give you a ride home."

Jessica looked at her. "Really? It's miles out of your way."

Constanza shrugged. "So what? Since you've been grounded, I've hardly seen you." She put her arm around Jessica and started walking her between the few remaining cars. "You never hang with us at study hall anymore."

"Oh, yeah. Sorry about that."

"It's okay. I know you have this weird affliction where you believe that study hall is for actual studying." She giggled. "And it's not like *I* would be jealous of Miss Gothoid over in the corner."

Jessica sighed. "Dess is pretty cool, really." Of

157

course, she couldn't imagine having a conversation about Jonathan's hand-holding phobia with Dess. And *forget* Rex or Melissa.

"Yeah. Super-cool," Constanza said. "But I guess she does know her trig. Isn't she one of Sanchez's math groupies?"

"Sort of."

Constanza opened her purse and pulled out a key chain jangling with a miniflashlight, a fingernail clipper, a rabbit's foot, and a host of keys. She squeezed it, and the powder blue Mercedes ahead of them let out a chirp.

"Whatever and who cares? We're going to spend this ride talking about *you* and your boy problems, Miss Day." Constanza made her way around the car.

Jessica smiled and opened the passenger door, relaxing a little for the first time since the physics test had hit her desk that morning. Running into Constanza had been her first bit of luck all day. For the next twenty minutes, at least, she wouldn't have to hear about darklings or slithers, ancient blood feuds, missing lore, or even ice-cream socials.

Inside, Constanza began to fiddle with the radio.

"So, your boy's PDA-shy in daylight. Sort of an affection vampire?"

"Yeah."

"Very common syndrome. And it's pretty clear what to do." Constanza started the car, put both hands on the steering wheel, and looked across at her.

"What?"

"Be patient."

"Patient?" Jessica's eyes widened. Patience wasn't the advice she'd been expecting from Constanza.

"Yes. Just let your anger mellow inside you, aging like a fine wine. Then when Jonathan does something that really pisses you off, let him have it with both barrels."

Jessica blinked. "Um, I got lost. Are these wine barrels?"

"Pay attention, Jessica. These are barrels of anger." Constanza sighed, thumping the steering wheel. "The problem with boys is, you can't tell them every time something annoys you. If you complain every single second that Jonathan isn't holding your hand, you look feeble and whiny and desperate. So you have to hit him with all his flaws at once. Which means . . ." She put the car into gear. "Waiting until he does something that he *knows* is bad and having a tally of all your complaints ready in your mind. Be patient, but be prepared—that's my motto."

Jessica shook her head as they backed out of the parking space. "You're probably right. I mean, about not bugging him. He'll freak if I'm all clingy. I'll just have to talk to him."

"Wait until you have the upper hand, though. Patience is a virtue."

"Uh, yeah, I guess." Although at some point, Jessica knew from experience, patience was also being a wimp.

As they reached the edge of the parking lot, a car swerved in from the street and screeched to a halt right in front of them. Constanza slammed on the brakes, and the Mercedes stopped with inches to spare.

It was Jonathan and Dess, looking very much in a hurry. His car was dirty, as if they'd been driving off-road, and Jonathan wore a wild-eyed expression.

He glared at Constanza's car, then squinted through the two windshields at Jessica.

"Jeez. Speaking of patience . . . ," Constanza said.

Jessica swallowed. Something serious had happened. "Look, I better go. He looks upset. His thing he had to do . . . maybe it didn't go so well."

"Sure, Jess."

Jessica opened her door. "I'm really sorry, Constanza. I'd love a ride home some other time."

"No problem. See you tomorrow. I want to hear more about this."

"Oh . . . sure." *If I can tell you anything at all.* Jessica wondered what she was about to find out. From the way Jonathan and Dess looked, last night had been bad.

Constanza laughed. "I mean, even if Jonathan is being a pain in the ass, you have to admit, the guy knows how to make an entrance."

13 | 11:45 P.M.

INTRUDER

Jessica lifted a corner of the shade to peer out, wondering if the movement could be seen from the bushes across the street. Her lights were off, of course, and she'd draped T-shirts across the pulsing eyes of her bedside clock and snoozing computer. The only light in her bedroom crept in beneath the door: the faint glow of the hall night-light.

She couldn't see anything outside—nothing human, anyway. Just intertwined tree branches, fallen leaves, and a few pools of illumination gathered under porch lights.

Somewhere out there, Melissa was searching, sifting through the few waking minds for one thinking stalking thoughts. *If* she and Rex were

162

actually in town tonight and not headed off to the edge of the badlands to tangle with monsters. Jonathan had told her the story as he'd driven her home from school—how they'd stumbled onto a house where darklings gave orders to human followers in midnight séances.

Jessica shuddered, trying to imagine the half-thing that made this communication possible, the kidnapped midnighter somehow melded with a darkling.

Jonathan had also passed on Rex's assurances that Jessica would be safe for a while; something about a stolen domino, which hadn't been completely convincing. What if the man with the camera already had his orders? What if he had a spare set of dominoes? Didn't seem like much to bet your life on.

Jessica knew she wouldn't be out of danger until the blue time came, when she and Jonathan could soar above Bixby to safety. She glanced at her watch: only twelve minutes to go.

A noise crept into the room.

It was the sound of creaking wood. And it was definitely coming from inside the house. Jessica dropped the window shade, turned, and froze.

Along the dim strip of light creeping beneath the door a shadow moved, accompanied by the faintest of complaints from the wooden floorboards.

Mom? Her mouth moved to form the word, but no sound came out. She tightened her lips. If it was her mother, she would knock or say something, wouldn't she?

Jessica waited motionless for what felt like a solid minute, her heartbeat rising slowly into her throat. The shadow under the door didn't move. In the darkness Jessica's vision began to conjure stirrings in the corners of her room. The light under the door seemed to grow in intensity, and the moan of the wind outside kept getting louder.

Were they waiting for midnight? That wouldn't make any sense if they were normal humans. Unless they planned to attack in the last minutes before the secret hour came, to bundle her up all ready for the darklings. But why? To join her with some darkling body to do their bidding?

Jessica chewed her lip. She couldn't just stand here.

Slowly she knelt by the bed, sliding out her weapons box. Ignoring the flashlight and lighter, she pulled out Anfractuously, the bicycle lock.

Made of heavy steel, it was suitable for both midnight and daylight threats.

She took slow steps toward the door, stood to the side, back against the wall, and raised Anfractuously above her head.

A loud *thump* filled the room; the bicycle lock had struck the wall behind her.

Jessica froze.

A whisper pierced the door: "Jess?"

"*Beth?*" She yanked open the door, revealing her tousle-headed sister standing there in pajamas. "You little sneak! What are you doing outside my door?" she hissed.

Beth walked into the room, looking around interestedly. "Well, mostly I was wondering what you were doing here *in*side your room."

"Shhh! You'll wake up Mom and Dad," Jessica whispered. Beth had spoken in a normal voice.

"So close the door."

Jessica groaned and glanced at her clock, but the numbers were obscured by the T-shirt she'd draped over it. If her little sister was still here at midnight, things were going to get tricky.

Beth followed her gaze. "Interesting. Is that to hide the light?"

"Shhh!" Jessica hissed again. She relented and closed the door. The last thing she needed was her parents joining them. "What do you want?"

"I want to know what's going on with you."

"What do you mean, Beth?"

"Well, the blinds are drawn, the lights are off, you're dressed, and you've got your bike lock in your hand. Going somewhere?"

Jess looked down at Anfractuously. "*This* was to bash your brains in with, actually."

Beth smiled sweetly. "Who did you think I was?"

"No one," Jessica said. "Just some retarded serial killer in pajamas. Now why don't you go back to bed?"

"You need to get your watch fixed," Beth announced. "It's wrong every morning."

Jessica paused, although she knew that pausing was always a bad idea with Beth. It gave her little brain time to think it knew more than it really did. "Yeah, I guess it's running fast."

"Yeah, but *exactly* an hour fast? Every morning?"

"I miss Chicago time," Jessica said, a trickle of sweat beginning to crawl down her back. Just how much had Beth noticed?

"Nice try. Chicago time and Bixby time are the same."

Jessica sighed. "Okay, Beth, you win. Every night I fly to New York on my broom to attend wild parties, and in the morning I sometimes forget to set my watch back to Bixby time. Satisfied?"

Beth sat down on the bed, nodding slowly. "Not completely, but at least we're getting somewhere."

"Where you're getting is into trouble. Leave. This is *my* room!"

"So call Mom."

Jessica took a breath and opened her mouth, but all that leaked out was another deadly pause, which was as unstoppable as Beth's growing smile.

"Didn't think so. On a related topic, Jess, I tried to wake you up Sunday morning. But mysteriously, I couldn't open your door."

"Maybe I locked it."

Beth snorted. "Your door doesn't have a lock. I *am* your little sister—I know these things. I suspect that you jammed this under it." She held up a doorstop, the one Jessica had secured her door with the night they'd spotted the stalker.

"That's mine."

Beth dropped it onto the bed with a smile. "Yes, it is. And when I find out what you're up to, *you* will be *mine*."

Jessica glanced at her watch. Six minutes. If the darkling groupies would just burst in now, she could jump into her closet, and in the confusion they would assume that Beth was her and whisk her off to the badlands, where she could annoy the darklings until they were forced to escape into yet another hidden hour or perhaps another dimension entirely. A win-win situation.

"Waiting for someone?" Beth asked.

"Yes . . . *you*. To leave."

"Someone who's coming at, oh . . ." Beth whisked the T-shirt off the bedside clock. "Twelve?"

Jessica just shook her head. Her heart was pounding too hard for her to say anything. Maybe if she stood very still and came back to this exact spot when the hour had ended, Beth wouldn't notice any minuscule changes in her position.

But Beth, it seemed, was noticing everything.

She sat on the bed, eyes sweeping the room. "You're majorly grounded, but there's always dirt on your sneakers in the morning. And rust and grease on your jeans. It's like you go out

168

Dumpster diving every night."

Jessica ground her teeth together. Beth must have been spying on her for weeks, probably since they'd arrived in Bixby. All the time she'd been worrying about her poor, friendless sister having trouble adjusting to the new town, the little sneak had been busy snooping.

It occurred to Jessica that she could really let Beth in for an eyeful. All she had to do was wait until midnight came and when it ended be standing just behind her or in another room entirely, vanishing before Beth's snotty, superior gaze.

Of course, if Beth saw her disappear, she might start talking about it. Mom and Dad wouldn't believe her, but if she told someone at school, the story might eventually get back to the other midnighters. Rex wouldn't be very happy about that.

Even worse, instead of being terrified, Beth would probably decide to start showing up *every* night at midnight, trying to figure out exactly what was going on.

"Did you think I wouldn't notice how lovehappy you are all the time?" Beth continued. "Or *were*, at least until you got all paranoid Saturday night. And now you're waving that thing around."

169

Beth pointed at the bicycle lock, still in Jessica's hand. "That guy you got busted with, Jonathan— he's been in trouble with the police a bunch, right?"

"Beth, you don't know what you're talking about."

"That's right, I don't. I've never met this guy; he could be a total psycho for all I know." Her eyes fell to the floor. "Jess, I'm worried about you."

Jessica blinked. "You're what?"

"Worried. About. You." Beth pulled her knees up onto the bed and hugged them. The superior smile had faded from her face. "You never got brought home by the cops before, or snuck around, or lied to me."

"Beth, I don't—"

"You lie to me all the time now, Jessica. I can tell." Beth looked straight at her, daring her to disagree. "You weren't like this before we came to this stupid town. I knew all your friends back then."

Jessica swallowed. It seemed so long ago, like another life, but she did remember. Before Mom and Dad had announced the big move to Bixby and the packing and good-byes had turned Beth into a full-time whiner, the two of them had always talked. Teased and argued mostly, but never lied to each other.

• "Beth. I don't mean to keep secrets from you. It's just that . . ." Jessica's voice caught. Beth's eyes were so full of longing; she needed something to cling to here in Bixby.

It would be so easy to tell her.

Guiltily, Jessica allowed herself to imagine the look of awe on her little sister's face. Beth wouldn't believe it at first, but Jessica could *prove* it in another two minutes, flitting from one spot to another in the blink of an eye. Beth would have to accept the truth, and Jessica would have an ally when she had to cover things up. There would be one less person in the world to deceive.

"Beth . . ."

"What?"

The words didn't come, of course. She would hate herself if she said them. For years the others had kept the secret from everyone—friends, family, the police who enforced Bixby's merciless curfew. It wasn't convenient, but what else could they do? Rex said that lots of people used to know about midnight, but look what had happened— one day the midnighters had all just disappeared. Secrecy was their only real protection. Her shades

171

were drawn and windows locked right now because someone out there *knew*.

And there were worse things than the man with the camera. Jessica's imagined vision of the half-thing came into her mind. Midnight wasn't just secret; it was full of horrors. She couldn't dump her nightmares on her little sister—it wasn't fair. The whole idea was stupid and selfish.

Jessica sighed and looked at her watch again. Forty seconds. "Let me show you something."

Beth's eyes widened. "Really?"

Jessica smiled—just one more lie tonight. "Really. Come here."

She opened the door to her closet, pointing into the darkness. All she really had to do was distract Beth for a few seconds; as long as she wasn't looking at Jessica at the stroke of midnight, her little sister shouldn't notice a thing.

Beth stood and crossed the room, a little suspicious now. "No one's in there, right?"

"Yeah, sure. I keep my new psycho boyfriend in the closet. Don't be a wimp. Look." Her watch said twenty-four seconds now.

Beth frowned warily but came. "Turn on a light or something?"

"Sure." She flicked the overhead light on, but Beth only frowned harder, like this was all too easy. "Come *on*." Jessica took her sister's shoulder and pulled her toward the closet. Fifteen, fourteen . . .

"What?" Beth stared into the darkness.

"Just look. Let your eyes adjust." Ten. Jessica took her hand from Beth's shoulder, stepped back out of her view. Beth turned to track her movement.

"You better not be pulling some—"

"Look *there*!" Jessica snapped. This was turning out to be trickier than she'd expected; maneuvering Beth was like herding a cat. And her watch wasn't always perfect to the second. There was only one way to be sure. . . .

"Jess, there's nothing in there but—"

Her little sister squawked as Jessica shoved her into the closet, stumbling against the hanging clothes with a clatter. She swung the door closed behind Beth until it clicked.

"Jess!" came a muffled roar. A solid thump followed, probably a kick.

Jessica leaned her weight against the door, watching the stroke of midnight come and go. That was the problem with quartz watches, Rex always said. They tended to lose a few seconds every day.

"You are so dead! If you don't open this door in five seconds, I'm going to scream."

Five seconds should be fine, Jessica thought.

"One, two, thr—"

The familiar shudder came, a ripple in the wooden solidity of the floor beneath her feet and the door against her shoulder, a simultaneous choking off of little sister and moaning Oklahoma wind. A distortion passed through the room, leaving everything still and flat and lit from within by a soft blue glow.

Jessica sighed. The coming scream was almost certainly unavoidable, and her parents might have already heard the ruckus. But it was Beth who had invaded *her* room, after all, refusing to leave. In any case, explanations and recriminations were all on the other side of midnight.

She left the closet door closed, unable to imagine a worse sight than a frozen prescream Beth face, deathly pale and furious. Arming herself with Explosiveness and Demonstration and pulling on her sneakers, Jessica unlocked and opened a window, swinging one leg across the sill.

Looking back at the room, she was momentarily proud of herself for resisting the temptation to tell secrets. She had done the adult thing and protected Beth from the truth. Maybe she would even apologize when her little sister emerged from the closet.

"See you in an hour, sweetie," Jessica called, and dropped to the ground outside.

14 | 12:00 A.M.

ACARICIANDOTE

"There!" Jessica pointed with her free hand, the motion sending the two of them into a slow spin.

Jonathan looked down. "I can't see Rex and Melissa anywhere."

"Me either. Just the car. Kind of hard to miss it."

Jonathan laughed. "Must take some kind of mindcaster voodoo, keeping an old piece of crap like that running."

He tugged her closer, taking her free hand in his. Their drifting rotation slowed as they descended, somehow canceled out by his motion. A flash of annoyance went through Jessica. That equal-and-opposite-reaction thing again. Jonathan understood it automatically, though that particular law of motion always seemed to leave her adrift.

Her irritation passed quickly, though. The moment felt too good to stay angry—falling like this, her head resting against his chest. She closed her eyes, sensing when they were about to land from the tightening of his muscles. Their legs intertwined for a moment as the ground caught them, knees bending and bodies pressing against each other for support.

They jumped again, Jessica following Jonathan's lead, keeping both of his hands in hers. She opened her eyes: the leap had been just high enough to clear the house between their last landing and the parked Ford.

As they reached the peak, he said, "You seem better tonight."

"Better than what?"

"This afternoon."

"Oh, that." There'd been a lot to digest, what with Darkling Manor and the half-being and something convoluted about Dess thinking that Rex and Melissa were . . . touching. "It's just been a long week, that's all."

"It's Monday night, Jess."

"My point exactly. But yeah, I am better now."

Things were always better with Jonathan in the secret hour. "Anyway, it's officially partly Tuesday."

They landed in the street near the car, Jonathan's clothes billowing a little as they corkscrewed down to a dead halt.

"Hey! I just realized . . . you're wearing a jacket!" She stepped back to look at him in surprise, normal weight settling across her.

Jonathan shrugged. "In case I have to walk home. You know, if we find the stalker or something and I wind up following him."

She smiled, looking into his eyes. Every night he was here, ready to protect her. Taking his hand once more, weightlessness rose in her like laughter.

"Jonathan, you don't have to walk home. If you ever get stranded here in town again . . ." She turned half away. "It's crazy to freeze to death. Just knock on my window next time."

"Your parents would freak."

"They won't know you're there."

He laughed. "So you'll hide me in your closet all night?"

Jessica's smile faded and she let out a groan. "Actually, my closet's kind of . . . busy right now. Long story." She dropped his hand and sighed.

With Beth acting the way she was, Jessica was about as likely to get away with hiding Jonathan in her room as she would Melissa's car.

The rusting Ford looked even more broken-down than usual tonight. One of the hubcaps was missing. "Where are they, anyway?"

"They probably haven't gone too far." He glanced at his watch. "Not in eleven minutes. Your closet's *busy*?"

She sighed again. "You don't have a little sister, do you?"

"No. But what's that—?"

"Hey!" Rex's voice called to them from across the street. He and Melissa emerged from behind a row of bushes, their black clothes almost invisible in the deep blues of midnight.

Jessica's eyes widened. The two were holding hands, swinging them like ten-year-olds on a playdate. Melissa was wearing gloves, of course, but the sight of the mindcaster in casual contact with another human being was shocking. And she was actually *smiling*.

Jessica dared a quick glance at Jonathan.

"Ix-nay on the inking-thay," he said softly, then called, "Find something?"

Rex shook his head. "Not a whiff. We've been driving around here since just after ten."

"Nothing on the air but TV drones and wet dreams," Melissa said.

"Oh," Jessica murmured. "Thanks for sharing."

Melissa giggled. Which was also a new and scary development.

"Looks like my grand theft domino has things on hold for the moment," Rex said.

Jessica frowned. Leave it to Rex to be convinced the threat was over because he had his hands on the flame-bringer domino. It figured. That was the way he saw the world: control the symbols, control everything.

"I wouldn't be so sure," Jonathan said. "All we really know is that they're not hanging around tonight. And anyway, midnight's not the natural time for them to pull something. If they really wanted to hurt one of us, wouldn't they do it in the middle of the day?"

"True." A thoughtful look crossed Rex's face. "And with Jessica, they're probably expecting her to come to them. An invitation to a party, maybe."

Jessica frowned. "What are you talking about?"

Rex looked at Jonathan. "You haven't told her?"

Jonathan looked down sheepishly. "Oh, Dess mentioned that to you guys?"

"Of course she did. Right away."

"Mentioned what?" Jessica cried.

Jonathan's dark eyes widened as he turned toward her. "Well, there was a lot of stuff to get through in one car ride. I was dumping so much on you already. Once I got you away from school, I figured you'd be safe until I told you tonight."

"Told me what? Safe from *what?*"

"Well, Dess and I found out who owns Darkling Manor. There was a gas bill in the mailbox." He swallowed. "It was addressed to Ernesto Grayfoot."

Jessica blinked, dizziness welling up in her. "It must be a coincidence."

"It's not exactly a common name, Jess," Jonathan said. "And this is an awfully small town."

"You don't know that they're related," she insisted, her voice hollow in her ears. Constanza was her only normal friend in town. . . . She *couldn't* be one of the darkling groupies.

"I only found one Grayfoot in the Bixby phone book," Rex said. "It's the number for Ernesto out at Darkling Manor. But the place is empty. Constanza's dad must be unlisted."

"So maybe Ernesto's from out of town!" Jessica cried. "From the other side of the country!"

"Or maybe he's Constanza's older brother."

"She doesn't have one." Jessica paused, suddenly unsure. When she'd spent the night at Constanza's house, she hadn't met any siblings, but a much older brother who lived somewhere else might not have been mentioned. And it surely was just a coincidence that she'd run into Jessica in the parking lot and then offered her a ride home. . . .

"Jess." Jonathan took her hand, but she pulled away. "We're not saying that Constanza's one of them. Just that you should ask her about her family. Find out what you can."

"We need to find Ernesto," Rex said. "Melissa needs another crack at that woman we saw at Darkling Manor. She has some kind of plans in her head, about something being constructed out in the desert."

Jonathan spoke softly. "Just tell Constanza you're doing a report or something."

"I've seen the name going back generations, even before the oil boom," Rex said. "If you say you're working on local history, it'll make sense to her."

"But it won't make sense to *me*," Jessica cried. "I don't want to use her. Constanza's my *only* friend. . . ."

There was an awkward moment's silence.

"I mean, besides you guys," she added lamely.

Rex and Jonathan just looked at her. She tried to make her mouth work, to come up with something that would change what she'd said.

"*We're* your only friends, Jessica."

The three of them stared at Melissa, unable to believe that she'd really said the words. Even Rex was struck speechless.

"We're the only ones who know how the real world is," Melissa continued. "I mean, Rex and I barely made it out of Las Colonias. When you first got here, almost getting killed was a nightly thing." She snorted, a measure of her usual contempt returning. "You think Constanza Grayfoot's ever faced anything like that? Ever had a darkling come after her?" She turned away. "So we understand you like nobody else. *We're* your friends."

Jessica's eyes fell to the street, where windblown leaves hovered a few inches above the asphalt. "I didn't mean you guys weren't my friends," she said softly.

"Don't sweat it," Melissa said. "Rex and I will look into this. Maybe follow her around after school lets out, do some mind reading."

"Sure," Rex added. "No problem."

"Thanks," Jessica said. "And yeah, I'll talk to her."

"I wish you'd told me this afternoon."

Jonathan didn't respond.

"It's just that I might not have been such a bitch in front of them if I'd already had time to think about it," she explained.

"I'm sorry," he said flatly. "For the tenth time."

Jessica sighed. The way she felt, she wouldn't have minded another ten. Not that it was his fault totally. Anyone who managed to look like a self-ish, immature bitch diva next to *Melissa* had to take some of the credit herself.

They sat together on the gravel roof of the Bixby Shop Mart, surrounded by the black shapes of exhaust vents and industrial air conditioners.

"I just don't know what to do," Jonathan said, finally breaking the silence.

"About what?"

"About you. *For* you, I mean." He picked up a

rock and threw it out over the empty parking lot. After it left his hand, it slowed gradually, as if falling through an invisible foam in the air. The rock finally came to a halt, joining the floating galaxy of gravel he had tossed out across the asphalt plain. Jonathan was different than the rest of them when it came to gravity. Something about time and space warping . . . something about *physics*.

She sighed again. "I still don't understand."

Jonathan threw another rock. "I mean, it was one thing when it was darklings. I could help you with that. I could fly you away. But this time the bad guys come from Flatland."

"Come from where?"

He frowned. "I thought you had Sanchez for trig. He makes all his advanced classes read this book, *Flatland.*"

"Oh, wait," she said. "Dess showed it to me. Flatland's this two-dimensional world, right? Where everyone's a triangle or a square, and this three-D sphere guy shows up." She threw a rock of her own, which soared through the others and crashed to the ground, skittering across the parking lot. "It failed to improve my understanding of trigonometry."

"That's the one," Jonathan said. "So when I'm

in normal gravity and I can't fly, can't jump, can't see the angles . . ."

"Can't look down on everyone?" she asked.

He threw another rock and snorted, his brown eyes flashing violet in the dark moon's light. "Sure, that too. All that stuff is Flatland. It's like being squashed down into two dimensions." He turned to face her for a moment. "I can't do *anything* to protect you from these guys. Melissa can still read their minds, Dess can still do the math, Rex can still . . . I don't know, look stuff up. But I'm useless."

"Useless?" She shook her head. "You're not useless."

"They could drive up to school tomorrow and haul you away, and I couldn't do a damn thing about it. Except possibly limp after their car." He stood, favoring one foot, and threw another rock, flinging it so hard that it disappeared into the darkness.

"Thanks for the mental image." Jessica frowned. "Is the Flatland thing why you never hold my hand?"

"What?" He looked down at his palm, which he'd been absentmindedly massaging. "We hold hands all the time."

She shook her head. Darkling groupie or not, maybe Constanza had given the right advice. Maybe now, when things were all screwed up anyway, was the right moment to talk to him. "Not in normal time. Not in Flatland."

Jonathan looked dumbstruck for a second, staring at his hand as if expecting it to confess something to him. "Really?" he finally managed.

"Really."

He sat down again, still wearing a baffled expression. "Oh, great. Something else I suck at in Flatland."

She groaned. "It's not that you aren't good at it. It's that you don't ever do it! It's like *we* don't exist there."

His muscles writhed for a moment under his jacket, as if his clothes were too tight or if something invisible were binding him. "Sorry," he muttered.

She lifted her shoulders. "That's eleven."

They were silent for a while, but at least Jonathan had stopped throwing rocks. The moon began to set before them, dark light glinting from broken glass on the parking lot, and Jessica realized they'd have to start home soon. She still had an about-to-scream Beth to deal with when midnight ran out.

What a great night this had turned into.

Jessica stared at the dark moon until her head began to hurt. She didn't want tonight to end this way. Taking Jonathan's hand, she softly began to massage it.

"I like you all the time, Jonathan," she said. "Twenty-five seven."

He smiled back at her.

"Anyway," she added, "if there's a useless-during-daylight club, I'm the president. Unless you tremble before the mighty power of the flashlight carrier."

He laughed, then looked into her eyes for a moment. She saw a decision flicker across his face.

"What?"

He reached into his jacket. "I brought you something."

"A present? Why? For complaining so much?"

"No. Because I knew you'd be upset about Constanza. And because I should have told you. I couldn't think what else to do." He pulled out a slender strand that glimmered blue, coursing fire in the light of the dark moon. "Like you and me, it has no powers whatsoever in normal time."

He handed it to her, a delicate silver chain, its links so small that it came like sand into her palm. Charms dangled from it; she recognized a tiny house, a curled cat, praying hands. . . .

"It's beautiful."

"It was my mom's. I took off a couple of . . . the miracles, those little charms, so there's thirteen now."

"Oh, Jonathan." She drew it around her wrist, closing the minuscule clasp carefully. "I promise never to throw it at a darkling. What's its name?"

"Acariciandote."

"Um, say again?"

"Acariciandote. It's Spanish. My dad doesn't speak it anymore, but Mom always did."

She tried the syllables slowly, wincing as they went terribly wrong in her mouth. "Does Spanish work on darklings?"

"*Gringa*." He shook his head, smiling. "Spanish was kicking darkling ass in Oklahoma about four hundred years before English got here."

"Oops, sorry. I never thought about that." She tried to say the name again, getting lost after three syllables. "What does it mean?"

189

"Funny about that." He took her hand. "It means 'touching you,' like when we fly."

She smiled. "Like always, you mean." She held the bracelet up to the light. "It's absolutely . . ." Jessica paused, staring past the dangling charms at the moon.

It was already half set.

"We've got to go." She stood. "I can't be late. My little sister's in my closet."

"Huh?"

She grabbed his wrist and pulled him into a dead run along the roof, heading for the edge. "I'll tell you on the way."

They sailed down Division Street, jumping low and hard, leaving sneaker prints on the long, flat roof of a northbound eighteen-wheeler. A wrenching turn toward her neighborhood sent them thrashing through the canopy of a huge oak, scattering leaves and twigs to the frozen winds. Even though Jessica's arms were covered with scratches, she laughed aloud, happy to be flying at speed again, just barreling along with the ground a blur below them. She felt her worries fall away for a few moments, stalkers and

Grayfoots and half-darklings lost in their wake.

They just made it, careening to a stop on her front lawn with five minutes of midnight left, barely enough time for Jonathan to make it home before the freezing wind leapt up again.

Jessica spun him to face her, feeling better than she had since the stalker had entered her life. She lifted Acariciandote, which gave off a faint tinkling sound, the charms still spinning from their flight.

"Thanks for this, Jonathan." She kissed him hard, pulling his feet up off the ground.

He smiled and looked away, shrugging.

"Now get home safe and fast. No walking!" She pointed him back toward town, giving him a push. "See you tomorrow in Flatland."

He laughed and started running. His long strides became half-block jumps until one fantastic leap took him into the air and out of sight.

Jessica watched after him and grinned. Her normal weight wasn't as crushing as it usually seemed when he left her. Maybe things would still be screwed up tomorrow in Flatland, but at least the cool metal of Acariciandote would be around her wrist, a reminder of midnight.

She took deep breaths, letting the thundering of her heart gradually slow while she knocked leaves and grass from her hair and clothes.

With thirty seconds to go, she climbed in through the window, remembering to kick off her shoes as she crossed the room.

"Okay, Beth. Do your worst." She took another deep breath, placing one hand on the knob of the closet door.

Midnight ended as it had begun, late by Jessica's watch, tarrying those same nine seconds before normal time rumbled up through the soles of her feet, blue light and silence draining from the world together.

"—ree, four . . . ," came a muffled voice from the closet.

Jessica pulled it open, revealing Beth with red face and clenched fists.

"Okay, you win," Jessica said, raising her palms in surrender. "Don't scream."

"I'm going to do more than scream, Jess!" she spat, pushing past Jessica and into the room. "When I tell Mom that you tried to lock me. . . ."

Her voice trailed away, the look of anger fading into one of confusion.

"What the hell, Jess?"

"What?"

"You look . . . You're not . . ." Sharp eyes scanned Jessica from head to toe, then Beth reached out to pull a stray leaf from her hair. "What the . . . ?"

"That's a leaf, genius."

"It wasn't there. You look different. What did you *do*?"

Jessica swallowed. She realized that she was still out of breath from the dash home. Her face was probably as red as Beth's. Her hands were scratched from the trip through the oak tree, and her hair had to be a mess.

And Beth was staring at the *bracelet*. . . .

"Oh, this," she said, hoping an explanation would reach her lips in time. "Yeah, this is what I wanted to show you. But I didn't want you to see where I hide it because it's a such a . . . big secret. Pretty, huh?"

Beth's eyes swept to the open window, and Jessica groaned inside. It had been closed and locked a few seconds before.

"You hide that bracelet . . . outside?"

"Uh, yeah, okay. You got me there."

Beth's eyes squinted even further. "You shoved

me in a closet so you could jump out the window to where you keep your bracelet? Are you totally *cracking*?"

"No. But you said something about Jonathan. . . ." Jessica struggled to remember. That conversation had been an hour ago for her, but only a minute had passed for Beth.

"Yeah, that he's been in trouble with the police."

"Right! That's it." She held up the bracelet to the light. "But I wanted you to see this. He gave it to me." The smile on her face was huge, idiotic, and beaming. "Isn't it great?"

"Yeah, sure," Beth said, her eyes still locked on Jessica's. "It's wonderful. And I'm glad that you hide it . . . outside. In the bushes."

Jessica sighed. "Its name means 'touching you.'"

"It has a *name*?"

"Sure." Jessica shrugged. "Anyway, thanks for coming by. I'm glad I got to show it to you." She hugged Beth hard. "See you tomorrow."

Jessica opened her bedroom door, and her little sister walked out, casting wary glances back, totally at a loss as to how she'd wound up so confused.

"I'll make sure you get to meet him soon," Jessica whispered.

Beth nodded once and bolted for her own bedroom on scurrying, silent feet.

15

2:42 P.M.

DEAD ZONE

The house didn't look like much. It squatted in darkness, out of repair and covered with twisting vines, shaded from the afternoon sun by the mushroom cloud of willow tree that dominated the front yard.

Dess looked at Geostationary again. This was the place. In fact, the equations that had led her here should have been obvious all along. Once she'd realized it was a base-sixty thing, the math had been easy.

Back in advanced algebra the year before, Mr. Sanchez had taught them how to convert into base two (turning regular numbers into ones and zeros), all the while claiming that this knowledge was going to get them computer jobs one day. Yeah, right. A few more machines in the Bixby High computer lab might've helped more.

But Dess always humored Sanchez, and practicing new bases was a pleasant distraction. It had kept her brain busy back in the days before Jessica Day had come along to keep everyone busy all the time.

After mastering binary (which had taken about 256 seconds), Dess had tackled base sixty because there were sixty seconds in a minute, sixty minutes in an hour. So Dess had it down cold that, for example, 2:31 a.m. was 9,060 seconds after midnight.

Of course, what would you *do* with that bit of trivia?

The answer had come when she'd started playing with her father's oil-drilling maps two Fridays ago. All of the secret hour lay within a single degree of longitude and latitude, the twelve-riddled 36 north by 96 west. But degrees, it turned out, were sort of like hours. They were divided into sixty minutes, and each of those minutes was divided into sixty seconds. That had been the big revelation: if coordinates used the same math as time, then the *place* where the secret hour happened could be sliced up into minutes and seconds, just like the hour itself.

Looking back, Dess knew she should have realized this before now.

From the mountains beyond Rustle's Bottom, she had often watched midnight roll in. Like dawn, it swept from east to west, carried by the rotation of the earth. And like dawn, it didn't hit in a perfectly straight line. There were bumps and ripples in midnight's arrival.

But the shadows that convoluted the secret hour weren't cast by mountain peaks or water towers. They were actually cast by numbers. All you had to do was start seeing the minutes and seconds that lay in a grid across the streets of Bixby, and it was obvious where the turbulence would arise.

Dess put Geostationary in the pocket of her coat, got off her bike, and pulled off her sunglasses. She was breathing hard. The moment her brain had finished the calculations, she'd practically run out of the school building, skipping last period and riding her bike here at about fifty miles an hour.

Now, though, Dess found herself in no hurry to approach the house. What sort of person would live in a spot like this? Just some random Bixbyite who couldn't afford anything better? Or something worse, like a coven of darkling groupies?

But then she noticed the thirteen-pointed star mounted next to the door and felt a lot better. Realtors always told new arrivals in Bixby that in the old days, the plaques showed which houses had fire insurance. This was only a half lie. The tridecagrams were insurance, all right, but not against infernos.

The star was a good sign. She couldn't imagine darkling groupies leaving a tridecagram stuck onto their house. Her eyes hunted for more reassurances and easily found them: the walkway was thirty-nine flagstones long, the chimney 169 bricks high. Perhaps this run-down shack had once been the headquarters of that Ladies' Anti-Tenebrosity League that Rex was always talking about.

Dess started to lean her bike against the old willow. But then she saw the marks and froze.

A foot long and at least an inch deep, three parallel gouges had been cut into the thick bark. Giant claws had swept through the old willow, like carpet knives lacerating flesh. The yellow-green sap had welled up like blood and congealed.

Judging from the size of the claws, the wound had come from a very old darkling of the saber-toothed variety.

She touched the marks; still sticky. She didn't need Rex to tell her this had happened recently . . . probably within the last two weeks.

Dess swallowed, the thought flooding through her again that she really shouldn't have come here alone. This place could be hiding anything.

A few moments after Jonathan had handed her the captured coordinates of Darkling Manor, the pattern of minutes and seconds had coalesced in Dess's mind. She understood now why Melissa had never spotted the unspeakable transactions taking place out in Las Colonias. There were dead zones in Bixby, places where midnight's arrival threw up imperfections, like bubbles trapped in Lucite. There Melissa's ability was useless, the shape of frozen time itself too tangled for her mind to penetrate. When Dess had done the math, the numbers on her new toy had led her here.

Right in the middle of the suburbs, not that far from where Jessica lived, this house squatted on the deadest of the dead zones.

Dess stood there for a while, trying to get her teeth to grip the worn-down nubs of her finger-nails. Finally, though, she grimaced and let her bike fall against the tree. It was broad daylight; no darklings lay in wait. And the thirteen-pointed star showed that one of the good guys had made this his home back in olden times. Dess had worked for days trying to understand how coor-dinates bent the rippled surface of midnight, and this discovery was hers to make. Alone.

She walked up the path.

The house was standing open behind a closed screen door. Dess pressed a button hanging from the door frame by a single screw, but nothing hap-pened. Lowering her sunglasses to squint through the crumpled and pitted screen, she made a fist to knock.

Out of the darkness, a pale face peered back at her.

They stared at each other for a moment. The old woman was wrapped in a dark red nightgown, worn so thin that it shifted in the barely percepti-ble breeze that pushed past Dess and through the door. The woman's eyes were wide open, the whites glowing in the darkness, but her expression showed more curiosity than fear.

"Come in," she said. "It's taken you long enough."

16   2:54 P.M.

AFTER-SCHOOL SPECIAL

Thirty seconds before the scream of the last bell rang out, Melissa's headphones were in place, her tape cued to her lancing song.

She leaned back, closing her eyes. Across Bixby High she could feel fingers gripping the sides of desks, books and pens gathered, backpacks zipped closed under the exhausted and complicit stares of teachers. The minds around her whirred with anticipated routes, the quickest way to lockers, to the nearest door and onto the bus, the fastest way *out*. The noise escalated maddeningly in the last few seconds and filled her head like a cafeteria chant pounded onto a table. . . .

Out, out, out!

Finally the scream sounded, and the building exploded around her.

"Ooooh," Melissa said. Last bell didn't compare to midnight's arrival, but it was still the second-best moment of her day.

She hit play and tipped her head back. Metal power chords detonated in her ears, drowning out the scrapes of desks and sneaker squeaks around her. She felt bodies struggling past each other in the halls, fingers attacking locker combinations, and unbottled conversations gushing through the halls.

Then the flow reached the doors and the pressure that had tormented her mind all day began to subside, like a lanced boil spilling its runny contents at last.

She sighed, opening her eyes. Mr. Rogers stood over her. The classroom was empty except for the two of them. She snapped off the tape.

"Melissa? Are you all right?"

"Never better." Her satisfied smile only disturbed him more. Last semester she'd trained her final-period teacher to deal with the lancing ritual. She hoped Rogers wasn't going to give her any trouble.

"Do you do that after every class?"

"No, just this one. I like to relax for a moment after the rigors of a hard school day. I hope that's all right with you, Mr. Rogers."

"You know, listening to music isn't allowed in classrooms."

Her eyes narrowed. "I don't turn it on until the last bell rings. When class is over. When *school* is over."

She could taste the answer before he opened his mouth. The rancid butter flavor of a petty mind grasping for control.

"Still, Melissa," he said, "this *is* a classroom, and I'd appreciate it if you waited until you were out in the hall before turning that thing on."

A sharp retort curled her tongue, but Melissa let it slide. These last few days her temper had become easier to control.

Besides, as her social studies teacher liked to say, there were always productive ways to channel protest.

"Certainly, Mr. Rogers," she said pleasantly. "Do you happen to live in Bixby?"

"What? Yes, over by the Dr. Pepper plant. Why do you ask?"

"Nothing. Just curious."

She smiled. Mr. Rogers lived close enough to visit, one of these nights during the midnight hour.

Asshole.

The empty bleachers reeked of defeat. Melissa never paid attention to football, but sitting here she could tell that the Bixby Tigers were losers and had been for a long time. Her mind was filled with futility and the bleak taste of cheering for a team that didn't stand a chance.

Wafting up from the hidden spaces underneath, she also caught the scent of secret pleasures, along with a lingering fear of getting caught. Lifting her sunglasses to peer down through the bleachers, she saw cigarette butts hiding in the slatted shadows. Melissa could always sense hidden places— the narrow alleys between temporary classrooms, the janitors' closets and basement doors that drew truants to them. They all had the same taste: sweet momentary freedom spiced with nervous glances over the shoulder.

She wondered what was keeping Rex. Bixby High was mostly empty, leaving only the tastes of band practice, a drama rehearsal, and the football team, who were doing mindless calisthenics on the field in front of her. Melissa closed her eyes, inhaling deeply to relish the peace of after-school depopulation.

Suddenly a picture began to form in her mind, a remnant from the scant minutes she'd been connected to the woman in Darkling Manor. Angie— that was her name—full of confidence and contempt for her partner. Melissa had fished only fragments from Angie's mind before the half-thing had chased them off, but here, waiting for Rex, the long benches of the bleachers triggered a fleeting image. It floated before her eyes now: the construction in the desert, a road stretching out into the salt flats until it simply . . . ended.

It was *huge*. And it had something to do with the halfling. Angie had never seen the nightmarish creature, of course. She was a stiff whenever it appeared. But she had communicated with the halfling through lore symbols and knew it bore some relationship to the thing being built in the desert . . . the road to nowhere.

"Hey!" Rex's voice called from below, scattering the half-formed picture in her mind.

The bleachers wobbled as he made his way up, hands in pockets to thread his long coat between the seats. He sat heavily beside her, kicking up his black boots. The sun glimmered along the metal loop of Conscientious around his ankle.

"Hey, Cowgirl."

"Hey, Loverboy." Rex smiled at the new nickname, as he always did now that the touching thing was working out.

A football bounced against the bottom row of the bleachers, wobbling to an uneven stop a few yards away. Calisthenics were over. The two watched a player in a Tigers uniform retrieve the ball and pause to give them a suspicious glance.

"Freaks!" he called, then turned and ran back to rejoin the other boys dressed in purple helmets and gold Lycra tights.

"Footballs are retarded," Melissa said. "They're not even *round*."

Rex shrugged. "That must help our team. It makes the game more random, after all."

"Why don't they just flip a coin?"

He looked at her. "Um, they do. At the beginning."

"Oh." Melissa sighed. Even Rex didn't understand how little she knew about pointless stuff like sports.

But Melissa had to admit that she could see the world more clearly lately. Bixby High wasn't as overwhelming as usual. Today had actually been decent until Mr. Rogers had been pissy about the lancing ritual. Now that the school was mostly empty, Melissa had even recovered from that unpleasantness. The bumbling idiots scattered across the football field were strangely interesting to watch, chasing the errant ball like a flock of ducks, even making the same sorts of noises.

She smiled. Touching Rex, letting her mind open to his, had changed her. It alleviated the pressure in her brain. It was like letting a few thousand barrels blow out of a pinched-off oil well. She found herself wishing they'd started a long time ago.

"So which one is she?" she asked.

Rex turned toward the cheerleading tryouts just getting under way on the sidelines. Girls in sweats or last year's uniforms were scrambling to obtain matching pairs from a frilly stack of pom-poms.

"She's one of the tall ones," Rex said. Melissa noticed that the cheerleading candidates were divided into very tall and very short. She wondered what height had to do with leading cheers. "She's half Native American and wearing a uniform. Red sneakers?" Rex started to raise his arm to point, but Melissa pushed it down.

"I got her. She's pretty."

"You really never noticed her before? She's, like, famous."

"I don't *notice* anything, Rex. Things either assault me or they don't."

Melissa closed her eyes. Nothing distinct was coming from any of the cheerleaders, just a blurry, competitive alpha-girl buzz—the sensation of beer foam going up her nose. And the testosterone-filled morons on the football field weren't helping reception either.

She opened her eyes.

"Still too crowded. Let's follow her after it's over." She spat between the bleacher slats to clear the accumulated tastes from her mouth.

"Sure," Rex said. "Just thought we'd try. But I don't want to lose her. She's our best shot at finding Ernesto Grayfoot."

Melissa shrugged. "Whatever. Once she's away from the pom-pom club, I should be able to trail her."

"You didn't get anything in the library?"

"Hardly." Melissa had slipped out of fourth

period to linger outside Constanza and Jessica's study hall. With classes in session, it had been a total waste of time. Only the minds of the two midnighters had come through—Jessica trying to get up the nerve to talk to Constanza and failing miserably, and Dess's brain whirring through the last phases of some mathematical solution. She'd ridden off after sixth period in a hurry, toting her new coordinates toy and beaming thoughts of maps and numbers in all directions.

Melissa remembered the image she'd seen earlier, the fragment from Angie's mind. "Hey, Rex, can we wait for Ms. Cheerleader in the parking lot? These bleachers are making my butt go to sleep."

He laughed. "Sure." A flutter of excitement moved in him.

"Yes," she answered his unspoken question, "there's something I want to show you." She pulled off a glove one finger at a time as they made their way down. "While I was waiting, something triggered my memory. I saw the picture from that woman's mind again, but clearer this time."

"The construction project?"

"Yeah." She paused at the bottom of the bleachers, pointing down the length of the lowest bench. "Whatever they're building in the desert, it's long and flat, like a road."

"A road? To where?"

Melissa shrugged. "To nowhere. It just stops."

"Darklings don't build things." Rex shook his head. "And they hate the highways that pass through the desert. But maybe the darkling groupies are building a trail to get out to some lore site."

"I don't know, Rex. It's pretty huge for a trail. The biggest thing I've ever seen."

He squeezed her shoulder. "Come show me. We'll figure it out once we've found Ernesto."

Melissa nodded and smiled, feeling Rex's quiet confidence cut through the buzz of football practice and mindless cheerleader pep. She put her arm around his waist as they walked back to her car, glad for the thousandth time that she'd tracked him down eight years before, running through empty, blue streets in her cowgirl pajamas, seeking the only other midnight mind that she could feel in Bixby. She couldn't wait to touch him again—at least they had something to do while they waited.

Following Constanza Grayfoot was going to make for a long afternoon.

MADELEINE

"Back in my day, there were maps. You didn't need to consult a polymath every time you built a house. Do you want tea?"

Dess blinked again, realizing that she hadn't said a word since crossing the threshold. Her eyes had adjusted quickly to the gloom, but her brain was overwhelmed by the clutter stacked everywhere: rusty tridecagrams, Bixby town seals, steel window guards thirteen bars across, fireplace grates with a fine mesh woven in patterns of thirty-nine. A vast horde of antidarkling antiques were piled against every wall, jumbled together into jagged metal sculptures that begged to have their angles calculated.

She started to reply, but from another room the wail of a teakettle erupted, sweeping from a low moan up to an angry screech.

"I'll take that as a yes," the old woman said. "Back in my day, young people didn't take so long to answer simple questions."

Dess closed her mouth.

Rex was going to freak when he saw this place. It made his historical collection look like some shabby roadside snake zoo. Here was a whole town's worth of midnighter heirlooms, the heritage of lost generations quietly rusting away. Dess wondered if there was lore here too, not just a few scraps of information written invisibly onto desert rocks, but a library as extensive as the rummage sale around her. She would have to ask. There was a lot she was going to ask, once she got her mouth working again.

"Milk and sugar?" The barked question and the rattling of a tray preceded the old woman's return. "Or is that too demanding a question for you?"

"Just milk." Dess hated tea, but it seemed too late to mention the fact.

"Very sensible," the old woman said. "Milk coats the stomach, and sugar rots the teeth. I never touch sugar of any kind." She smiled broadly, revealing two uninterrupted rows of gleaming white. "You wouldn't guess I haven't seen a dentist in forty-nine years."

Dess swallowed. "No, I sure wouldn't."

The tea tray rattled to a stop on the table before Dess, and the woman sat across from her, grasping the strings hanging from the pot to bob the tea bags vigorously up and down. "Can't trust myself when they turn on that laughing gas. Might as well hire the Goodyear Blimp to advertise where I am."

These words spun in Dess's brain for a moment, then cohered in a moment of clarity.

"You're a mindcaster," she said.

"And you have a fine grasp of the obvious." The woman pulled the tea bags from the pot and dropped them with a wet slap onto a saucer. She poured two steaming cups, adding milk generously to both.

For a moment, silence descended over the tea party. The old woman sipped delicately, and Dess warmed her hands on her cup, lifting it once to sniff. The floral scent of the brew revolted her. The only tea she liked was iced tea, with so much lemon and sugar added that it was basically lemonade with caffeine.

She wondered if the woman could sense her distaste or if the dampening effect of the house was too strong.

How long had she said? Forty-nine years . . . the number Rex always gave for when the last lore had been recorded. But she couldn't have been sitting here in this run-down house all that time, could she?

The woman seemed to be waiting for her to say something.

"Um, my name's Dess."

"Of course it is," the woman snapped. "I know all your names. But it's polite of you to say so, Desdemona. I'm Madeleine."

"Pleased to meet you," Dess said. She felt her manners creaking into gear under the woman's sharp gaze.

"And you. Although I know you all quite well, of course."

"Of course . . ." Dess frowned. "So you can taste us from in here? You can mindcast, even though it's a dead zone?"

"Dead zone? What sort of chicken-fried baloney is that?" Madeleine lifted her spoon and stirred her tea forcefully. "This is a crepuscular contortion, the finest in Bixby. As I said, we had maps in my day. There's one around here somewhere. You might want to see it, my dear." She stood and strode from the room, her teacup rattling on its saucer.

Dess let out a long sigh and leaned back, her brain spinning again. She pulled out Geostationary to confirm exactly where she was, soothingly expressed as raw numbers rather than words, chicken-fried or not. A few moments of staring at the coordinates began to settle her thoughts, and she finally allowed a smile to creep slowly across her face.

She had made her discovery, and it was a doozy. All their lives there had been another midnighter, a hidden remnant of a previous generation right under their noses. While they had stumbled around blindly, a living witness to Bixby's secret history had been right here in town.

It was time to start asking questions. If Rex were here, he'd want to begin at the beginning: What happened forty-nine years ago? Why had she hidden all this time? And how had she managed to disappear so completely? Did she really never leave the house?

"Ah, here it is!" Madeleine's voice echoed through the house. There was a rustle and then a thump as something fell in the next room. She returned, a long roll of paper in one hand, the rattling teacup and saucer in the other.

She sat with a noise of contentment, handed the roll of paper to Dess, and poured herself more tea.

As the map unrolled, the questions that Dess had meant to ask evaporated. Laid out on the worn paper was Bixby, but not the Bixby familiar from the usual gas station map or her father's oil-drilling elevations. Printed in faded ink and cluttered with antique decoration was the bright grid of midnight, the minutes and seconds tangled around each other into dead zones and vortices. The pattern suggested by the coordinates of Darkling Manor was spelled out here in comprehensive detail. This map showed Bixby in the secret hour, the Bixby of her dreams.

Dess swore softly, realizing that she recognized these lines and swirls and shapes. "You've been mindcasting this to me while I was asleep."

"I expect that you must earn top marks at school, young lady." Madeleine smiled as she stirred her tea. "There are always rewards for those who state the obvious frequently and with conviction."

Dess took a deep breath. One question had been answered in full—the woman could seriously mindcast from inside this dead zone, or crepuscular conundrum, or whatever it was. The dreams that had led her to her father's GPS receiver and finally this house had been in crystalline, insistent Technicolor. She'd been pulled here like a dog on a leash.

"You wanted me to find you."

"I had rather hoped you would sooner, but I suppose with your lack of education, you did as well as could be expected."

Dess's eyes narrowed. "Lack of education? I'm in advanced trig!"

Madeleine smiled. "I would hope so, being a polymath. But I don't refer to your education at Bixby High, inadequate as that may be. I mean all of you, poor orphans, struggling to make sense of the secret hour." She lifted the cup to her lips, voice fading. "So alone."

Dess dropped her eyes from the woman's expression and stared into the piles of scrap that surrounded the little tea table. The metal looked as if it had been stacked in haste, without rhyme or reason, but not recently. Rust had joined the pieces together, and a coating of dust obscured every surface. Madeleine had been here for a while. And, as she'd said, *so alone.*

"Do you stay in here . . . all the time?" Dess asked.

The old woman smiled to herself. "I used to get out more. Before Melissa was born, the days were not a problem, as long as no one recognized me." She chuckled. "When I was young, I had a wig and a terribly ugly pair of glasses. Of course, these days I can only leave when Melissa is in school. Poor girl."

Dess frowned. Madeleine's answer had only raised more questions. Wigs? Who was she hiding from?

At least the last part had made sense.

"That's why Melissa's never tasted you, right?"

"Of course. Normally she could spot another mindcaster like an oil field fire on a dark horizon. If it weren't for Bixby High, I'd be stuck in here all day long." The old woman shook her head. "And mind you, Dess: she must never know. Everything in Melissa's mind will eventually make its way out into the desert. At midnight, no one's thoughts are her own."

Silence fell over them again. Dess realized she should be finding out more and almost wished that Rex were here. He was fond of timelines, ordered sequences of events. *Begin at the beginning,* he would insist. But what was the beginning here? History was so messy, like some endless equation where every step only led to another batch of variables. She sat still for a moment, trying to pull the right question from the tangle of her mind.

"So . . . what happened?" she finally said.

The woman sighed. "They won."

Dess blinked and took a sip of tea. It was lukewarm and bitter, but it cleared her head.

"It was the oil boom that did it," Madeleine continued. "Bixby was a family before all those people arrived, all that money. We knew who could be trusted and who couldn't."

Dess tried to imagine Bixby back then, but all she could conjure was a grainy, black-and-white music video with a lot of just-plain-folks drinking lemonade, quilting, and waving to each other from fire trucks. But somebody must have been doing trig, making weapons, and kicking darkling ass.

And they'd have worn sunglasses, wouldn't they? Midnighters' eyes couldn't deal with full-strength sunlight. Did they even *have* sunglasses back then?

She shook the vision from her head. "Sixty years ago, right? Rex always says that's when it changed."

"A clever boy, your Rex." Madeleine smiled. "Bixby had survived the dust bowl and the Great Depression; it was ready money that brought us low. Of course, as a young girl, I thought it was exciting. New faces, clothes from a store, our own movie theater. But after a time, we didn't know our neighbors anymore." She clenched her teeth. "I remember the summer when it happened."

A cool and invisible finger traced Dess's spine. "When they came and got everyone?"

The old woman lifted an eyebrow. "Oh, no, not that. I'm talking about air-conditioning."

"Huh?"

"In the summer of 1949, I had just turned eleven. We played all day until it grew dark, which in summer was very late. Young children and teenagers together, while the adults sat on the porches, visiting. Everything was in the open, everyone could see each other." Madeleine drew her arms around her shoulders. "But then one evening we were playing, and we looked up and all the adults had vanished."

Dess swallowed. "Darklings?"

"No." The old woman shook her head sadly. "Air-conditioning. It was the first really hot night that summer, and they'd all gone inside, shutting up the doors just as tight as they could. Instead of our parents and neighbors, all that remained to watch us was a faint blue glow coming from the windows."

"A blue glow? Like midnight?"

"No. Television."

"*What?*"

"Try to pay attention, dear," Madeleine snapped. "That summer, all that oil-boom money had been spent on air conditioners and televisions. It was the beginning of the end."

Dess cleared her throat. "Hang on—you're saying you lost to the darklings because of *air-conditioning*?"

Madeleine lifted a finger sternly. "And television. You can't discount television. You see, Dess, after that first evening the adults stayed inside, watching Mr. Jack Benny instead of looking after

223

our childish games." She raised her eyes and looked directly into Dess's, a thin smile on her lips. "The games changed that summer. Certain children had always wanted to play a different kind of game. Do you know the kind I mean?"

Dess swallowed. For a moment Madeleine's face had looked exactly like Melissa's, changing the way hers did when the silence of midnight descended, suddenly cool and remote.

"Um, I don't think so."

"I think you do. The games certain children enjoyed were of cruelty and dominance and, most importantly, exclusion. Now they had their chance."

Dess said softly, "Sounds kind of like Bixby High." She leaned back and took a drink of the bitter tea, wondering if the old woman was kidding, or crazy, or actually telling the truth. *Airconditioning?*

Madeleine nodded. "That was the beginning of Bixby High as it is now. On school days I can hardly taste anything but that place." She sighed. "That poor girl Melissa. It's a wonder she hasn't done worse things than she has."

Dess leaned forward, her voice firm, trying to

get Madeleine back to her story. "But that's not all that happened. I mean, Rex says the lore just *ends*. You guys didn't stop fighting the darklings because you were busy watching TV, did you?"

Madeleine shook her head slowly. "It happened seven years later, but the end had already begun that summer. Three children learned the secret. In one of the unseen games we played, a young midnighter revealed the truth."

"Why?"

She seemed to want to shrug, but it came out as a trembling of her shoulders. "To curry favor, to be *included*, I suppose. Thousands of years of secrecy lost because no one was watching.

"In any case, once these three daylighters knew the truth, they started a new game. They went out into the desert every night and arranged stones, hoping to send messages to the beings they knew were out there."

Dess nodded. "Kids still do that. They try, anyway."

"The tradition is an old one. Even I can feel them sometimes, their terror or disappointment coming across the desert just after midnight. But these three were more determined than most.

They wanted to play this game to the end. For years they tried to learn what meaning the moving stones had, and when that failed, they brought a young seer out into the desert with them one night. A gift for the darklings."

Dess put her teacup down sharply, and the lukewarm liquid sloshed over the rim, staining her fingers. "The halfling."

Madeleine nodded. "An appropriate term, I suppose. There was never a name in the proper lore for what she became. I knew her as Anathea."

"But you're a mindcaster. Why didn't you know what was going on?"

"None of us did. Early on, the three had moved to Broken Arrow—outside the range of our powers. They never came to Bixby, just as I fear to leave this house. They made their plans in secret and became very rich."

"Rich? The darklings pay well?"

"In a way, yes. The oldest of them know what lies in the desert, the veins of rock, and the ancient hollows of water. Like a metallurge." She smiled at Dess's confusion. "A talent you've never heard of—there are many others, poor girl. Suffice it to say that the darklings can taste the earth, just as they taste your clever little mind at midnight." Madeleine narrowed her eyes, and Dess felt a chill pass through her. "So the three were paid. Oil for blood."

"Oh." The word *oil* sent a chill through her. She remembered the name on the letter that Jonathan had found at Darkling Manor. "Were any of those kids called Grayfoot, by any chance?"

"Very good." Madeleine's excellent teeth appeared in the dying light of the afternoon. "You may have a chance yet, young lady."

Dess frowned. "But I thought the darklings hated oil wells."

"They do. But the darklings also tell the Grayfoots where *not* to drill. They use their human allies to preserve their own places."

Dess nodded slowly. "And eventually these . . . allies came and got you."

"With their hired help. It only took one night, in the wee hours after midnight, and we and our closest daylighter allies were all but finished." She swept her eyes around the cluttered room. "We were prepared for an attack from darklings, not from men. All this metal . . . useless."

"At least you escaped."

Madeleine nodded. "I had snuck out of my parents' house that night to play some of those games I mentioned earlier. We came here, knowing this was the safest place in the secret hour, a contortion so deep that the darklings didn't know of its existence." She rapped a bony knuckle sharply against the grain of the table. "And still don't, knock on wood."

"We? There are more of you?"

Madeleine shook her head slowly. "There were. One left Bixby a few days later at high noon, and we never heard from him again. The others grew old and died, one by one. Here in this house."

Dess took a deep breath, the musty smell of the room suddenly taking on a disturbing flavor. She had expected to find a mystery here, some strange new terrain of midnight amid the tangled minutes and seconds. But this place held only tragedy, isolation, and lingering death.

Madeleine smiled, her expression reminding Dess of Melissa again. "You did ask, my dear. I can't be blamed for answering."

Dess snorted. "Hang on, *you* called me." She

frowned. "Why did you call me, again?"

"Because I'm tired of hiding." Madeleine took a sip of her tea. "And I have also become quite sure that without my help, none of you shall survive."

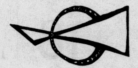

18
10:42 P.M.

CONSTANZA

Constanza Grayfoot led a busy life.

In one afternoon she'd led them to the veterans' hospital on I-35, on a long visit to the stores of downtown Bixby, and through the tempest of the Tulsa Mall. And now, nine dollars in gas money later, they had wound up where they should have started—down the street from her house, waiting for midnight to fall.

Only one problem: they were practically unarmed. Rex stared out the front windshield at a stunted, gnarled mesquite tree, the most immediate sign of the nearby badlands.

"This is not good."

"I thought you said the house was clean," Melissa said.

"It is." In a few slow drive-bys Rex had determined that Constanza's house didn't have a lick of Focus on it. If her family was working with the darklings, they were doing it somewhere else. "But won't they feel us out here?"

Melissa shrugged. "If they're looking for us, they will."

"Yeah, well, I blew all my weapons on Sunday night. This is not a great time for a rumble."

"We can always do another brilliant improvisation," she said. "And Categorically Unjustifiable Appropriation is in the trunk, as yet untouched by inhuman hands. By the way, I'm still waiting for you to stick it back on my tire. Any day now would be fine."

"We should wait," Rex said. "Drive back into town now and come back after we get some more weapons from Dess."

"From Dess?" Melissa laughed. "Haven't you noticed? That girl's too busy with her own projects to make anything for us. She's about as useful as Jonathan these days."

Rex shook his head. "Dess'll be pitching in soon enough. We're going to need her to find whatever's out in the desert. Until then, she can play with all the maps she wants."

"You think Dess can turn the pictures I got from Angie's mind into coordinates?"

"That might be complicated." Rex looked at her and frowned. "You might have to . . ." He didn't bother to finish. They were miles from the mind noise of central Bixby, it was late at night, and the emotion was strong in him; Rex knew she could read the thought.

She smiled and reached over to touch his arm with a gloved hand.

"Don't worry, Loverboy. I wouldn't think of besmirching your honor that way."

He smiled back at her but felt his face flush. There was no point in denying the stab of jealousy he felt at the thought of Melissa touching Dess, sharing her mind as she'd shared it with him. It had been bad enough that time with Jonathan out in the desert. *But there was no choice,* Rex reminded himself. If she hadn't, they'd all have been darkling meat.

Speaking of which . . . He looked at his watch.

Over an hour. Enough time to get back to home and safety before midnight. "Maybe we should come back with Jessica. We wouldn't need weapons with her around."

"Ah, the mighty flame-bringer. Too bad she's grounded."

Rex sighed, wondering if any seer in history had ever had to deal with such a motley crew of midnighters.

"Of course," Melissa continued, "she could have spent the night with Constanza this weekend. Then she'd be here waiting for us, flashlight in hand. Only she'd be way too chicken now. Too bad you and Flyboy had to blab."

Rex stared at her. "What else were we supposed to do? Just 'forget' to tell Jessica about Ernesto Grayfoot? Let her spend the night out here, not knowing the danger?"

"Yeah, you're right. Jonathan would have told her anyway." Melissa chuckled. "Plus it's *wrong* to keep secrets. And as far as secrets go, you wouldn't want Jessica to witness any serious mindcasting, would you? She might wonder why her parents let her go to that party last week."

Rex just kept his mouth shut, not rising to the

bait. Melissa had changed so much these past three days. She could almost tolerate school now, had kept her cool even in the Tulsa Mall, and had picked up Constanza's scent every time they'd lost her on the road. Her mind seemed clearer all the time.

But certain things hadn't changed. Rex knew firsthand how caustic she was on the inside, still wounded from sixteen years of physical isolation. Not to mention the eight years of loneliness before the two of them had met, a childhood spent fighting off the collective mind storm of humanity all alone. He wondered if Melissa would ever recover from being born the only mind-caster in Bixby.

He looked at his watch. "Well, it's not that late. We could call her from that Seven-Eleven back on Forty-four and tell her and Jonathan to come here tonight."

The smile on her face flickered again with amusement. "Requesting help from Flyboy?"

"He saved your life, I seem to remember."

The smile faded. "Oh, that. My secret shame." She let out a long sigh. "Fine. Here's a quarter."

★ ★ ★

The kitchen window opened easily, but climbing in turned out to be tricky. Especially while carrying Categorically Unjustifiable Appropriation, which Rex had brought along just in case there wasn't time to make it back to the car. When he blindly planted his foot in a sink full of dirty dishes, the clatter echoed throughout the house.

"Christ, Rex," Melissa said from behind him. "It's lucky you're not a real burglar. You could wake the dead."

"I'm thinking more haste than stealth, Cowgirl. Taste anything yet?"

She lifted her nose to the air, her eyes catching the rising arc of the moon with a violet flash. "They're curious, but nothing wicked this way comes. Yet. And Jonathan's headed toward Jessica's right on schedule." She frowned. "That's funny. I can't taste Dess anywhere."

"Maybe she found one of her blind spots," he said. "Anyway, come on."

The house was even bigger than it had looked from the outside, the living room long enough to hold a bowling alley. As Melissa stopped to plunk out a few notes on the grand piano in the corner, Rex searched for signs of Focus. But the house was clean on the inside too.

He smiled. Maybe they would get out of here without a rumble.

"Upstairs?" he suggested.

When they found Constanza's room, Melissa let out a laugh. "*This* is Jessica's only friend?" She shook her head. "I don't know why we bother trying to compete."

Rex had to chuckle. Clothes were scattered everywhere, as if a whirlwind had emptied the two huge closets. One entire wall was covered with mirrors, in front of which a frozen Constanza posed, trying on one of her purchases of the day. The floor was littered with discarded price tags, any one of which represented Rex's clothing budget for the decade.

"She's up late," he said.

"Why sleep when you can look at yourself in the mirror?"

"Just be careful with her."

Melissa snorted. "I'll try not to damage the shopping lobe."

Rex laughed but turned away as her hands reached for the motionless figure. He could do without seeing Melissa's expression of delight as she entered Constanza's mind. It was different with stiffs, of course, a one-way intervention completely unlike what the two of them shared. Even during daylight hours, if Melissa accidentally touched a normal human, it only heightened her usual sensitivity. The only true connection happened between a mindcaster and another midnighter.

Still, he didn't want to watch.

The upstairs hallway led him to another bedroom, even larger than Constanza's. Two frozen figures occupied the bed, and Rex retreated from the room after one look at their pale, blank faces.

The last room on the second floor was a study, the desk crowded with papers and books. Rex sat down and began to leaf through them, looking for phone numbers, letters, or anything with the name Ernesto on it. Most of the papers had to do with oil drilling, federal regulations, and financial forecasts, long columns of numbers that possibly even Dess would have found boring.

After a few minutes, however, a bound sheaf caught his eye. The front page read:

237

He took a slow breath, recalling the image that Melissa's touch had left in his mind in the parking lot this afternoon. The long black highway, absolutely straight, stretching out into the glimmering white of the salt flats, ending in the middle of nowhere.

"A road in the desert . . . ," Rex murmured. He remembered seeing an op-ed piece in the *Bixby Register* over the weekend, someone complaining about a new runway being built outside of town.

Of course. The groupies weren't building this thing; they were trying to *stop* it from being built. Darklings hated human intrusions into the desert; highways, pipelines, and oil derricks forced them even farther out into the badlands. And anything built by Aerospace Oklahoma would bring advanced metals and fancy machines along with it—just the sort of new technologies that had chased the darklings into the secret hour to begin with.

Rex opened the folder and skimmed the report.

It argued that the runway was actually being built to allow Aerospace Oklahoma to test experimental aircraft, huge planes whose thundering booms would wake up everyone in town in the middle of the night.

He raised an eyebrow. Rex doubted that anyone would ever want to land a plane near Bixby unless it really *was* an emergency.

He remembered the stolen thoughts that Melissa had shared with him: in Angie's mind, the road in the desert and the halfling were strongly associated. But what could a runway have to do with a half-midnighter, half-darkling creature? They had to find Angie again or someone else who knew.

Rex searched the report, but the name of its author was nowhere to be found. He delved deeper into the desk, opening drawers and searching pigeonholes, no longer trying to conceal the fact that it had been rifled. There had to be more here, a list of names related to the report or some indication of a sponsoring organization, anything that would show who else was involved with the darkling groupies. But other than the one folder, he found only oil business documents, a few personal letters, a massive credit card bill, and a party invitation. Nothing more about an emergency runway, and nothing that mentioned Ernesto Grayfoot. There were maps and geological data that Dess might be able to make sense of, but he couldn't tell what was important.

Finally Rex sighed and let the papers drop from his hands. He couldn't make much headway through the mass of paper in what was left of the secret hour, not without help. But maybe knowing about the emergency runway would help focus Melissa's casting. Constanza's parents must have something useful in their heads.

Rex stood, clutching the folder in one hand, and turned toward the door.

Melissa was standing there, her face grim.

"What is it?" he asked. "Does Constanza know something?"

"Not a clue about darklings or anyone called Angie. But I found Ernesto Grayfoot in there. They're cousins, I think."

"Okay, that's a start. I want you to . . ." His voice faded into silence. Melissa had closed her eyes, swaying on her feet. "What's up?"

Her eyes opened slowly. "They're coming, Rex."

Fear clutched his stomach, like the time his

father had pointed a loaded gun at him, dead drunk. "The halfling?"

"Not the halfling, nothing that exotic. Just three old darklings . . . hungry ones."

He looked at his watch: it was twenty-five minutes into the secret hour. "Where the hell are Jonathan and Jessica?"

Melissa cocked her head, searching the psychic web of the secret hour for the familiar taste of their minds. "Miles from here. Over by Aerospace Oklahoma."

"Headed this way?"

"No. Just sitting there. They're . . . confused." She opened her eyes. "I thought you said you talked to her."

"I said I left a message. She wouldn't let me talk to Jessica."

"You left a message? *Who* wouldn't let you talk to Jessica?"

"The girl who answered the phone. But she said she'd tell Jessica right away. I think it was her little sister."

19

DIRECTIONS

The razor-wire fence stretched in both directions out of sight, shimmering with pale fire in the dark light of the fully risen moon. Jonathan remembered their flight through the Aerospace Oklahoma complex two weeks before, the relentless frenzy of their pursuers. He'd almost lost Jessica that night when their hands had slipped apart and she'd fallen to the ground. The memory sent a nervous shudder through him.

Of course, these days those same creatures were scared of Jessica, now that she knew her talent. Even this close to the badlands, they hadn't seen a slither all night.

"Anything coming back to you?" he asked.

Jessica nodded slowly, pointing east. "The fence was on our left, so we were driving that way."

"Yeah, that makes sense. That road leads to Rustle's Bottom."

"Great." She smiled happily, gesturing in the opposite direction. "So Constanza's must be back *that* way."

Jonathan took a deep breath. This was taking forever. "I thought you spent the night there."

"*Once*, okay? Constanza drove me to her house from school. I didn't pay that much attention to where we were going."

"No kidding."

"I was kind of preoccupied. You know, about to discover my mystical destiny and everything?"

"All right, sorry." Great, it was going to be another night of apologizing. "Let's keep moving."

They turned and held hands, launched themselves down the empty highway, long strides eating up the distance. The coils of razor wire to their right flashed past ominously as their speed increased.

"I don't understand why Rex thought I'd know where Constanza's house is. I've only been in this town a month." She sighed. "Even if it seems like years."

"It's all right, Jess. We'll find it." Jonathan hoped she would keep her mind on flying. One false step and they'd find themselves plowing into the top of the fence—razor wire at sixty miles an hour wouldn't be pretty.

"I could have called Constanza or something, but Beth didn't give me the message until she got off the phone to Chicago. Five minutes before midnight. Little twit."

Jessica sank into silence, her expression tight. Jonathan wondered if Beth would be such a pain if Jessica didn't do things like lock her in the closet. Another few leaps and they had cleared the perimeter of Aerospace Oklahoma, the pulsing coils of razor wire dropping behind them. Finally.

"Look, Rex and Melissa are probably okay. I bet they just wanted to show us something. What did your sister say, exactly?"

Jessica was silent until they had landed and jumped again, angling past an old VW Bug frozen on the highway. "She said, 'Rex and Melissa are at Constanza's. They need you.' That doesn't sound optional."

Jonathan snorted. What it sounded like was Rex giving orders. "Come on. You know how cautious

Rex is. He wouldn't go this far out at midnight without serious weaponry. Maybe they brought Dess along."

"I hope you're right. Let's just get there."

"It would help if we knew where *there* was."

"I'm trying, all right?"

They climbed a highway overpass, and Jonathan groaned at the view before them. The highway extended out toward the badlands, with a dozen or so turnoffs between here and the other end of Bixby County, every one of which led to long stretches of housing developments. From up in the mountains in normal time, you could see them glittering, the black river of asphalt spinning off into bright eddies of streetlamps and backyard security lights. But here at midnight, nothing glowed except the dark moon. Constanza's house could be anywhere in the blue expanse of desert.

However frustrating this was, at least they were flying. His sore throat was gone, his ankle had stopped hurting, and last night he had started to clear things up between him and Jessica. If Rex hadn't left his cryptic little message, this would have been the perfect hour to spend time in some high place with her, alone.

Thank you, Rex and Melissa.

Jonathan wondered how those two could have gotten themselves into trouble again so soon, forty-nine hours after their last scrape. Were they *trying* to get killed? Last night Melissa had seemed different, as if Rex's calm, collected sanity was slowly seeping into her. But maybe the opposite was happening too, and Melissa's madness was bleeding into Rex.

Since Jonathan had touched her, feeling what it was really like inside her head, he'd wondered if at the core of her bitterness lay a genuine death wish, a desire to permanently escape the torment of never having her brain to herself.

Suddenly something flashed through his mind.

"Decatur Street?" he said softly.

"Yes!" Jessica cried. "I was *just* thinking that. I remember now. That's the exit she took."

Jonathan swallowed. "That's weird."

"So you knew where she lived all along?"

"Me?" Jonathan laughed. "Yeah, right. Like I spend a lot of time with cheerleaders."

He pointed off to the right, tugging Jessica toward an exit ramp. They leapt across a quartet of gas stations arrayed around an intersection, coming down onto a rough, undeveloped field. Rainbow cacti dotted the field like spiky basketballs, and Jonathan slowed their pace. He'd clipped a cactus once in the secret hour—as sharp as razor wire, with the added bonus of spines that broke off and stayed in you.

From the top of their next jump Jonathan saw a dark cluster of houses in the distance.

"Look familiar?"

"Yeah. I think that's her neighborhood. She's not just a cheerleader, you know."

"Sorry," Jonathan muttered. "I'm just saying, I had absolutely no idea where Constanza lived. I'd never given it a thought until tonight."

"But you just said—"

"I know." He could feel the last few jumps settling into his mind, the way the angles always did. But this familiarity made no sense. Somehow he could see the approach to Constanza's house as clearly as the trip to Jessica's every night, every open field and rooftop, all the landings between here and the two-story mansion sitting on the biggest lot of the development.

But he'd never been here before. Not once.

★ ★ ★

A haze appeared on the horizon, a crooked column like the dust devil they'd seen three nights before. But this one was much larger and in motion, the black and fluttering shapes of slithers forming a whirling vortex over the house.

"Crap. Looks like they did need us."

"I hope we're not too late." Jessica pulled out her flashlight and put it to her lips. Jonathan heard her whisper above the screeching, "Demonstration."

The cloud wheeled in the air before them, starting to bleed away into the desert, the beating of leathery wings roaring like a hundred flags in a high wind. He wondered if the darklings had already left, their ancient minds sensitive enough to have felt the flame-bringer coming and smart enough to flee.

"Um, Jonathan . . . could you?" Jessica held out her wrist.

He smiled and said, "Acariciandote," slowly and clearly to the bracelet.

"Thanks," she said. "I'll learn. Promise."

"I'll give you lessons." Jonathan pulled his chain over his head and murmured, "Rubbernecking." It was good to have it ready, even if he probably wouldn't need it with Jessica around.

At the peak of their next leap the flashlight sprang to life in her hand, its blinding beam cutting through the swarm of flying slithers. Jonathan's eyes jammed shut, seared by the astonishing intrusion of white light into the cool, eternal blue of the secret hour. Matching the horrific screams that filled the air, a last image remained burned into his vision: slithers bursting into flame at the light's touch, a fiery wedge exploding across the black horizon, the dark moon itself paling in comparison to the power of the flame-bringer. Then the smell of burned flesh reached his nose.

Jonathan coughed and forced his eyes open.

Mercifully, Jessica had turned Demonstration off. The flock of slithers had been split by the beam, leaving two chaotic masses careening across the desert. A blotchy haze marked the place where the light had passed through the swarm, like the drifting puffs of smoke left over after the finale of a fireworks show.

Jonathan tried to blink away the spots before his eyes. "Warn me next time?"

"Sorry." She squeezed his hand. Through the streaks burned onto his vision, he saw that her eyes were wild, her expression electrified from the surge of power that had coursed through her. His hand tingled where their palms were pressed together.

He blinked again: Acariciandote was glowing on her wrist, the little charms as bright as diamonds.

They settled on the lawn of the big house. Dead slithers lay around them amid the sparkle of metal. Jonathan knelt and picked up a power drill, the steel bit blackened by fire.

"They put up a fight, at least."

"Rex!" Jessica called. "Melissa?"

A hissing noise answered them, a wet and shuddering sound that carried a foul stench across the lawn. A massive shape lurched from between Constanza's house and the next one over, a welter of legs thrusting out in all directions as the thing struggled to keep itself upright.

Jonathan gagged at the smell, his eyes watering as they beheld the creature.

It had been a tarantula not long before, most of its mass gathered in a bulbous body. But it was trying desperately to transform, the legs receding into the beast, its body stretching, writhing like a giant hairy earthworm. A wet, flailing wing emerged from its back, half formed and sickly. The darkling hissed at them again, and a stream of viscous liquid shot from its mouth onto the ground a few feet short of Jessica.

It was dying.

"Close your eyes," she said.

"No problem."

The scream deafened him at first; then Jonathan heard the burst of flame, felt its heat drying his exposed flesh like a bonfire out in the desert. He didn't breathe for an endless time, then finally was forced to fill his lungs with the smell of the ancient, dying darkling.

When he opened his eyes, coughing as he struggled to inhale, there was nothing left of it, just a blackened patch of lawn and a glimmer of metal. Jonathan squinted through the tears in his eyes.

A hubcap lay in the grass where the darkling had been.

"That's what wounded it," he said.

"*Wounded it?*" a voice called. "I think Categorically Unjustifiable Appropriation gets the kill."

Melissa and Rex stumbled around the side of the house, their faces and hands blackened where improvised weapons had burst into blue flame.

"Just because you showed up in time to hose

251

down the remains, don't go taking credit, Jess."
Melissa's eyes were bright, her voice on the edge
of laughter. The sweat on her face glistened like a
knife.

Rex looked sick to his stomach. "Never again,"
he said softly, slumping on the front porch. He
looked up wearily. "So you *did* get my message."

Jessica nodded. "Barely. Next time, leave
directions."

Rex thought for a second, then said, "Oh."

"We wouldn't have made it at all, except at the
last moment Jonathan remembered where
Constanza lived."

"I had no idea," Jonathan said.

Melissa was staring at him, her eyes narrowing,
tempering the crazed look on her face. "But then
suddenly you did," she said softly.

He returned her gaze and nodded. She knew
something about what had happened in his head.

"What were you guys doing out here, anyway?"
Jonathan said.

"We spent all day following Constanza," Rex
answered, "trying to find out what we could about
Ernesto. It was a bust, so we figured we'd try the
secret hour."

Jonathan frowned and looked at Melissa. "You can do that? Read people's minds when they're frozen?"

"Best time for it," she said softly, her smile sending a chill down his spine. "Turns out Ernesto's her cousin. That's about all I got before things got hairy. And scaly."

"Speaking of scales, do we have to clean this up?" Jessica asked. Dead slithers and the remains of the darkling were scattered in dark blotches all around them. The smell had been mostly burned away by Demonstration, but the lawn was still faintly sticky underfoot.

Rex let out a dry laugh. "It'll vaporize once normal time starts up again. That porch light should get the job mostly done. Sunrise will finish it off."

Jonathan looked up at the moon. "Oh, yeah, normal time. Maybe we should discuss this tomorrow. I've got about fifteen minutes to get back to Jessica's and then to my house."

Rex nodded. "At lunch, then. Except I've got a history test the period after."

"Like you need to study for that." Melissa laughed.

Jonathan stared at her again. Unlike Rex, she

seemed full of energy, as if she had enjoyed the rumble. Even the death throes of the darkling hadn't left Melissa with her usual migraine-addled expression. She seemed to be changing day by day. Was she somehow growing more powerful?

He took a step toward her, lowering his voice. "Something came into my head on the way here. Directions. We wouldn't have found you in time without them."

"I know," she said simply.

"You put them there. . . ." Jonathan swallowed dryly. They'd been *miles* away. "You cast something into my mind, didn't you?"

Melissa shook her head slowly, the look on her face softening, as if she were lost in thought. "That's the crazy thing, Flyboy," she said quietly. "I tasted it, but it sure as hell wasn't me."

20

12:16 A.M.

MEMORY LANE

Dess strained to push her bike faster, hoping that the batteries in her headlight didn't totally croak before she made it home. The shuddering little pool of light that traveled just ahead of her had started out pretty dim, and it was fading out like Tinkerbell full of poisoned cake. She should have started home ages ago; the parentals were going to freak that she was out past midnight.

Good work had been done today, though. Dess patted the lump of Geostationary through her coat. Her mind felt clear for the first time in a week, finally purged of the maelstrom of her dreams. At last the equations had done what they always did, resolving into rules and patterns and

255

meaning. Once again her mind had given her the answers.

A frown flickered across Dess's face. The answers . . . They seemed fuzzy now. She remembered a pattern of some kind that stretched across Bixby. A base-sixty thing, having to do with minutes and seconds. But why had she been out here riding her bike until after midnight?

Her smile returned. Not to worry. That special Dess-triumphs-again glow was sitting pretty right in the middle of her chest. She couldn't remember all that clearly what she'd done since leaving school, but that figured. She'd been abstracted, lost in the world of pure math. And the answers were fuzzy because sometimes the really complicated solutions took a few run-throughs before your brain had them down cold.

What was the trick to it again? That's right, there it was. . . .

"Lovelace," she said aloud.

A door opened in her mind, and the bitter taste of milky tea flooded into her mouth. She remembered. . . .

"Damn." The headlight wavered for a few seconds.

The ramshackle house squatting in the center of the dead zone, the old woman, the secret history of Bixby pouring out of her as the sun went down. But like any good secret, Dess had to hide it from the rest of them, especially Melissa.

Then she shivered in the growing cold, remembering what had been bugging her, the reason she'd switched the memories off ten minutes ago, why she wanted to hide them even from herself.

Madeleine had started out crotchety and maybe a bit spaced-out but had gradually become much scarier, even . . . *Melissa*-like.

But that wasn't fair. Even if her story had scared the bejesus out of Dess, the woman wasn't anything like Melissa. For one thing, growing up in Bixby hadn't left Madeleine a mental cripple. Somehow she had borne the gift of mindcasting without going nuts. She was definitely sane.

Well, maybe not *sane* sane. There was the little matter of air-conditioning. Television, Dess could deal with—Madeleine wasn't the first old person to rag on TV to a slightly nutty extent. (The thought made Dess frown as she wondered if the house had cable or not. Another shiver passed through her—stuck inside for forty-nine years without the Discovery Channel.)

Still, crazy or not, you couldn't deny that Madeleine spoke from experience. She'd actually been there when the darklings had eliminated a whole generation of midnighters. If she wanted to blame air-conditioning . . . whatever.

Car headlights were approaching, and Dess pedaled harder. She was keeping to back roads, trying to avoid being seen. It wasn't curfew that had her nervous but the final part of Madeleine's story. . . .

When the car passed out of sight, Dess let out a sigh of relief. Her headlight was fading badly now; maybe she should just turn it off. Invisibility might be safer.

The old woman had watched Rex and Melissa for the last sixteen years and Dess for fifteen, always wondering why the darklings hadn't bothered to pick them off. It wasn't just their wild-animal indifference or the fact that none of them had ever amounted to much of a threat—not until Jessica had showed up, anyway. Midnighters were good to eat, after all.

But what Madeleine had slowly realized was that the darklings actually *wanted* a few midnighters around, as long as they were isolated, disorganized, and ignorant of history. Midnighters were useful, in case anything ever happened to the precious halfling. Midnighters could be harvested.

Another pair of headlights appeared in the distance. It was a van, white and generic, the kind of anonymous piece of crap you'd rent for a kidnapping. As it drove closer, the cold Oklahoma wind grew teeth, biting into Dess's coat and tearing through goose-pimpled flesh straight into her bones.

One of the windows was opening. . . .

The van roared past, an empty beer can clattering on the street behind her.

"Missed!" she called through gritted teeth. "Assholes."

Her pounding heart gradually slowed, and she reached up and flicked off the headlight. Staying dark was safer after all. Now she *really* remembered why she had been waiting to think about all this until she got home. It was just too damn spooky on the open road at night.

She murmured the other half of the mind trick: "Ada."

The door in her consciousness swung closed

again, leaving one last memory fading before her mind's eye. As she had left Madeleine's house, the old woman had reached out and touched her on the cheek, asking her to say the name of someone important to her from history, and something huge and powerful had surged across Dess's mind.

A door. That was what it had been—a barrier to protect her new knowledge from Melissa's prying because what Melissa knew, the darklings would know soon enough. They could taste each other across the desert all too well.

Then the door closed completely, shutting out the terrible thoughts about harvesting and lonely old ladies and air-conditioning, leaving only one imperative: *Don't let Melissa touch you.*

Dess laughed. Sure, like Melissa ever touched anyone if she could help it.

She struggled along in the dark for a while. Cars passed, but she ignored them, feeling only the happy glow of math well done, equations resolved into rules and patterns and meanings. Her mind felt clear for the first time in a week, finally purged of the maelstrom of her dreams. . . .

A fallen tree branch snapped under her front

wheel, and she cursed. Why exactly was she riding along in the dark?

She switched on her headlight. Dim, but better than nothing.

21 | 11:16 A.M.

UNANTICIPATED ILLUMINATIONS

"So when we got there, there were like a thousand slithers in the air. And this *demented* old darkling." Jessica's stomach turned as she remembered the thing's death smell. "Melissa had pretty much killed it already with this hubcap, but I finished it off."

"Ah, the mighty Categorically Unjustifiable Appropriation is finally put to use," Dess said. She leaned back against the locker next to Jessica's, a smile lighting up her face.

"Yeah, the thing was totally in a bad way," Jessica said. She looked down at her palm, still tingling from holding Demonstration. All morning aftershocks had surged through her, sending shivers up her arm. In the nights after discovering her talent Jessica had experimented with lighters, flash attachments, and highway signal flares, but nothing gave her the buzz of an actual rumble.

She took a deep breath, and the crowded hallway of Bixby High came back into focus.

"So, you got another flashlight name for me?" she asked. "Something . . . light?"

Dess closed one eye, giving the matter a microsecond's thought. "How about Decaffeinated?"

Jessica giggled. "Not that kind of light, silly. More like . . . luminescent. Hey, does that work?"

"Nope. Only eleven. Coronaphobiac?"

"Which would mean . . . ?"

"Someone who's afraid of eclipses."

Jessica raised an eyebrow. "How do you *know* this stuff?"

"I listen, read, watch the Discovery Channel, and the tridecalogisms kind of . . . stand out."

"Hmm. Coronaphobiac? Still not quite what I was going for." Jessica opened her locker and she regarded the pile of books unhappily. "No time for trig today. I promised Rex I'd grill Constanza about her family." She picked up the social studies textbook. Maybe if she brought it along to the library, Constanza would assume she was writing a report about local history.

"You should ask her if any of them live in Broken Arrow."

Jessica looked up. "Why?"

Dess shrugged. "Just an idea. If Melissa hasn't heard their thoughts all these years, they probably stay out of town."

"But the snake pit's darkling central, and that's in Broken Arrow, isn't it?"

"Broken Arrow County, yeah. But the town's farther east, just beyond the limit of the secret hour. The perfect place for darkling groupies to set up shop."

"Okay, I'll ask her." Jessica smiled. "Hey, all that map stuff you've been doing is paying off."

Dess returned the smile. "You'd be surprised." She looked past Jessica, suddenly frowning, and said, "Ada."

Jessica turned. "Who?"

"Melissa and Rex, I mean."

The two were coming down the hall, Melissa

in headphones but sharper eyed than Jessica had ever seen her in school. Rex looked well rested, about a thousand percent better than he had the night before.

"Headed up to the library?" he asked.

"Yes," Jessica said. "No stone in Constanza's brain shall remain unturned."

"That should take about five minutes," Melissa muttered.

Rex rolled his eyes in apology. "By the way, did we forget to say thanks last night? You know, for the lifesaving."

Jessica shrugged. "It was implied—by the not being dead. Sorry we got lost on the way."

"You made it in time." He glanced at Melissa. "Somehow."

"Oh, right." Jessica turned to Dess. "That was the weirdest part of the whole night. While we were looking for Constanza's house, Jonathan and I both suddenly had this brain flash and knew exactly where it was. It was totally random."

"Random?" A puzzled look came over Dess's face, as if there was something on the tip of her tongue. Jessica suspected she was about to get a lecture on the deadly sin of using math terms loosely.

But Dess said, "Unanticipated Illuminations."

"Huh?"

"A new name for your flashlight." Dess smiled, as if at a private joke, the puzzled expression never quite leaving her face.

"You would not believe what happened last night."

Jessica stared into Constanza's wide eyes and found that she simply couldn't resist. "More demonic vandalism?"

Constanza's mouth opened. Closed. Opened again. "Who told you?"

Jessica shrugged. "I just guessed. Or maybe I heard something in the hall?"

Constanza shook her head. "No way. I haven't told *anyone*. Except Liz. And Maria. But, like, no one."

"Wait a second." Jessica forced her own eyes open wider. "It didn't happen to *your* house, did it?"

Constanza looked both ways down the hall, silent for a moment as a few freshmen went by on their way into the library. "Okay, this has to stay a total secret, Jessica."

"Not a soul."

"So, my dad wakes up last night because he smells something really nasty, and in his study he sees that someone's gone through his desk. So he's running around turning all the lights on, and the kitchen's all messed up, and his tools are lying spread around all over the lawn. And the grass is all burned, like someone built a bonfire on it, but with a totally dead-rat smell."

"Eww." Jessica winced. After all the excitement the night before, she hadn't thought much about what it would be like to wake up in the aftermath. And she hadn't realized that Rex and Melissa had been rifling through anyone's desk. Of course, was that any worse than rifling through someone's brain?

"And guess when this all was," Constanza said.

Jessica blinked. "No way."

"Way. Right at the stroke of midnight."

The late bell rang, and Constanza jumped.

"Girls?" Ms. Thomas's voice came from inside. "Please cross the threshold or you *will* be tardy."

Constanza sighed, peering in at the long table full of her friends. "I promised my mother not to spread this all over school because it could be a total real-estate-value downer. But I don't know how I'm going to sit there and not utter a word. I mean, Liz and Maria are sitting right there, just *dying* to talk about it."

"Well," Jessica said, "you could help me with something instead." She waved her social studies textbook in the air. "Do you know anything about your family's history?"

"So, the Grayfoots were a Bixby family until they got chased out?"

"Yeah, that's the way my dad tells it." Constanza looked over at the big table, eyes narrowing as she checked for the hundredth time that Liz and Maria weren't busy spreading rumors about last night's vandalism. She turned back to Jessica. "My grandfather's totally psycho about going anywhere near Bixby. He never even drives through. If he has to head out west, he goes up to Tulsa and then over."

"But you guys live here."

She snorted. "Well, my father moved here when he was eighteen, just to piss off his old man. They always fought the whole time he was growing up, so Dad came here to escape. Granddad stopped talking to him for years, until I was born, basically. And even now my father says they don't tell him everything about the family business. My cousins know a lot more about what's going on than Dad does. They're all suck-ups and never go into Bixby either."

Jessica nodded. Of course, anyone in the clan who knew the truth about midnight would also know about mindcasters and would stay out of Bixby. She wondered how old Constanza's grandfather was and how he'd learned about the secret hour so long ago.

"That's the problem with being born rich." Constanza sighed. "You've got to toe the line or you get cut off. That's why I want to be an actress, so I can make my own money."

"So when did this all happen? I mean, how long ago did the Grayfoots leave?"

"Ages. Like when my grandfather was a teenager. So, fifty-something years? There was a lot of money in the oil business during the boom, and the Anglos didn't want us Native Americans to make any. Whatever happened, my grandfather was totally traumatized. He never talks about it."

Jessica took a deep breath. Fifty-something years ago—about the same time that the lore had mysteriously ended.

Of course, the story as Constanza had learned it made sense too. Rex talked a lot about how Oklahoma history was one big long land grab. The rest of the country had shipped its native populations onto reservations here, back when it was a useless dust bowl. Then the moment the whites had wanted the land, all the treaties had gone up in smoke, and the last Native American territory had become the forty-eighth state. The discovery of oil had only made things worse for the tribes.

Maybe the truth was a mix of both stories. Jessica wondered if the Ladies' Anti-Tenebrosity League had ever invited any Native Americans to its ice-cream socials. According to the lore, the ancient people here had fought the darklings for thousands of years, but maybe they'd been cut out of the secret society after white settlers took over the town. According to Rex, that was pretty much the way everything else had worked back then.

Had the lore ended and Bixby lost all its midnighters just because of broken treaties and old scores being settled?

"Sounds horrible," Jessica said. "But also really interesting. Thanks."

Constanza picked up Jessica's textbook. "But wait, you're taking world history. Who are you writing this for again?"

Jessica glanced at the book. A world map stretched across its cover, the Oklahoma flag nowhere in sight. "Um, I'm not really writing a report. I just got interested because I met this guy . . . well, didn't really meet him. I doubt he'd remember me. But I think he was related to you. . . ."

"Who?"

"Uh, do you have a cousin named . . . Ernesto?"

Constanza laughed. "*Ernesto!* What? Did he hit on you?"

"No!" Jessica felt herself blushing, thinking, *Stalked, yes . . . hit on, no.*

"Oh, don't be embarrassed." Constanza giggled. "He hits on everyone, but he's a sweetheart, really. In fact, if you want to meet him properly, he's picking me up from school today."

Jessica swallowed. "He is?"

"Yeah, we're all headed out to Broken Arrow to stay with Granddad for a couple of days. The old guy's even more freaked out than my parents because of the you-know-what last night. Brings back bad memories."

"Sure, bad memories. Ernesto's coming *here*?"

"Yeah, he sneaks into Bixby sometimes to visit me. He even owns an investment house out in . . ." Constanza's face grew thoughtful. "Las Colonias! How spooky is that?"

"Very." Jessica leaned back in her chair, a prickly feeling coming over her. Her stalker was coming here, to school.

"So, you want a ride home? You'll like him. And he's a total babe, isn't he?"

"Um, no. Jonathan's driving me home today." Jessica hoped he'd brought his father's car.

"Where'd you meet Ernesto, anyway? And why all the interest?"

Jessica shrugged. "I guess it was in Broken Arrow or Tulsa? He was taking pictures of . . . something, and I just overhead his last name. So I thought I'd ask you."

"About my entire family history?" Constanza shook her head, laughing. "Well, aren't you full of surprises, Jessica Day." She winked. "I'll tell him he has a secret admirer."

"Great." Jessica managed to smile.

22 | 12:11 P.M.

DIN

The lunchroom produced an incessant whine in her head, like the sound of a buzz saw going through a box of rats. Melissa could hear the keen of spinning metal, the tearing of defenseless cardboard, and the screech of little mammals scrambling to get on top of each other. Strange—the dessert was chocolate pudding today, which usually tamped down the desperation until the sugar rushes hit. It was probably the gray, slimy chicken livers filling everyone with trapped and panicky thoughts.

Eight more months of eating this crap! she kept hearing.

Melissa turned up the volume in her head-phones, but the screeching guitars only made things worse. She closed her eyes and visualized a barrier around her mind, but it crumbled under a fresh onslaught of anxieties: the chocolate pudding was running out.

She'd been letting her guard down lately in school, expecting things to be easy, as if connecting with Rex was going to save her from Bixby High. That was what happened when you let somebody in—everybody else tried to get in too.

Of course, maybe it could also work the other way around. . . .

Melissa gritted her teeth and turned the tape player off. At first, the whirlwind in her head redoubled without the edge of heavy metal to cut it. But Melissa took a deep breath and let herself stop fighting the cacophony of voices. That was what had finally worked with Rex: allowing the flood of alien thoughts to sweep through her, trusting her own mind to still be there when the assault was over.

For a horrible moment she felt herself being erased, overwhelmed by the crowd, drowning in their petty squabbles over prime seats and chocolate pudding. But slowly, just as when she and Rex touched each other, she came back to herself, regaining her footing despite the storm.

Melissa opened her eyes and held out a hand in front of her face. It hardly trembled, though her fingers were bone white from desperately clenching her fist the moment before. She took another deep breath and, for the first time ever in the cafeteria, pulled the headphones off.

No one noticed. They were all listening raptly to Jessica.

"The rest of her family never comes into town. Constanza's grandfather threatened to cut them out of his will if they ever set foot in Bixby. They're totally afraid to even drive through!"

Well, Melissa thought, *Jessica has finally gotten up the nerve to ask Constanza Grayfoot a few simple questions. Give the girl a round of applause.*

"All of them live over in Broken Arrow," Jessica continued, then shot Dess a puzzled glance. "Like you said they might . . ."

Even through the lunchroom bedlam, Melissa tasted the strange response that bubbled up in Dess's brain—satisfaction at having been proven right, followed by momentary confusion. Then her thoughts subsided back into the mass.

Interesting.

Jessica plowed ahead. "Anyway, the main thing is the timing. Her grandfather left Bixby about fifty years ago, right when the lore stopped."

She paused to beam at Rex, extremely proud of herself for noticing the obvious. At least in the din of the cafeteria Melissa didn't have to taste Jessica's enthusiasm. Last night her metallic flame-bringer flavor had gone off the charts, choking Melissa like a mouthful of new pennies. In fact, Melissa had felt midnight itself shudder, all the way out to the old, fetid minds in the mountains.

The darklings had every right to be afraid of Jessica Day: her talent tore straight through the fabric of the secret hour. And she enjoyed the hell out of it. Her green eyes were still wild and gleaming as she delivered more of the profound intelligence she'd collected.

"Because he moved here, her dad doesn't get told much about the family business. There's only one Grayfoot who ever comes here from Broken Arrow. And guess what his name is."

They all sat looking at her stupidly.

"Ernesto?" Flyboy finally managed. It was so *cute* when couples finished each other's sentences. And what was with Jessica? She was touching Jonathan like a monkey picking nits to eat. His vague discomfort with the touchy-feely contact didn't rise above the din, but you could see it on his face.

"Exactly." Jessica leaned back and draped her hand over Jonathan's shoulder.

"Well, that all makes sense," Rex said. "But Constanza's father isn't totally in the dark. I found something interesting on his desk." He pulled out the folder he'd pinched and went on to explain the vision Melissa had prized from Angie's head.

Melissa stopped listening and wondered if anyone was going to bring up the really big question about last night: How the hell had Jonathan and Jessica found their way to Constanza's?

Melissa had felt the two shooting down the highway, their minds tentative and frustrated, like new freshmen trying to figure out the way to the temporary classrooms. Then suddenly something had clicked into place, filling both their heads with surety and purpose. A flash of inspiration out of nowhere, dumping the information into their empty heads.

Whatever had done the job had left no trace of itself, but for that fraction of a second Melissa had tasted something new out there. . . .

Momentarily adrift in the perplexing memory, her control slipped, and the cafeteria's mob mind overwhelmed hers for a few awful seconds. She forced herself to relax and ride out the tempest.

When she returned to herself, Dess was saying, "There's no runway on any of my maps."

"It hasn't been built yet." Rex shrugged. "I don't even know where it's going to be."

"Hang on, I think my mom knows something about it," Jessica said. "She's on some committee at work."

"But what does a runway have to do with Jessica's stalker?" Jonathan asked. "Or the halfling, for that matter?"

"We don't know yet," Rex admitted. "But it's pretty obvious that the Grayfoots are involved in all three."

"So what do we do?" Dess asked.

"Jessica, you should find out what you can about the runway from your mom," Rex said. "But we also need to go back to Constanza's house. There are tons of papers I didn't have time to look at. And maps and other stuff that Dess might be able to figure out."

"Constanza's house?" Jessica complained. "What, last night wasn't enough of a disaster for you?"

"And now the darklings will be expecting us," Dess added. "And the Grayfoots know we're on to them, thanks to you two."

"Yeah, okay," Rex said. "Us going alone was stupid. But this time all five of us will be there. The darklings won't dare mess with us if Jessica's there from the stroke of twelve. And with more people we can search faster, hopefully without wrecking the place."

"What do you mean, 'from the stroke of twelve'?" Jessica asked. "Flying out there takes a while."

"There won't be time to fly," Rex said. "That close to the desert, we'll need you around at midnight if we want to steer clear of another rumble."

"You don't expect me to spend the night at Constanza's, do you?" Jessica's fear of the Grayfoots cut through the lunchroom din, tasting of sour milk. "They're not even staying there right now, you freaked them out so bad."

"That's fine," Rex said. "You can spend the night with Dess. Melissa and I will pick you up before midnight. We'll all drive over together."

"What about me?" At the thought of being left out, Jonathan was clinging to Jessica's arm now.

"Fly or drive." Rex shrugged. "It's your choice."

No one said anything. Melissa could taste doubts in all of them, but they were more afraid of doing nothing. They'd all started to get paranoid about the darkling groupies.

"All right, then, this Friday?" Rex said, smiling. "All five of us together at midnight again?"

Nobody disagreed.

"Well, *yee*-ha," Melissa said quietly, but none of them heard her over the noise.

As Melissa walked with Rex to his history class, the maelstrom dropped off behind them, her mind calming in slow stages. Compared to the cafeteria, the rest of school was a cakewalk, and her senses sharpened with every step.

Melissa had once read something on a bus station bathroom wall: *What doesn't kill me makes me stronger.* The sentence had stuck with her, partly because it was about the stupidest thing she'd ever read. Things that didn't kill you could leave you maimed, or deaf and blind, or just plain crazy. None of which would count as stronger in Melissa's book. But the bathroom guy had a point. Sometimes not dying, like not being erased by all these years of the mind noise of Bixby High, might have a payoff. Riding out the mayhem in the cafeteria instead of fighting it had left her head clearer, and Melissa had to admit that she felt a little stronger.

As they walked, she tasted a nervous glimmer in Rex's mind.

"Relax, Loverboy. Since when have you ever had trouble with a history test?"

"I'm going to kill the test," he said. "I'm a lot more worried about finding out what's going on in time."

"In time for what?"

"We left a mess at Constanza's. I've overheard rumors about it all day. The Grayfoots must know we're on to them now. They'll act against one of us soon."

"Maybe," she said. "So we ransack Constanza's house, like you said."

He stopped and looked at her. "You were listening?"

She smiled. "I always listen. Or try, anyway. So how hard can it be to find out what they're up to?"

Rex sighed. "Very. We don't know what we're looking for, and the Grayfoots may have already cleaned up any evidence in Bixby. If we don't find anything on Friday, that leaves us with going to Broken Arrow, where we're not protected by the secret hour. And with Jessica's parents the way they are, we can't take her anywhere in real time."

"We can fix the way they are, Rex."

He shook his head. "We've done enough of that."

Melissa tasted the sour flavor of Rex's festering guilt—a perfect example of something that, while not killing you, could leave you very, very screwed up. "Okay, whatever. Maybe Dess can help. Her latest project seems to have wound down. Not much brain activity today except feeling smug about herself. She'll be looking for something to sink her teeth into. We can show her what we found in Angie's brain."

"Right . . . but what if you have to . . . ?"

She felt it in him again, the same cloying emotion that had flickered through him before the rumble last night, possessive and resentful.

She slowed as the emotion overwhelmed her mind, put one hand to her head. "Rex, chill out." People pushed past them, the jostling shoulders punishing her delicate flinch response.

"Sorry." He pulled her out of the flow and leaned her against the wall.

She opened her eyes and breathed hard. "Like I'd even *think* of doing that." The thought of Dess's buzzing little calculations crowding into her brain made Melissa ill.

But Rex just stood there, biting into his own lip hard enough for her to feel it. "What if that's the only way to show her what you got from Angie's mind?" he asked.

Melissa sank back against the lockers, wishing he would stop obsessing about this. His brain traveled the thought on well-worn grooves, like the mind of someone who'd spent all night memorizing a single formula. She focused her mind on the hard knuckle of a combination lock pressing into her back.

"Not just the images," Rex went on, "but the

stuff Dess can use. I can't hold all those numbers in my head. It's mostly mathematical symbols I don't even know the names for. You might have to touch her to—"

"Stop it!" she cried. His emotions were twisted around her guts, as if a boa constrictor had crawled inside her and started squeezing. Melissa could hardly breathe, the mind noise of his jealousy raging like the cafeteria, every bit as invading and much more *personal*. She gagged on the taste of it, and the world disappeared for a moment.

And she saw what was buried in Rex's mind, so deep he could barely glimpse it himself. This wasn't really about Dess. It was about that night two weeks ago, when she'd had to take Jonathan's hand. It had been horrible—she could still taste the acrobat's surprise at what he'd seen inside her, his insipid pity rolling into her head as they'd flown. But in Rex's mind it boiled down to only one thing: before allowing him into her mind, Melissa had shared herself with Flyboy, whose existence was one long affront to Rex's authority.

When she opened her eyes, Rex was holding her, his head turned to keep the bare skin of his face away from hers. The hall had almost emptied, but people were looking at them.

Melissa pushed him away. *Crap.* Her face was wet.

"I wouldn't do that to you, Rex. That time with Jonathan sucked, all right?"

"You might have to."

She looked into Rex's eyes, letting his emotions flood through her without resistance, wondering if he understood how many times she'd been given a headache by some idiotic lovers' quarrel that felt *just* like this: purposeless and obsessive and vain. Melissa had been force-fed a diet of overheard jealousy in these halls for years. The last thing she needed was the same thing from Rex. Didn't he realize that if she'd learned anything from sixteen years in other people's heads, it was that betraying your friends was a fool's game?

The bell rang. Rex was late for his test.

"You might have to," he repeated.

She shook her head. "Try and make me."

23

TRANSORBITALS

Beth Spaghetti Night returned unexpectedly.

Back in Chicago, Beth had made dinner for the family every Wednesday night for the last four years. Since she was nine years old, she'd made the same sauce, used the same gauge of spaghetti (no. 18), and enforced the same simple rule: others were allowed in the kitchen, but only Beth could touch the food before it was time to eat.

When the familiar scent of long-simmering tomatoes slunk into Jessica's room, she stared at her desk calendar for a puzzled moment, then threw down her physics book and ran down the hall. Her little sister turned from the bubbling pot and shot her a look to inform her that the rule was still in force.

Jessica leaned against the door frame and smiled. Beth Spaghetti Night had been one of the small, important things lost in the move, like the VCR manual or her father's windshield scraper, almost forgotten among all the other dislocations.

But somewhere inside, Jessica now knew, she'd missed it.

"Smells good," she said.

"Is good," Beth replied.

Jessica wanted to cross the kitchen and hug her sister, but the smell and sight of Beth at work seemed too fragile to disrupt. Besides, getting that close to the stove might imply an infraction of the rule.

"Don't pretend you're in a bad mood, Beth."

"I'm not."

"Not pretending or not in a bad mood?"

"Not *either*." Beth turned to glance at Acariciandote on Jessica's wrist, as if to reassure her that no amount of pasta should imply she'd been forgiven for the closet incident.

Jessica sighed. "I said I was sorry."

Beth didn't respond. Two days of silent treatment had been her only retaliation for the night before last, but it was slowly starting to get to Jessica. This was the supreme advantage held by little sisters who screamed a lot: it made their silence all the more terrifying.

But a moment later Beth turned and said the unthinkable: "Want a taste?"

Jessica was paralyzed for a moment. But when her sister extended her arm, she forced her feet to cross the kitchen, trying to suppress a suspicion that the spoon was actually coated in extra-strength Tabasco, or battery acid, or worse. She blew softly, and a tiny drop of red rolled off to spatter the white tile floor. It certainly looked and smelled like spaghetti sauce. Jessica closed her eyes and wrapped her mouth around the hot, thickly coated wooden spoon.

It wasn't finished yet, but the familiar buttery flavor of almost-too-many reduced onions filled her with relief. This hadn't been an elaborate revenge plot after all.

"It's great."

Beth nodded. "Told you." She turned back to the pot. "So can I meet this guy?"

Jessica blinked. "Jonathan?"

"Duh."

"Sure. Of course. You could've today. He drove me home from school." The last words brought up a momentary image of Ernesto Grayfoot, but Jessica forced it from her mind, not wanting to wreck the moment.

"Next time he comes by, have him say hi. You know, if I'm not locked in a closet or something."

She smiled. "Okay, Beth." *Forgiven at last.*

The tinkle of keys in the front door caught both their ears, and the subject was dropped. But Jessica felt it between them, a shared secret after all.

The sounds of approach stopped short at the kitchen door, and Jessica turned to enjoy her mother's look of surprise. A grocery bag slumped against her hip, jutting celery stalks suggesting some planned meal now being hurriedly abandoned in Mom's head.

"Oh . . . I bought . . ."

"*Not* on the counter."

Jessica lifted the offending groceries from her mother's grip and removed them to the safety of the living room.

"Mom, could I spend the night at Dess's this Friday?"

"Who's Dess?"

Beth turned from her cooking. "You have a friend called Dess, Jess?"

"Yeah, it's a mess," she said with a grin. "Her real name's Desdemona. She's in my trig class, and it would be really great if we could hang out and, you know, *study*?" Jessica leaned both elbows on the kitchen table and smiled, wondering if her emphasis on the last word had been too obvious. The study angle was the easiest way to work her mother's guilt. It had been her idea to sign Jessica up for all advanced classes after the move.

But Mom's engineering side took over. "Didn't you already spend Sunday studying with Rex?"

"Yeah, that was history."

"Yes, but you used up your ungrounded day to go over there, Jessica."

"No, 'history' as in last week."

"I thought your father said it counted as this week's." She pointed at the calendar on the kitchen wall, where the weeks started on Sunday and ended on Saturday.

Jessica squinted at it. "No way! Sunday is the week*end,* so that week ended and now it's this week."

Her mother opened her mouth but only an exhausted sigh emerged. She spread her hands. "Sure. Fine."

Jessica felt a forward jolt inside, as if she were in a car that had braked too quickly, her arguments piling up on each other like unbelted kids in the backseat. (First law of motion, her new physics lobe informed her.) Beth turned from the not-yet-boiling water to deliver a steely glare. Mom never would have given up so easily on a technical point back in Chicago, before the long days at Aerospace Oklahoma had begun to wear her down. Instead of a flush of victory, Jessica just felt sorry for her.

She tried to smile. "Oh, great. Cool. So, how's work?"

A soft sigh. "Workable."

"That's it? Come on, Mom. You're there like twelve hours a day. There must be something to tell." Jessica shrugged. "How's that runway doing?"

Her mother looked up, a little puzzled. "The runway?"

"Yeah, aren't you on some kind of committee?" Jessica tried to sound casual, as though she always had conversations about emergency runways. "It's just that these kids were talking at school"—not technically a lie—"about how some people in town don't want you to build it?"

Her mother nodded tiredly, then leaned back until her head rested against the kitchen wall. "At school too? Christ. That's what I've been dealing with all day. Suddenly the whole town's gone nuts over this thing. I thought being on the committee was going to be a breeze."

"So, tell me all about it."

"Well . . ." Her mother frowned. "I've told you about air brakes, right?"

"Yeah, that was right after the birds and the bees," Beth spoke up.

"Sure, Mom," Jessica said, ignoring her sister. "That loud, scary noise right after you land, which is the engines reversing to slow the plane down."

"Exactly. Well, and don't get scared about this, because it almost never happens . . ."

"Safer than driving. Right, Mom?"

She ignored Beth. "But sometimes the air brake mechanism fails in midair. A light goes on in the cabin, so they know before landing, but they have to fly the plane to a special runway that's really, really long. They put them all over the country but mostly in the middle. And they're building more now because extra runways are really important if . . . well . . . if you suddenly have to land every plane in the country all at once. You know?"

"Yeah, Mom," Jessica said reassuringly. "Beth and I know about boys, we know about drugs, and we know about terrorism."

Her mother smiled tiredly. "Well, okay, I guess. As long as you're saying no."

"Two out of three," Beth mumbled.

Jessica shot her a look, but the pot had burst into a boil, and the rasp of spaghetti sliding from its box promised that Beth would be busy for another few minutes. She turned back to her mother.

"So how could anyone be against it?"

"No one was. And then suddenly there are all these ads in the *Register*. We think the whole movement's an invention of this Broken Arrow oil family who want to drill out there. They must be crazy, though." She kicked her leatherwork satchel on the floor next to her. "Our geologist says there's nothing out in the salt flats worth drilling, mining, or even looking at."

Jessica's eyes drifted toward the satchel. "Geological reports? Cool."

"Pardon me?"

"I mean, um, they might be interesting to look at," she said. Maybe not for any normal person, but Dess would die for a glimpse of something both maplike and numberish that had to do with the runway. She and Jonathan could fly over there tonight, and Dess would have half an hour or so to devour them. "It's just that everyone's talking about it at school. Maybe I could do a report or something."

Her mother laughed and gave the satchel another contemptuous kick. "Knock yourself out. But the Grayfoots aren't admitting that this is about oil. They've got city hall worked up about sonic booms and experimental crashes, like we're building the runway to test transorbitals or something."

"Sure, I think I heard that too. Hey . . . transorbitals?" Jessica said softly, her fingers lifting from the table one by one.

Her mother nodded. "Yeah, I told you about

those. Airplanes that go into low orbit? They can fly from New York to Tokyo in just—"

"Thirteen!"

"What?"

Jessica's triumphant smile faded, and she saw that Beth had turned around to stare as well. "Uh, it's just that 'transorbitals' has . . . um, thirteen letters."

"What?" they both asked.

"What is that fantastic smell?" Donald Day boomed from the kitchen door, dropping his golf bag to the floor with a clatter.

"I'll set the table," Jessica said quickly. "Let me get this out of your way."

She pulled the heavy satchel from the floor and hauled it into the living room, setting it beside the exiled non-spaghetti-related groceries. She noted its exact location for later reconnaissance and hoped that her mother would suspend all homework in celebration of the first Oklahoma edition of Beth Spaghetti Night.

24

TEA PARTY

"Ada," Dess said.

She saw the knowledge go. One moment the crumpled house held fascination and promise, the sight of it filling her with intrigue and the thrill of secrecy. A few seconds later it was just another house, its curtained windows signifying nothing, like the scores of other run-down places she'd ridden by on the way here without a second glance.

Except that standing there, not remembering anything, Dess did give it a second glance. The exact geometry of its broken eaves and sagging porch triggered something inside her, a sudden, inexplicable need to speak a name aloud.

"Lovelace," she whispered.

The door in her mind reopened, and Dess wavered on her feet. The secret history of Bixby flooded back into her mind—the kidnapped seer and hidden survivors, the crepuscular convolution and the battle lost to air-conditioning—along with memories of maps and charts she'd studied here, everything she'd learned from the veiled archive. And rising from this flood of knowledge was the pleasure of remembering that all of it had been revealed to her and her alone.

Dess smiled. Opening and closing the door in her mind was cool. Maybe one more time . . .

"Quit fooling around out there! You're giving me a headache."

Dess jumped at the booming call from the house. What was it about grumpiness and mindcasters?

She walked up the leaf-strewn path and through the screen door without knocking. Getting yelled at counted as being invited in.

"Be careful not to bump your head," Madeleine said, pulling on a rope that hung from the ceiling. The attic stairway descended, like the gangplank of a flying saucer belonging to aliens who were really into rusty springs. When the bottom step touched the floor, the old woman climbed up with quick, confident steps.

Dess looked dubiously at the loaded tea tray she held.

"Well, come on. Don't let it get cold! If I can make it up here, surely a young person like you can."

Dess scowled at the unfair comparison. She hadn't seen Madeleine carrying anything heavier than a scrolled-up piece of paper. But she placed one foot on the wobbly stair, bringing a tiny complaint from the ancient springs. Another step up and she found her balance, the objects on the tray beginning to chatter like windup teeth.

"Come on, girl! Don't dawdle."

Why anyone would want to build a house with an attic here in Oklahoma, Dess didn't know. It would be a killer heat trap in summer and relentlessly fill up with dust year-round. She kept climbing step by step, reaching the top with only one moment of blind terror when her center of gravity shifted, the tray pushing her backward like a heavy hand before relenting and allowing her to proceed.

Once Dess had cleared the hatch, Madeleine

lifted the burden from her arms and said, "Been a *very* long time since I've had my tea up here."

"Gee, I wonder why," Dess muttered.

But as she took in the attic, her annoyance turned to surprise. Dess had expected a junkyard, like the rest of the house, multiplied by its attic-ness. But it was almost empty up here, no furniture, nothing except a stack of cushions in one corner. A few shafts of afternoon sun lit the dusty air, shining through chinks in the small, painted-over windows. The beams of the roof met overhead, leaving barely enough space to stand.

With a crouching walk, Madeleine carried the tea tray to the corner with the cushions and began to arrange the dishes, calling out, "This may explain things." She tossed the rolled-up piece of paper to Dess.

Unscrolling it, Dess immediately recognized the angles of the house, a three-quarter plan drawn back before the place had started to sag. It was like Madeleine's map of Bixby, marked with the eddies and swirls of midnight, but scaled to show incredible detail. Dess frowned and pulled out Geostationary, checking the digits with the highest precision, effortlessly converting the plan's quaint feet and inches to the device's meters and centimeters.

She looked around the attic again, seeing its dimensions clearly now, and her eyes fell on the corner occupied by the tea tray. Of course, just there, where Madeleine had placed her own cushion . . .

"This is where you mindcast from!" Dess cried.

"I knew your grasp of the obvious wouldn't fail you."

Dess ignored the jibe and stared at the diagram, sinking into its geometries. No wonder they had built an attic onto the house! This was the spot from which the crepuscular contortion opened onto the rest of midnight, a one-way mirror behind which Madeleine was hidden but from which she could observe without revealing herself and maybe even . . .

"Hey, did you help out my friends night before last? Put something in their heads?"

Madeleine paused, a cup half poured before her, and shot a cold glance across the attic. "It couldn't be avoided."

Dess raised her eyebrows. "Uh, I think they appreciated it, actually. Or would have if they'd known what the hell was going on. Rex and Melissa were dead meat until Jess showed up."

"Agreed. Come here and sit down." Madeleine poured out more tea. "Milk, no sugar, correct?"

"Sure," Dess said, making her crouching way to her cushion, the scent of tea turning her stomach. Some mind reader. Madeleine didn't even know she hated tea, even up here in mindcaster heaven, the mother of all psychic duck blinds. Although maybe because Dess was up here herself, her mind was shielded too. Which was a reassuring thought.

"To reach out that far, during midnight . . ." Madeleine shook her head. "They'll have tasted me."

"Melissa sure did. Jonathan and Jessica too."

"Not *them,* you simpleton. The old ones in the desert."

"Jeez, sorry." Grumpier and grumpier.

"They'll be looking for me now." Madeleine looked up and caught her eye, deadly serious.

Dess nodded. No wonder she was in such a crappy mood. Rex and Melissa's little foul-up at Constanza's had cost Madeleine her psychic cover.

Forty-nine years of secrecy blown because they hadn't bothered to leave a clear phone message.

"Yeah, those two don't have their heads screwed on very tight these days," Dess said. "They've been doing the psychic nasty with each other, which has got them acting all . . . weird."

Madeleine shot her a glance. "I know about that too, of course. And thinking there's something wrong with a mindcaster touching another midnighter is a bunch of old chicken-fried baloney. It's helping Melissa gain control." She shook her head. "If only I could have guided them, they might have begun long ago."

Dess frowned, remembering that Madeleine had touched her as well, reaching out casually as she'd left here Tuesday night. A few seconds contact between fingers and cheek was all it had taken, and the mental garage-door opener that hid her new knowledge from Melissa had been installed.

Dess watched the milk swirling into her tea—a collision of two galaxies, one light, one dark. "Well, you weren't guiding anyone; you were hiding."

She looked up, expecting a tongue-lashing.

"Indeed," was all Madeleine had to say.

Dess took a drink of tea: a burst of acid combined with an unsettling hint of flowers. She pursed her lips. Why did she always wind up drinking the stuff? Darn peer pressure.

Madeleine stirred her tea, the tinkle of metal and porcelain filling the attic. "They'll be much more fearful of you now, if they suspect you're no longer orphans. They may move against you sooner than I had expected."

"*Move* against us," Dess repeated dryly. Rex kept saying that too, like this was a chess game.

"Yes, that's why I called you here today."

"Called me . . . ?" Dess snorted. "I had the wacky notion that coming here was *my* idea." Last night Jessica and Jonathan had shown up during the secret hour with a stack of Aerospace Oklahoma geology reports, including a detailed map of the planned runway. During study period this morning Dess had suddenly realized she should cross-reference Jessica's information with the archive here.

But maybe Madeleine had put that inspiration in her mind, just like she'd shown Jonathan the route to Constanza's.

Dess frowned. If this was a chess game, she

had just been demoted to pawn. Which sucked. The whole reason she'd worked so hard on coordinates and midnight was to have her own thing, a piece of midnight separate from the other four, just as they had their private couple realities.

She took a long drink of tea, its acid taste suiting her mood.

"Are all you mindcasters so manipulative?"

Madeleine raised an eyebrow. "Manipulative?"

"Uh, yeah. Maybe the darklings don't even care about you anymore. Maybe you just hang out up here because you enjoy pulling people's strings. And occasionally—*reluctantly*—reaching out to help us."

"Help you? I don't merely help you, young lady. I *made* you."

Dess blinked. "Come again?"

Madeleine placed her teacup and saucer firmly onto the tray, with a look so intimidating that Dess shifted on her cushion. *Could a mindcaster really do anything to you with her touch?* she wondered. Madeleine had installed a mental block in her brain with a brush of her fingers—could she just reach across the tray and hit the erase switch, leaving her a dribbling idiot? Dess's fingers flexed, reaching for the comforting weight of Geostationary in her jacket pocket.

"How many seconds in a day, Dess?" Madeleine said softly.

"Eighty-six thousand, four hundred," she replied automatically. "Duh."

"And how many new students at Bixby High in the last three years?"

Dess shrugged. "I don't know . . . ten?"

"And how many of those happen to have been midnighters?"

A shock went through Dess. *Two . . . Jessica and Jonathan.*

"Oh my God." Her head began to spin, calculating the odds. It all depended on how close you had to be born to straight-up midnight to see the secret hour. But even if a person born within a full *minute* on either side became a midnighter, there'd still be only one in every 720 people, not two out of ten. And if you had to be born within a second or so, the odds went soaring to about forty thousand to one, which made the chances of two midnighters showing up in a row around 1.6 billion to one, in which case two out of ten was . . . pretty darned unlikely.

Dess realized with growing horror that she'd done the thing she hated most, ground her teeth over every day, and constantly railed against whenever anyone would listen. . . .

She hadn't done the math.

"So much for my famous grasp of the obvious," Dess muttered.

She thought of Jessica's mother and her lucky new job at Aerospace Oklahoma, Jonathan's father and his trouble with the police that had forced him to move from Pittsburgh . . . like anyone would move to Bixby to get *away* from cops.

She glared across the tea tray. "You've been jerking people around."

Madeleine smiled.

"And what about us three?" Dess continued. "All born in Bixby within a year of each other? That must be a stochastic fluke right up there with the dinosaurs getting beaned by a meteor!"

"I have to be very quiet at midnight," Madeleine said softly. "But years ago I could cast freely during the rest of the day. When a woman is in labor, her mind is very open to suggestion. If she pushes at just the right moment . . ."

Dess felt sick to her stomach. *Pawn* didn't even

cover it. She took every mean thing she'd ever thought about Melissa back because right here, right now, she was sitting and having tea with the biggest queen bitch of all time.

"It only works one time in a hundred," Madeleine said. "After my successes, I was exhausted."

"But Jonathan and Jessica moved here from hundreds of miles away. . . . Are you saying you can mess with people all the way in Chicago?"

"From within this contortion I can feel potential midnighters all over the continent, so I knew Jessica was special. And at my age I no longer need to touch daylighters to change their minds. But I did the real work here in Bixby, making sure that certain executives at Aerospace Oklahoma formed a good opinion of Jessica's mother."

Dess narrowed her eyes. "Didn't her father lose his job about the same time?"

"He was about to." Madeleine snorted. "It doesn't take a mindcaster to make a company called sockmonkeys dot com go out of business."

Dess's skin was still crawling; the feeling of being manipulated . . . *created* by someone made her want to flee right down the rickety stairs and out the door. But she had to ask one more question: "Why?"

"To save Rex and the lore."

"What do you mean, save Rex?"

"He's older than you and Melissa, and he was born naturally at midnight, a seer. He was my chance to create a new generation. Alone, Rex would have drifted off into insanity and irrelevancy. He needed the rest of you to lead and to protect him from the darkness."

Dess remembered Rex's tales of seeing marks that no one else could see, thinking he was crazy and that the frozen blue world was a dream. She recalled her own awful isolation before Melissa had finally found her. A whole lifetime of being a lone midnighter would have been terrible.

Of course, Madeleine would know all about facing the secret hour alone. . . .

"So you yanked around the rest of us just for Rex?"

"Mindcasters have always recruited midnighters from far away, Dess," she said. "It has been done this way for thousands of years. The ancient tribes would send war parties to kidnap young children with the gift. And in the last century there would be telegrams with offers of employment. My own mother was brought here as a schoolteacher when I was an infant. This is a dust bowl, Dess. It has never been a populous place."

"Oh." She sipped, her mind still reeling. "I just hadn't . . . done the math."

There was a long silence, in which Dess concentrated on not feeling like a puppet. Bixby was so small—of *course* they'd have to bring in midnighters from outside. Otherwise you'd never have more than one every few decades, feebly poking around the secret hour alone, unsure if any of it was real or not.

Letting her mind drift, Dess found herself disturbed by the faint but growing possibility that she was starting to *like* hot tea. She wondered if Madeleine was reaching out with her mind right now, changing the neurons in Dess's head one by one until her taste buds fit the right configuration.

Or maybe drinking tea was like discovering some horrible new fact, and like bad news: eventually you just got used to it.

"So what should we do to survive?" she said after a while. "I mean, I wouldn't want to waste your sixteen-year investment."

"That's the spirit," Madeleine said. "And my request is very simple: you have to end the threat of the Grayfoots forever."

Dess snorted. "Oh, is that all?"

"Easier than you might think, Desdemona. Anathea is wasting away."

"Why? She only lives one hour a day, so fifty years has only been a couple of years for her, right?"

"They took her too young. The human half of her body is being consumed by its darkling side. When she dies, the darklings will have no way to communicate with their human allies. And with the flame-bringer here in Bixby, the darklings wouldn't dare move against any of us. I might even be free again."

Dess's eyes widened. Maybe this had been Madeleine's real motivation all along. It wasn't about saving Rex; it was about raising her own private army to free her from the castle of crepuscular contortions.

"So we just wait for the halfling to die?" she asked.

Madeleine shook her head. "They will try to make another, with my Rex. But you must make sure they never do, Dess."

She swallowed. "How?"

Madeleine tipped her head back, eyes closing. For a moment she looked like Melissa when she was casting—her expression sensuous and yet inhumanly distant. "Joining a human being with a darkling is a tricky business. The place where Anathea was transformed must be special, as unique as the spot where we sit now. You must take Jessica there and raze it to the ground with the power of the flame-bringer. Once white light has burned there, it will be ruined." She opened her eyes. "They'll never make another halfling again."

"Okay," Dess said. "Tell me where."

Madeleine shrugged. "I'm afraid it isn't on the old maps, and it's as hidden as we are here. You'll have to find it yourself."

Dess chewed her lip, remembering the maps and folders that Jessica and Jonathan had brought over the night before, the black bolt of the runway jutting into the desert, its simple geometry mixing with the swirls and eddies of midnight. And suddenly, without knowing precisely where her target lay, Dess realized what had gotten the darklings in such a panic.

"You know about the runway?" she asked.

Madeleine nodded, smiling slowly and regally, her expression like that of a cat.

"Why, Desdemona. Isn't it a pleasant feeling when your grasp manages to exceed the obvious?"

On the way home, Dess wondered why she was helping Madeleine.

The woman had yanked her around like a dog on a leash, manipulating her dreams without asking. She'd boarded up a portion of Dess's memory and nailed it shut to protect herself from the darklings. And she'd messed with Dess's *mother* when she was at her most vulnerable, prodding her to give birth at the exact moment of midnight.

And she'd done it to hundreds of others too, a host of 11:59s and 12:01s that hadn't quite hit the bull's-eye, all to build her darling Rex a posse.

A car passed, kicking up gravel that pinged through the spokes of Dess's bike. Her shadow was long in front of her, the last rays of warmth on her back bleeding away. It was going to be another dark, cold ride home.

Thinking of home, Dess wondered for a moment what her life would be like if she'd been one of those 11:59s. Would she know numbers like she did? Maybe polymaths were people who were good at math anyway, who just happened to be born at midnight. But without the secret hour, it wouldn't be the same. Sure, she could still build bridges, design computer games, or get rockets into space, but in normal time math was just a tool for engineering. And something beautiful on its own, of course, a frozen music of values and ratios and patterns.

But in the blue time *math kicked ass.*

Being born without that would've sucked. She'd be just another kid who lived beside a trailer park. Sure, one who got easy A's in trig and who knew that one day she was going to leave this crappy town behind and make lots of money in the stock market or something.

But she would never have forged a weapon like Resplendently Scintillating Illustrations and slain a darkling with it. In the daylight world there were no darklings to slay.

Maybe that was why she was helping Madeleine. She might be a manipulative bitch, but Dess couldn't imagine living in any other reality than the one those manipulations had created. In a way, Dess owed the old mindcaster something.

Like her life, such as it was.

So at the door, when Madeleine had asked Dess if she could touch her again, she'd said yes.

"Just a little piece of knowledge, protection in case Melissa ever tries to touch you. Something to throw in her face."

Dess stopped pedaling, her bike wobbling. She let it roll to a stop, concentrating on the ground and breathing hard, trying to keep her stomach under control. But in the end she let the bike fall and ran into the roadside grass, puking up lunch and stomach acid at the memory that Madeleine had given her.

Had they really done that? Back when they were twelve years old?

Dess shook her head, tearing up a handful of dry spear grass and wiping her mouth on it. Her stomach was mostly empty now, but she didn't want to deal with this all the way home. It was almost dark and the wind was picking up.

"Ada," she said, and the memory slipped mercifully away. She could feel it just out of reach, however, ready for her if she ever needed to burn Rex and Melissa to the ground.

25 | 8:44 P.M.

DOMAIN OF SPIDERS

"Here's your meds, Dad."

Rex knelt before his father, holding out the tiny paper cup of pills with both hands. White-rimmed eyes lowered from the TV set to meet Rex's, filled with the usual anxiety and suspicion. But his father's trembling hand took the cup, brought it to his mouth, and tipped it back. Rex reflected that dry swallowing was one of the few new tricks his old dog of a father had learned since the accident.

"That's real good, Dad."

One less thing to think about, anyway. Melissa was coming by at ten to drive him to Constanza's, and with an extra yellow in the mix, his father wouldn't be causing any trouble between now and well past midnight. Rex didn't like altering his father's prescriptions, but left alone in the wee hours, the old guy was more of a danger to himself than one extra sedative would ever be.

"You seen my . . . ? You seen my . . . ?"

"Around here somewhere," Rex said, rose, and turned away.

In the kitchen Daguerreotype was waiting by his food dish, rubbing his jaw against the corner of the counter.

"Clever Dag," Rex murmured. The old tom always ran in here when the sound of pill bottles being opened reached his ears. "That's right. Daddy's got his meds, now Daggo gets his."

He wound the key of the sardine can, the dense smell of oil and fish spilling out and sending the cat into an ankle-rubbing frenzy. Rex peeled one slimy sardine from the crush and waggled it by its tail. Daguerreotype lifted a paw halfheartedly, then meowed loudly and looked reproachfully at his bowl.

"Not the time for games, is it, Daggy?"

"Mrrrreeow," came the reply. Eating was serious business.

Rex flipped the sardine into his own mouth and pulled out six more as he chewed, dropping them into the bowl from knee height with an oily *splat*. He watched the cat's ravenous assault for a moment, then wiped his hands, picked up the phone, and dialed.

"Yeah?"

"Is Dess there?" he asked.

"It's me, Rex. The beagle has landed."

"What?"

Dess sighed. "Jessica's been here all afternoon. We'll be ready for you at ten-thirty, all weaponized, like I said. Do you need to talk to Jess? Because we're busy doing something here."

"No. That's fine. See you in . . ." He turned his wrist to note the exact time.

"See ya, Rexy."

The line went dead. Rex sighed. This trip to Constanza's had seemed exciting when he'd gotten the idea—all of them together at midnight for the first time since Jessica had discovered her talent. But now that the evening was upon him, all Rex could contemplate was having to juggle their five personalities all night long, on top of not getting anyone killed.

"Why weren't you born at midnight, Dag? Then you could do my job."

The cat paused to look up at him, then dove back into the dish.

The phone call was another thing out of the way. He'd already talked to Melissa, and Rex didn't see the point in calling Martinez. With Jessica headed into danger, Jonathan would be there on time, if not early.

He went to his room to prepare.

Dess was bringing weapons, so Rex packed light. Into his backpack he stuffed the runway report he'd pinched from Constanza's father, a compass, extra batteries, a ragged twenty-dollar bill for gas, and a snakebite kit (useless for slithers, but useful for snakes). Finally he stuck an extra flashlight into his coat pocket—mostly for when it got dark, but written on its side in block capitals was the name INTENTIONALLY, just in case Jessica could use it in a pinch.

Forget reading the lore or seeing the marks of midnight, Rex thought. This was his real job: making sure that *somebody* bothered to be ready for anything. He stuffed a bottle of rubbing alcohol and bandages into the backpack.

The sounds of a car pulling up outside caught his attention. He frowned. It was more than an hour until Melissa was supposed to get here, and what he really didn't need tonight was one of his mother's surprise visits. She drove down from Norman sometimes on the weekend to dispense advice (and sometimes money, more usefully) and to convince herself that she hadn't totally bailed after Dad's accident.

Rex walked silently down the dark hallway back to the living room. His father wasn't asleep yet—his milky eyes shone in the restless glow of the TV—but the extra yellow had worked quickly enough that there was no passing mention of spiders. The empty terrarium brushed along Rex's shoulder in the flickering light, imagined shapes dancing behind its scratched sides. An idea half formed in his mind that it was darker in the living room than usual.

He peered out the window, praying that his mother's Mary-Kay-pink Cadillac wasn't occupying the front driveway.

There were two vans in the street, their side doors rolled open and disgorging figures in dark colors. Six or seven of them, moving quickly in the

320

darkness, spreading out across the lawn, surrounding the house.

Rex watched, stupefied. Pointlessly and too late, he realized why the living room was so dark. The stark white rectangles that usually flooded through the front windows were absent. The lonely streetlight that cast them had been broken.

It took an effort of will to turn away from the astonishing sight of the attackers. As Rex retreated down the hall—first walking, then running—his brain admitted only slowly that the things he'd seen out the window were not part of a movie or a dream. They really had come for him.

He should have known it would come to this. Melissa had said that the halfling was sick; the darklings would need to create another before she died or lose their link to their human allies forever. They must have wanted to get rid of Jessica before sending the groupies after him, but Rex had made that tricky by messing with the dominoes. Now they were desperate, with only one course of action left: taking Rex Greene to the desert and changing him there.

In his room he pulled on his coat and grabbed the backpack, turned off the desk light, and took two steps toward the door, then realized he was barefoot. His eyes swept the floor of the unlit room, struggling to pick out his boots from among the piles of papers and books and discarded clothes.

Not here. That was right, they were by the back door.

He ran to the kitchen with soft steps, trying to listen for his attackers. Maddeningly, there was no sound at all, no passing cars, not even the moan of autumn wind in the trees. Rex flicked off the lights in the kitchen and peered over his glasses. Even in darkness the boots stood out with the bright detail of Focus from stomping slithers out at Constanza's house.

He sat on the floor, back braced against the outside door, and pulled them on.

Finally he was ready to run.

Rex sat there, wondering how far he'd get. He was panting already, and the figures out the window had been so fast, their movements so graceful and confident. He remembered Melissa's words: *Get some poison.* Rex had let himself think she was just being overdramatic. But the realization rose slowly and horribly inside him that maybe he should have listened to her after all. . . .

The house was still silent, the night disturbed only by the sounds of a baseball game from the television. At least his father would be almost unconscious by now.

Not a light in the house was on. Rex's one advantage was his midnighter's photophobia. He could practically see in the dark.

A sound reached his ears, finally. A knock at the door.

Rex closed his eyes. The knock came again, stronger, and his father made a small sound of irritation: *Somebody get that.*

Why were they knocking? For a moment Rex allowed himself to believe that his paranoia had gotten the better of him. Maybe it was just two vanloads of lost tourists asking for directions. He swallowed, fighting the urge to answer the knock. It would be so much easier to pretend he didn't know who they were and why they were here. Just go and open the door to them.

No one would ever know he'd just given up.

Rex rose slowly to his feet and peered out the kitchen window. The backyard seemed empty except for its usual heap of junked car parts. But movement caught Rex's eye. His old tire swing gently swayed from side to side.

They were back there too.

Another knock came at the door. Impatient now.

Rex lifted the telephone from the receiver and held it to his ear. The little shell of plastic was utterly silent; like the streetlight, they'd taken out the phone line.

He crouched again, remembering all the times he'd had to escape his father's wrath, all the tricks he'd known before the accident. There'd been a way out onto the roof through his bedroom window, but it was blocked now by bookcases. The hiding place under the kitchen sink was still there, but four years' growing had left him too big to fit.

Then Rex remembered the crawl space under the house, where his dog Magnetosphere had always slunk away to be cool in summer and finally to die. The thought of the damp, cold space made Rex's skin crawl. And how could he get down there, anyway? He'd have to find a way outside first.

Then he recalled the bathroom window.

Rex had often retreated to the bathroom when

his father started to get a head of steam up. It was the only room in the house with a lock on the door, and the window was just the right size for a kid to crawl through. But that was four years ago. Rex wondered if he could still fit.

Would his attackers have stationed someone in the narrow side yard? There was no side door, and no other windows faced that way.

He stood, fighting memories of childhood fears. It was his only chance. And Rex was too old to still be spooked by his father's lies: he knew damn well that under the house was *not* where spiders came from.

Rex's steps were no longer quiet. His boots clumped down the hall to the bathroom and set the boards to creaking. When he'd reached the silence of the tile floor, he paused to listen again. The knocking had stopped.

Then the sound of rattling metal reached his ears from the living room. The doorknob was being jimmied or picked. The sound set his teeth on edge, and Rex almost wished they would simply burst through the door instead of taking their time.

Of course, they had surrounded him, cut him off from any help. Why should they rush?

He unlocked the bathroom window and slowly pushed it open, straining to keep it silent. Shrunken by the autumn cold, the wood slid easily. With one foot on the toilet, Rex pushed himself up and stuck his head out.

The narrow stretch of side yard was empty. The darkling groupies had covered the front and back, not expecting Rex to go under the house. Rex heard the panting of the Guddersons' dog next door, and smiled. Of course the trespassers would give the mean old rottweiler a wide berth. The animal was always listening for any reason to start up a righteous barking.

He pushed himself farther out and found that his shoulders passed through the window diagonally. If they fit, surely the rest of him would make it. The image of being stuck halfway filled his mind, but Rex shook it out of his head.

He pulled himself in and lifted the backpack through, dropping it softly to the grass. Then, with both feet up on the toilet and his hands on the windowsill, Rex paused. . . .

The dominoes, the lore signs he'd stolen from Darkling Manor—he hadn't thought of any reason to bring them tonight, so they were sitting on his desk, ready for the taking. Even if he got away, the darkling groupies would recover them. They'd have the symbol for the flame-bringer again, and they'd be able to go after Jessica. She'd always been their real target, after all.

He stood there for another few seconds, trying to hear past the mutterings of the TV. Were they inside yet? Was there time to go back and get the dominoes? The bathroom was next to his room; it wouldn't take thirty seconds.

Rex sighed. He couldn't endanger Jessica to save himself. He lowered one foot and then the other softly to the floor.

Out in the dark hall again, he saw nothing. But his father made a soft sound, one he knew from years of interpreting the old man's grunts and moans: confusion over an unfamiliar face. They were inside.

Rex took the few steps to his room, wincing at the soft thud of his boots against the floor. He scooped up the darkling dominoes from his desk, then paused again. Lying on the desk was Spontaneously Machiavellian Deceitfulness, a letter opener that Melissa had given to him a month ago. As a daylight weapon, it was useless.

But if he was captured tonight, it might serve to carry a message. . . .

He grasped the opener and pressed the cool metal against his forehead, focusing all his terror and anxiety into it. He imagined himself stripped and mutilated, his flesh melded with a darkling's, his mind enslaved to help his enemies.

Then he placed the blade's point against the soft wood of the desk and pushed as hard as he could until it stuck upright, quivering like a shot arrow when he pulled his hand away.

A noise came from the living room, a muffled protest from his father. Rex swallowed. They wouldn't do anything to the old man, would they? Of course, they didn't know how drugged up he was, how unlikely to raise any sort of alarm.

Rex closed his mind to any thought of his father. If restraining the old bastard was keeping them busy for a few extra moments, so be it.

He slipped out of his room and took two steps down the hall. One stride from the bathroom, his boot connected with a soft and plaintive shape.

"Brrrrp?"

Rex halted at the bathroom door. "Dag, shhh," he whispered.

A footstep sounded behind him, from the far end of the dark hall. Rex didn't turn. With the window open to moonlight, he knew he was silhouetted against the bathroom door.

"Rex Greene?" a voice called.

The time for silence was over.

He stepped inside and slammed the bathroom door, locked it, then jumped up onto the toilet and threw himself into the window's maw.

Halfway through Rex reached a sickening point of equilibrium, his front and back halves balanced, the windowsill digging into his belly, blood rushing to his head as he teetered forward. The moment stretched out, unresolved by gravity. . . . His hips were caught.

Then Rex realized: his shoulders had barely fit through diagonally, but now his body was square across the window. He tried to twist himself, to rotate the forty-five degrees he'd need to squeeze on through, but his struggles dislodged the loose window sash, which fell closed, wedging him in even tighter.

A muffled crash reached his ears—the bathroom door bursting in. His attackers had also dispensed with silence.

Rex felt a firm hand grasp his ankle and flailed with his feet while his fingers clawed for purchase at the house's aluminum siding. One boot connected solidly, and a hideous grunt spilled out through the window. The collision pushed him a critical few inches forward, and his hips were free.

The ground was rushing up at him. . . .

"*Uhnn.*" His shoulder exploded with pain, his head clouding as the world turned over itself. After a moment of disorientation Rex found himself on his back, the breath knocked out of him. He raised himself painfully on one elbow to look around. No dark figures, no sound save the jingle of the metal tags on the growling beast next door.

Then a voice cried from the window, "He's in the side yard! This way!"

They couldn't fit through the window, but they could see him. They would watch him crawl under the house. But maybe it would take too long to drag him out, especially if the whole neighborhood had woken up. . . .

He lashed out with his boots at the fence between his house and Guddersons', beating the wood like a drum only inches from the rottweiler's head. Vicious barking started instantly, as if the animal had been waiting all night for an excuse to start howling.

Rex scrambled the other way, pulling himself through the narrow gap between aluminum siding and earth, his head and upper body plunging into the cold, damp world beneath the house. This had been his father's constant threat, exiling young Rex into this shadow place where old, sick Magnetosphere had crawled away to die, this place where tarantulas bred and multiplied in the darkness.

He felt naked, as if he were about to grasp a biting, hairy spider with every desperate handful of dirt. Even his midnighter's vision was useless in the utter blackness. Brittle dead things scratched his face, leaves and branches that had blown here to rot. He was almost all the way under the house. They wouldn't waste time following him down here with the dog next door going crazy . . . would they?

Then he felt strong hands take his ankles.

Rex lashed out, trying to connect again. But more hands took hold, two on each foot, pulling him back out so fast that his coat and shirt rode up, his bare stomach sliding across the dirt. His fingernails skittered across the hard earth uselessly. Twisting half around, he reached up to grasp the floor beams of the house, but they were covered in a damp mold, as slick as algae-coated rocks in a stream.

He gave up, thrusting his hands into his pockets to grasp and scatter the darkling dominoes into the blackness.

And then he was out, the sudden moonlight shining on their sweating faces, at least four of them huddled around him, one reaching a hand down toward his face. But the Guddersons' dog was still barking. Maybe all he needed to bring out the whole neighborhood was a single, blood-curdling scream.

Rex took a deep breath.

Chemicals filled his lungs—a dentist-office, mortuary smell that overwhelmed him, his cry instantly silenced, his mind set floating. But in the brief transit between wild panic and blank unconsciousness, Rex felt a feathery and drugged satisfaction: they wouldn't find the dominoes.

Jessica was safe. No one else but he would dare crawl into that dark space, still haunted by Magnetosphere's ghost, the cold and dank and vile domain of spiders. . . .

26

SPONTANEOUSLY MACHIAVELLIAN DECEITFULNESS

Melissa couldn't wait to get to Rex's and taste his calm presence beside her in the car. Friday nights were the best time to drive out toward the desert, leaving behind the collective frenzy of Bixby wondering why it wasn't having fun. At least on school nights most of them would be headed for bed by now, not driving around half drunk looking for distractions that didn't exist.

But when Melissa pulled up outside the rundown house, she couldn't feel Rex inside.

She glanced at her watch and honked the horn.

"Come on, Loverboy. It's not *that* cold." Usually he was outside waiting, five minutes early or not.

The black, sagging bulk of the house remained motionless.

She honked again. *Christ, it's dark on this street.*

The risen moon glimmered across the shingled roof, but there wasn't a single light on inside, and some redneck had shot out the streetlight overhead. Had Rex fallen asleep?

"Loser," she muttered, switching off the engine and opening her door.

Walking up the path, Melissa caught the flicker of a TV inside. Great, the old man was awake. She'd thought Rex was going to ice him, like he usually did for important expeditions. Stalkers, mysterious runways, and the halfling—they had enough on their plate without aging psychos getting in the way.

She reached for the bell but paused. The knob hung slackly from the door, as if the last shred of the house's spirit had finally fled, leaving behind only broken bones. It spun loosely in her hand, the door swinging inward at the slightest pressure.

A chill began to crawl up Melissa's spine. The

cold metal tasted of nervous excitement, acrid as the smoke of a charcoal fire laced with too much lighter fluid.

"Hello?"

Her midnighter eyes could see perfectly in the TV flicker. Rex's dad was sprawled grotesquely in his chair, mouth open and drooling. There was an odd smell coming from him—a real one, not in her mind. It was sharp and chemical, like paint thinner. She could hear the old man snoring softly.

Melissa walked quickly past, toward Rex's room, keeping her hands in her pockets. The bathroom window was open at the other end of the darkened hall, filling the house with damp cold and the icy glint of moonlight.

"Rex?" she called hesitantly. If the old man wasn't dosed, she didn't want to wake him. But she wanted an answer, some sort of noise from Rex before she opened his bedroom door. She still couldn't feel him yet, which was wrong. His taste should be on her tongue now that she was this far inside the house. His mind always came through clearest, as if he had his own channel.

Unless he was in a deep, dreamless sleep. Or else was . . .

Melissa pushed at his bedroom door with her foot, hands balled into fists in her pockets.

The room was a jumble of black shapes, piled papers, and mounds of clothes, bookshelves pressing in at her from every wall.

But the bed was empty, a tangle of white sheets glowing in the darkness, and Rex's backpack was gone from where it always hung on the back of his desk chair.

Maybe he'd already split, some frantic phone call from him just missing her. But what emergency could have dragged him away from the work they had to do tonight? And in whose car?

She stepped into the room, pulling her hands out into the cold air, spreading her fingers to feel the cluttered resonances of the space.

A plaintive whine came from the doorway behind her, a blur of soft, inquisitive thoughts carrying hunger and annoyance.

"Come here, Dag." Melissa knelt, her long dress gathering in a velvet pool around her, and reached out her hand. Daguerreotype padded to just within reach and then began licking her fingers. The cat's mind tasted uneasy, as if his tiny kingdom had been invaded, and recently enough

337

that his fuzzy little brain hadn't yet smoothed over again.

Melissa rose from her crouch, tasting the air. Something biting and anxious came from the desk. She made her way through the disorder, spotting the source of the taste glimmering in a patch of moonlight.

Spontaneously Machiavellian Deceitfulness waited for her there, splitting the wood of the desk. She'd given it to Rex the week before school started—a letter opener, that silly intersection between knives and office supplies.

Her hand closed on it, and a shadow cast of his mind rushed into hers—panicked and fearful, hunted in his own home, certain of an awful fate if he were caught. They were here, already inside, creeping through the darkness to surround and take him. The emotions boiled off the thin piece of metal quickly, and then it was cold again, but they left no doubt in her mind.

Melissa pulled her hand away and moaned.

The groupies had him, her Rex, and tonight the darklings would turn him into one of them.

27

WEAPONS OF
MATH DESTRUCTION

"What's base sixty again?"

"It's like base ten, except the ones place goes up to fifty-nine, and a hundred's worth thirty-six hundred."

"Huh?"

"Thirty-six hundred," Dess repeated. "Sixty squared, silly."

Jessica looked down at the shield, an elegant spiral snipped from the side of a trash can and shaped to wrap around the wrist. It was for Jonathan, a sort of wing to help him with midair maneuvers. Numbers ringed the edge, but not the

339

normal Arabic kind. They were Phoenician numerals, simple strokes like 1's clustered with sideways V's, organized into something that Dess kept calling "base sixty."

Jessica pushed a pencil toward her. "Just write it down; I'll copy."

Dess rolled her eyes but put the pencil to paper, the figures spewing from its point as fast as thread from a sewing machine.

Jessica ran her fingers across the wing, anxious to get working again. This afternoon she'd discovered that she enjoyed soldering, loved watching the pinpoint of heat turn wire into drops of molten metal, and didn't even mind the puffs of smoke that smelled like a cross between new car and old bonfire.

Hanging out with Dess was cool.

On the way here Jessica had been a little nervous about spending the night with the polymath. The only times they'd hung out were in study period or the secret hour. She had no idea what Dess did for fun in normal time. The bus ride had taken forever, and the neighborhood they'd wound up in . . .

Maybe *neighborhood* wasn't really the word for

it. It was mostly trailers, like the temps at school, the double-wide kind you saw lumbering down the highway plastered with orange hazard triangles. But resting on cinder blocks as these were, hooked up to pipes and wires like hospital patients, they didn't look like they would ever move again.

Dess lived in a real house, although something about it didn't feel completely solid. When the wind blew, which it did pretty constantly out here, the cold penetrated the walls, the whole frame creaking like a ship in rough seas. The floors rang with a hollow sound as they walked.

But Dess's room was fascinating. Dess *made* things. Metal constructions cluttered every surface and hung from the ceiling, welded clumps of scrap iron and weightless filigrees of paper clips and thumbtacks. The deep purple walls were covered with watercolor paintings and a big blackboard scrawled with calculations in red chalk.

"That's you!" Jessica had said when they'd walked in. A self-portrait of Dess with longer hair hung on one wall—black, white, and gray Legos fitted together to form the blocky image.

"Duh."

On a long bench crowded with incomplete

weapons and a soldering iron, Jessica saw a mechanical ballerina clothed in black, its gears spilling out across the wood.

"And that's Ada Lovelace," Dess said, then winced, as if saying the name had given her a headache. "She was the first computer programmer, back before they had computers."

"That must have been tricky."

Dess shrugged. "Imaginary computers are better, anyway. I've messed around with the ones at school. They seem mostly to worry about punctuation."

Jessica frowned. "Mine doesn't."

Dess's eyes widened. "You've got a computer?"

"Yeah. My dad was always bringing them home, back when he had a job."

"Whoa." Dess nodded slowly, as if stunned by the revelation. Jessica got the same uncomfortable feeling she'd had at Rex's house on Sunday—she'd never felt rich before coming to Bixby.

She picked up the soldering iron to escape the awkward moment. "So this is where the magic happens, huh?"

"Yeah." Dess smiled. "You know, Rex and

Melissa blew all their weapons the other night, and I'm supposed to make more. You know how to solder?"

Jessica shook her head. When she'd first fallen into the secret hour, the three of them had given her a crash course on metals and tridecalogisms, mindcasting, and antidarkling numbers. But she didn't really know how the angles of a thirteen-pointed star warded off slithers, or which alloys the darklings were most scared of, or what made a weapon powerful other than its name.

Maybe it was about time she learned more about how this stuff really worked.

"Not a clue. Show me."

They had worked all afternoon, absorbed in the smell of solder and tungsten, ignoring the sounds of Dess's parents coming home. Her mother had finally knocked on the door to call them to dinner, and they'd eaten quickly and in silence while Dess's father steadily drank beer and watched the living room TV over Jessica's shoulder. She could feel Dess wanting to get back into her room, back into the safe space of numbers and constructions that she had assembled out of the junk around her.

But as she ate, Jessica began to notice Dess's touches in the rest of the house. The lights all had dimmer switches, there were·extra phone jacks and electrical sockets in every room, and the kitchen windows were colored with stained glass in beautiful antidarkling patterns. After dinner Dess's father had asked about the latest credit card bill, and she'd launched into a long explanation about transferred balances and how they wouldn't have to pay for another month.

He smiled and said, "That's my girl."

Dess beamed for a moment, as proud as a kid with straight A's. And then the parentals had gone to bed incredibly early.

"They work Saturdays," Dess explained.

"My mom does too."

Then they'd hit the soldering irons again, the room silent save for the hiss of metal melting. Rex called at about nine to make sure everything was in readiness, but Jessica was so engrossed she hardly listened. The shield for Jonathan was slowly taking shape, its decoration forming a pattern that had seeped into her mind over the slow repetition of tiny marks. Even the base-sixty thing didn't give her a headache anymore, as long as she didn't think too hard about it.

She was lost in the numbers when, about an hour later, the phone rang again.

"Jeez, Rex, wake up my parents," Dess answered, then a puzzled look came over her face. "Melissa . . . ?"

There was a long pause, and Jessica could hear the girl's voice from the other end, frantic and stumbling as she rushed through some story.

It didn't sound at all like Melissa.

"Okay, we will. See you soon." Dess hung up the phone, dumbstruck.

Jessica leaned back from her soldering iron, eyes stinging from the smoke. "Who was that?"

"Melissa. You've got to call Jonathan. Tell him to get his ass over here now." Dess thrust the phone toward her. "Oh, man."

"What happened?"

Dess shook her head, as if unable to believe her words: "Rex is gone."

"Gone where?"

"Taken. His house was broken into, and he's gone. And he left a message for Melissa: they got him." She shoved the phone firmly into Jessica's hand. "Call Jonathan. We need him *now*. Melissa was at a pay phone. She's already halfway here."

"But who—?"

"Call Flyboy!"

Jessica looked at the phone, the base-ten numerals on its buttons momentarily mysterious to her. She dialed Jonathan's number with trembling fingers.

He answered after one ring.

"Come to Dess's . . . quick. Rex is gone."

"Jessica? Gone where?"

"Kidnapped." She looked up into Dess's wide eyes for confirmation and found her stunned gaze returned.

"Rex was kidnapped? By who?"

"Just come here. Fast. I need you. Please . . ."

"Okay. I'll be there as fast as I can." He hung up.

"Lovelace," Dess was muttering. "Lovelace. Listen, Jessica? You've got to do something for me when Melissa gets here."

Jessica stared at the silent phone, unable to think. "Do something?"

Dess took her shoulders and spoke slowly and carefully. "You have to tell her. They took Rex out

346

to the desert, to where the runway's being built. That's the only place they can change him. We need to get out there and find him before midnight. Can you tell Melissa that?"

Jessica swallowed. "Sure. But where are you going?"

"Nowhere," Dess said. "I'll be right here. But you have to remember. *You* have to tell her."

"Why? I mean, Melissa will listen to you more than she will me. She doesn't even *like* me. And you're the one who knows about maps and stuff."

Dess closed her eyes, her right thumbnail between her teeth. "But I won't remember."

"What?"

"I *can't* remember, or Melissa will find out. . . ." Dess shook her head and muttered, "Crap! I can't tell you either, or she'll taste it in your head. This is not going to work." She started swearing, a muttering rant in low, even tones.

"Dess, what's happening? What's wrong with you?"

"There's something in my head, something I have to hide from Melissa. But I'm pretty sure I know where Rex is, okay? He'll be somewhere on the runway site. That's where they make halflings, so they'll take him there. That's why the darklings don't want the runway built. It'll run straight through the place where they make halflings!"

Jessica felt nausea rising in her at the thought of Rex transformed. At least the darklings had only tried to kill her, not turn her into something inhuman. She squeezed her eyes shut and opened them again to clear the picture from her mind. "How do you know this, Dess?"

"I can't tell you, or Melissa will see it in your mind. She can't know where I got the information, understand?"

"Uh, no."

"Listen, the darklings feel Melissa more than they do the rest of us, Jess. We have to keep this secret from her. Okay?"

"*What* secret?"

Dess pulled away, her hands shaking. "Earth to Jessica: if I *tell* you, it won't be a secret."

Jessica groaned and sat on the bed with her head in her hands. Dess had lost it. If Rex's disappearance was freaking her out this bad, Melissa was going to be a basket case. Jessica wished that Jonathan were here already, but he was miles away, all the way on the other side of town.

"Listen," Dess said, her voice under control again, "this is just like the base-sixty thing. You don't have to understand it, you just have to do what I say." She grabbed a piece of paper and quickly sketched the runway, each end marked with rows of numbers that spilled from the pencil. "Just tell me to take you to the runway. I'll still know where it is because you showed me the map; she didn't."

"She who?" Jessica asked. "Melissa?"

"No. Someone else." Dess wrote *REX* in huge letters across the paper and thrust it at Jessica. "Tell Melissa I drew this, and I'll agree with you because it's true . . . I think."

"You think it's true that you drew this?" Jessica asked, the paper slipping from her hands.

"No, I think I'll know that I . . . because I'll remember drawing this. . . . Oh, screw it. Just tell her to drive us to the runway!"

Jessica lifted the paper from the bed and stared at it, mysterious numbers and all. Dess was going nuts without Rex around, and Melissa had sounded just as bad.

Jessica took a deep breath, trying to recall the sensation she'd gotten from wielding

Demonstration against the darklings, the power flowing through her. She had taken a lot on faith since arriving in Bixby—trusting rows of thirteen thumbtacks to protect her, believing in a history that wasn't in her textbooks, banking on a flashlight to save her life. But so far, she'd survived.

She had to trust Dess now, even if the girl wasn't making any sense.

"Okay," Jessica said in a calm, firm voice. "I'll tell Melissa we're going to the runway. Because you said so."

"Great. Good."

"In the meantime let's finish these weapons, okay? We might need them." Anything to keep Dess occupied until Melissa got here.

"Sure. Just one more thing . . ."

"What?"

Dess stared at Jessica, her eyes bright with panic. "Don't think about this conversation when she gets here. Don't let Melissa taste anything I've been saying to you. If she knows, the darklings will know. Just . . . don't . . . think about it."

"Sure thing." Jessica nodded slowly and turned to the shield again. *The darklings will know* what? As Jessica worked to finish the shield, she wondered how you didn't think about something, how you kept it from your mind without it being in your mind in the first place that you weren't supposed to have it in your mind. . . .

Thinking like this was far worse than base sixty.

Jessica was still busy not thinking about the thing she wasn't supposed to think about when Melissa's car slid to a stop outside.

28 | 10:44 P.M.
TARANTULAS

"Ada," Dess said softly, and felt the door shut.

The knowledge slid from her mind, but with Melissa outside waiting, the transition wasn't clean. Though memories faded, the anxiety that filled Dess didn't disappear but was cast adrift. Her brain felt disjointed, full of unresolved worry, plagued by loose ends of uncertainty and fear.

"What the hell?" she muttered.

"She's here," Jessica said, lifting Jonathan's shield. "I'm done. You?"

Dess looked down at the bench before her, at the pile of throwing disks made from paint-can lids marked with high multiples of thirteen in Phoenician.

"Uh, yeah," she said blankly. Why did she feel this way, so worried and strung out? Oh, right, *duh:* Rex was missing. The groupies had got him and he was darkling meat unless they found him by midnight. Dess blinked, wondering why her head wouldn't clear.

Man, she thought, *I get* way *too caught up in work sometimes.* No wonder half the geniuses in the history of mathematics couldn't tie their own shoes.

She started shoving weapons into her duffel bag. "Let's move before she starts honking and wakes up my parents."

"We're going to wait for Jonathan, right?"

"Sure." Dess snorted. "But you get to explain that to Melissa."

Jessica scowled. "So I get to explain everything, huh?"

Dess glanced at Jessica. What the hell was she talking about?

They swept the finished weaponry into the duffel bag, and Dess dropped Geostationary into her pocket. She'd opened the window and was halfway out when Melissa let off a long blast of her horn. The barking of angry mutts spread across the trailer park like a fire in a dry field.

"Thanks, Melissa," Dess muttered. At least it was Friday night, and her parents would be expecting to get woken up a few times. There were always fights and loud music in the trailer park during the witching hours.

They ran, duffel bag clanking, across the front lawn to the old Ford, threw open the door, and piled into the back. It took a moment for Dess to realize that the front seat next to Melissa was empty.

Of course—Rex always rode shotgun.

She swallowed. Outside of rare glimpses in the school hall, she couldn't remember ever seeing Melissa without Rex by her side.

The mindcaster's knuckles were white on the steering wheel. Without looking back, she said in a small, anguished voice, "What do we do now?"

Dess paused. Where the hell would the darkling groupies take Rex, anyway? Back to Broken Arrow? She squirmed in the seat, trying to shift the duffel bag. One of the poles from her dad's tent, Daughterboard, was jabbing into her stomach, and she still couldn't think straight.

"Okay," Jessica said, all cool and collected,

"Dess thinks that they'll take Rex out into the desert. To where the runway's going to be."

"I do?" Dess asked.

Jessica shot her an annoyed look. "Yes, you *do*. That's why the darklings are afraid of the runway, remember? It's going to steamroll the spot where they make halflings." She pulled a piece of paper from her pocket and thrust it at Dess.

"Oh, yeah. This." She remembered drawing the map based on the stuff Jessica had borrowed from her mother. But would the darkling groupies really take Rex there?

"Maybe . . ." Melissa's voice came from in front. Her forehead rested against the steering wheel. "The runway was in Angie's head, and it seemed like it had something to do with the halfling." She put the car in gear.

"Hang on!" Jessica cried. "We have to wait for Jonathan."

Melissa thumped her palms against the steering wheel. "We can't wait. I can't just sit here doing nothing."

"He'll be here in ten minutes."

"So what? He's useless!"

"What?"

"He can't fly until midnight," Melissa said. "And we've got to find Rex before then."

The car started to move.

"Wait!" Jessica yelled. "He's *not* useless!" She pushed her door open. "I'm staying here to wait for him."

Melissa stepped on the gas, gravel spitting up around the car. "No, you're not. *You* we might need if we get stuck out there late."

"Then we need him too!"

"No time," Melissa said. The car surged ahead, pressing Dess back into her seat. Jessica looked over at her, eyes wild. Her door was still open, as if she were ready to jump. The thought of going out to the desert with a crazed Melissa and no Jonathan was clearly not making her too happy.

"Be careful, Jess!" Dess reached across and grabbed her arm. Through the still-open door the road was rushing past, a blur of gravel and patchy asphalt. Jessica tried to pull away, and Daughterboard managed to jam itself between Dess's ribs with a vengeance. "Ow! Come on!"

Jessica stopped fighting. The car was moving way too fast now.

"Make her stop!" Jessica said in an intense

whisper. "Or I'll tell her everything!"

"Huh?" Dess kept her grip on Jessica's arm. Had she gone crazy?

"If you don't make her stop, I'll tell Melissa the thing I'm not supposed to think about!"

"What are you talking about?" Dess asked. With Rex missing she could understand Melissa losing it, but why had Jessica gone nuts?

"I'll tell her!" Jessica whispered.

"Tell her *what*?"

The car slewed to a halt, throwing them both forward against the seat back with a thud. A choking dust cloud rose up through Jessica's open door before it slammed shut with the car's momentum.

Melissa shut off the engine and turned slowly, locking her eyes onto Dess. She made a sniffing noise.

"You know something about Rex," she said softly. "Something . . . secret."

Dess scowled. "Did you both double up on crazy pills this morning?"

"You do," Melissa said. She glanced at Jessica, who sat there wide-eyed and glaring. "You told Jessica. She stinks of not thinking about it."

"Told her what?" Dess said, fighting not to

cough from the dust roiling through the car. "Have you gone totally nuts?"

"And I can taste it on you," Melissa said. "Something like . . . tea." She wrinkled her nose. "With milk."

A sharp pain shot through Dess's head. "I hate tea."

"I've tasted this before," Melissa muttered; then her eyes brightened. "The other night, when Jessica and Flyboy got help finding their way. You know something about that, don't you?"

Dess crossed her arms in front of her. "You have totally lost it, Melissa."

"No, I think I'm about to find it." Melissa took her hands from the wheel and stared at her. "How do you know where Rex is? Tell me."

"Do I look like a darkling groupie? I mean, what Jessica said might be true, but how should I know?"

Melissa closed her eyes. "You do know, somewhere in there. But it's hidden . . . by someone clever." She opened her eyes and shook her head. "Man, Rex knew this would happen. How spooky is that?" She started pulling off one glove, finger by finger.

Dess slunk back into her seat, feeling something nauseous rising inside her. "Don't you dare touch me." Her stomach rolled over at the thought.

"I have to do this, sweetie," Melissa said. "They've got Rex, don't you understand? Plus keeping secrets is *wrong.*"

"Ada," Dess whispered, not sure why the name had sprung to mind, demanding to be spoken.

"I'm not going to be alone again," Melissa said. The glove was off.

Dess's stomach heaved, and something rose up in her mind, an awful memory out of nowhere, something she'd been given to protect herself.

"Just relax." Melissa reached out.

"Or what?" Dess spat. "You'll make me like Rex's father?"

Melissa's hand froze, her face suddenly pale. The words from nowhere had worked; they'd brought her to a halt.

"What—what do you mean?" Jessica stammered.

Dess could see the old man now—the empty eyes, the drool glistening on his half-shaven chin. The realization sank in. "You did that to him. And Rex helped you."

Melissa bit her lip. "That was an accident."

"An accident?" Dess felt her voice rising—anything to keep Melissa on the defensive. "You left him a vegetable by *accident*?"

There was a pause. "More or less. We didn't know what we were doing."

Jessica shrank into her corner of the backseat, eyes wide. "You can do that? You guys never told me. . . ."

"We never told anyone." Melissa's eyes narrowed at Dess, the fingers of her bare hand flexing. "Not even little Dess. But someone told you."

"How could you?" Jessica cried. "To Rex's *father*?"

"It was easy," Melissa spat. "You should have seen what he was doing to Rex."

"Jesus," Dess said. "I *know* the guy was a bastard, but . . ."

Melissa shook her head slowly. "I'm not talking about the beatings, Dess. Hell, there are times I want to knock Rex around myself. But he couldn't take the tarantulas. . . ."

"The what?" Dess whispered, but she remembered the terrarium, empty for the whole time she'd known Rex. She'd always thought the tarantulas had only existed in the old man's mind.

"The hairy spiders. Rex's father wanted to make him a man instead of some book-reading pussy. He used to force Rex to stand still while they crawled all over him." Melissa made a soft, strangled sound. "That's the first image I ever got from him, you know? The first time we ever touched, when Rex and I were eight years old. Tarantulas. His mind was rotten with it. That's why I never . . . That's why it took so long to touch him again."

It was silent in the car for a while. Even the dogs outside had settled down, as if they were listening.

"Rex wouldn't have survived if we hadn't done what we did," Melissa finally said.

"Jesus," Jessica said.

Dess's mind had gone blank. She couldn't bring herself to imagine it, didn't want to try. All that was left in her head was something thrumming again and again, blocking every other thought: *Keep her talking. Don't let her touch you.*

"And I was young," Melissa said. "I didn't know how to do it back then. I won't hurt you, Dess." Her voice was almost pleading.

"But I don't know anything." Dess turned to Jessica for help.

"Don't, Melissa," Jessica said. "She doesn't want you to. You can't."

"So we just let Rex die? *Worse* than die?" Melissa shook her head and seized Dess by the arm with her gloved hand. The other reached out toward her throat. "I'm sorry."

"Ada," Dess said, breathing hard, the name gushing up out of her. "Don't touch me."

"Melissa!" Jessica cried, but shrank farther away, pulling herself into her jacket, terrified now of the mindcaster's touch. "We'll go now. Whatever you want. We don't have to wait for Jonathan. Just don't . . ."

Melissa shook her head. "You know where Rex is."

Something huge rushed up inside Dess and jerked her limbs, made her flail like a puppet. "Ada, Ada . . ."

And then it happened: Melissa's cold hand grasped her chin, and a wave of emotion cascaded through her. Stomach-crushing panic and anxiety, the overwhelming fear that she would lose him— her Rex, her Loverboy—and be alone again, forever. Eight years of isolation rolled through Dess, alone against the invasion of ten thousand minds . . . the way Melissa had suffered before finally tracking Rex across the dark terrain of midnight, running the streets barefoot in cowgirl pajamas.

And inside herself Dess felt things crumbling, barriers bending under the weight of Melissa's mind—the run-down house and the empty attic, the old maps that showed Bixby's psychic currents. And finally Madeleine, her lined face forbidden to think of, bringing up the bitter taste of tea as sharp as stomach acid in her mouth . . . A jolt shook her body.

Here, cling to this, Dess.

Another wave flooded into her mind from Melissa, but this time there were numbers . . . blessed ranks of steady digits, eight across like the precise coordinates of Geostationary, as sweet as a cold washcloth pressed to her head in a fever. They wrapped themselves around an image of the emergency runway, carried on the name Angie. They began to dance, transformed by the math of minutes and seconds, the ripples and convolutions playing across Dess's hostage mind.

Good, find Loverboy. That's all that matters.

Dess trembled, stripped of her secrets and her will, until finally she raggedly said, "Lovelace," in surrender, and the last of the barriers fell away.

Seconds later the math was done. . . .

Melissa's hand slipped from her face. The mindcaster fell away into the front seat, breathing hard.

Dess heaved, trying not to puke. Her stomach hurt and, much worse, her mind felt trashed, strewn with Melissa's fears and loneliness, all the debris of her rotten life.

"Man," Melissa said quietly from the front seat. "You've been busy."

"I hate you. That was mine, not yours."

Jessica's cool hands touched Dess's cheek. "Are you okay?"

She opened her eyes and looked into Jessica's. Despite how much she still hurt and how disgusting the whole thing had been, her head felt clearer than it had for days. All those barriers Madeleine had built inside her . . . Melissa had swept them away. Dess knew the secret history again, completely and without encumbrance.

"Mindcasters," she said. "They suck."

"You're telling me?" Melissa murmured softly from in front. "She left us alone all these years. . . ."

"Dess, are you okay?" Jessica repeated.

The cool hands felt good against Dess's fevered skin. "Not great." She took a slow breath. "But I'll live. And I know where they've taken Rex. The exact spot was in Angie's head."

"I thought so," Melissa said softly.

Headlights swept through the car, turning the rearview mirror into a glaring, horizontal eye.

"Crap, it's just after curfew," Melissa muttered.

"Maybe it's Jonathan," Jessica said.

"Maybe," Melissa said. "If it's the cops, Rex is dead."

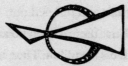

29

11:07 P.M.

DARK ROADS

The old Ford was stretched across the road like it had spun out. The lights were off and the engine silent. He couldn't see anyone through the windows.

"Christ," Jonathan said. He brought his father's car to a halt and jumped out, certain that he was too late. First there'd been no answer when he'd tapped on Dess's window. Then he'd spotted long skid marks on the gravel road, marking where a car had accelerated wildly away from the front of her house.

And now this. Melissa's car abandoned half a mile down the road.

The darkling groupies had gotten them all.

But when he reached the Ford, Jonathan saw shapes huddled inside. Melissa was splayed across the driver's seat, head listing to one side. Jessica and Dess were crouched halfway down in the back, holding each other.

And no Rex. Was he really gone?

"Hey, Flyboy," Melissa said, cranking her window down. Her face was as white as death. "Good to see you."

The back door opened, and Jessica tumbled out. She threw her arms around him, her face streaked with tears.

"What the hell happened?"

"Just a little navigation issue," Melissa said. Her voice was ragged. "But I think it's sorted out."

The other back door opened, and Dess stood and stared glassily at him across the roof of the Ford. "I know where Rex is. We've got to go." She walked toward his car, shaky on her feet.

All three of them looked terrible.

"Come on," Jessica said, slamming the door behind her and pulling him toward his father's car.

"Shouldn't someone ride with Melissa?" he asked. "She doesn't look so hot."

"Just get in the car and drive," Dess said.

* * *

They headed toward Aerospace Oklahoma, Melissa following and Dess in the front seat next to him, her eyes trained on the glowing GPS receiver. Jessica sat in the back, leaning forward to keep touching him, clinging to him as if she'd just been rescued from a burning house.

On the way, Dess told them about Madeleine, the old mindcaster she'd found hidden in Bixby three days before. Jonathan could hardly believe it—there'd been another midnighter in town all this time. The secret hour was almost too much sometimes. Flatland might be two-dimensional, but at least the rules didn't keep changing every ten seconds.

"She didn't leave her house for fifty years?" he asked, horrified at the thought. Having to stay inside for a week when he was sick drove him crazy.

"Forty-nine," Dess said. "She could go outside sometimes, as long as she was in disguise. If anyone recognized her, the Grayfoots might hear she'd shown up again. And then after Melissa was born, she only went out during school hours."

"What's going to happen now?" Jessica said.

"Now that the queen bitch knows?" Dess shook her head, her eyes never leaving the GPS receiver. "I don't want to think about it. As soon as we rescue Rex, we've got to warn Madeleine. Or maybe she'll taste it herself."

"But I thought the darklings couldn't find her because of where her house is," Jessica said.

"Yeah, but I know the exact spot, inside and out." Dess's voice was dry and exhausted. "Like Angie knew where to take Rex, you know?"

Jonathan glanced back at Jessica. "Um, not really."

"Coordinates *mean* something to me, something solid, like emotions have a taste for mindcasters," Dess said. "The location's in Melissa's mind now. She took it from me. The darklings will get it from her sooner or later."

Jonathan frowned. "Hopefully later."

"Well," Dess said, "if we bash Melissa's brains in before midnight, it won't be a problem."

There was a long silence. Jonathan felt Jessica's arms tighten around his chest, and he focused on the white lines of the road.

"No takers?" Dess sighed. "C'mon, guys. I'm just kidding."

Jonathan swallowed. They hadn't told him exactly what had gone down in the car or why it was spun out half a mile down the road from Dess's house. Just that Melissa had touched Dess, giving her the coordinates where Rex had been taken. And that her touch had opened the whole Madeleine can of worms.

But there had to be more to it than that, Jonathan realized. He still got the shakes when he remembered Melissa touching him. Dess couldn't have been thrilled about sharing minds with her, and Jessica wasn't psyched about having watched either.

For that matter, Rex was going to freak.

If they got to him in time.

Jonathan looked at his watch: 11:33. They weren't even at Aerospace Oklahoma yet. Flying, he could cut straight through town and be there in minutes. But if the darklings were going to do something to Rex, even a short time after midnight might be too late.

"Turn off," Dess said.

Jonathan slowed, squinting out into the darkness. There weren't any streetlights out here. "Um, where?"

"Right here." She pointed into the desert. "We need to go that way."

"Yeah, but a road would be nice."

Dess hissed softly. "According to Jessica's mom's maps, there should be an access road right . . . there." She groaned. "Or maybe there *will* be. Maybe it isn't built yet."

Jonathan brought the car to a halt, surveying the lightless desert stretched out before him. "Look, we can drive on salt flats no problem. But that's scrub, loose sand, and cactus. You want to get stuck?"

Dess sat beside him in silent thought. Melissa's headlights pulled up behind, filling the car with light.

"Keep driving," Dess finally said, "but turn off the moment you can."

30

FIRST LAW OF MOTION

"There!" Jessica cried, pointing.

The road came into view, not much more than a pair of tire-wide ruts in the dirt. They'd finally found a way onto the flats. She reached forward to take Jonathan's shoulders as he made the turn, shivering again with relief that he'd shown up when he had. Jonathan might be a pain about Flatland sometimes, but he was also the only one among the midnighters who wasn't crazy—the only one who made her feel safe. The moments trapped in the car with a raving Melissa and a schizoid Dess, speeding away without him, had made Jessica pretty positive about that.

The razor-wire fence of Aerospace Oklahoma

372

was a couple of miles behind them, the brightly lit construction sites visible across the dark badlands. They'd had to drive all the way past it before finding a way into the desert.

"Watch out for security," she said. "They do all this top-secret stuff out here."

"Rent-a-cops," Jonathan muttered. "Just what we need."

The car bucked on the uneven road, and Jessica let go of Jonathan and leaned back, bracing herself against the backseat. She glanced over her shoulder at Melissa's headlights, half hoping the old Ford would have plowed to a stop in the loose sand. But the car followed, still close, like a determined bloodhound on their trail.

Jessica looked up at Dess in front, her face softly lit by the glowing readout of her device. She hadn't said much since telling them about Madeleine. Jessica wanted to talk to her, to make sure she was really okay. Of course, she'd had two mindcasters messing with her brain, so maybe *okay* wasn't the word. But the moment the two of them were alone, Jessica had to say how sorry she felt. She'd been the one to reveal Dess's secret. And then she'd just sat there watching, too afraid to move, while Melissa had done that to Dess. . . .

The car slid violently to one side, its engine roaring as the tires lost traction for a moment on the sand. Loose stones pinged the metal frame underneath her. Jonathan fought with the wheel, and they bolted forward again.

Through it all, Jessica saw, Dess never took her eyes from the GPS receiver. "We're almost at the flats," she said.

"I can see them," Jonathan replied.

A moment later the car leveled out, suddenly riding as smoothly as if they'd found asphalt.

"Welcome to the Bixby Emergency Runway, south end," Dess announced.

Jonathan floored the accelerator, pressing Jessica back into the seat. An expanse of moonlit white glowed before them, the salty remains of an ancient sea, as flat as a parking lot.

Melissa's car screeched up behind them, then pulled up alongside. Through the rear window Jessica could see huge tails of dust rising from the two cars, white and crystalline, sparkling in the moonlight.

"Does that thing have a clock?" Jonathan asked Dess.

"Accurate to within a millisecond," she said.

"Good. Tell me when to brake. I don't want to go through the windshield."

Jessica swallowed. "What?"

"We don't know what happens if you're riding in a car at exactly midnight," he explained. "We might maintain our momentum when the car freezes. Or maybe not."

"For some reason, none of us has ever volunteered to test the theory," Dess said dryly.

"That damn first law of motion again!" Jessica groaned. "How far are we from Rex?"

Dess calculated for a moment. "Eight kilometers—five miles to you kids—and there's three minutes and twenty seconds left. We need to do ninety miles an hour."

There was a pause, then Jonathan said, "It's floored and we're barely making seventy."

"We'll be short by a mile point eleven," Dess said softly. "And this thing won't work in the secret hour."

"We'll be close, though," Jonathan insisted, "and we'll be flying."

Dess looked out the window. "Looks like queen bitch has the scent."

Jessica followed her gaze. Melissa was pulling ahead.

Dess counted down from ten.

"Nine . . . eight . . ."

Jessica checked her seat belt again, wishing they weren't cutting it so close. They weren't that far from the place, and whatever the darklings planned to do to Rex had to take some time. But Dess and Jonathan were hell-bent on getting as close as they could before the witching hour struck.

And she had to admit that seventy miles an hour was eating up the distance even faster than Jonathan could fly.

"Three . . . two . . . one . . . *brake!*"

She jolted forward and the car swerved, the tires letting out a shriek as they locked up on the salt. Jessica's seat belt bit into her shoulder, and a huge cloud of white rose up around them, blotting out the moon. The car swung like a fairground ride until the cloud filled the front windshield—they'd spun 180 degrees and then some.

Before they'd skidded completely to a halt another jolt struck, as suddenly as if the car's tires had stuck in flypaper. A wash of blue swept across the white expanse, and the seat belt cut across Jessica like a knife, her head slamming against the backseat.

Then everything was still, an absolute silence fallen over the roar of engine and screech of tires.

"Ow!" Jessica cried.

"What?" Jonathan asked, turning around. "I didn't feel anything."

"You're kidding." Jessica moaned. It felt like a bear trap had closed on her shoulder.

"Must be an acrobat thing," he said.

"Almost as bad as mindcasters," Dess mumbled as she unhooked herself, rubbing her shoulders and neck.

They piled out. Jessica coughed, tasting the suspended cloud of salt that swirled up from the car's distorted and frozen tires. She saw an equally motionless cloud ahead, marking where Melissa's car had hit the wall of midnight.

"You can fly us both, right?" Dess said, hoisting the clanking duffel bag over one shoulder.

"It won't be as fast," Jonathan said.

"We need you, Dess," Jessica insisted. She wasn't leaving anyone behind out here. "Take his left hand."

With Jonathan in the middle, they lined up facing the direction they'd been driving. The first jump went badly: Jessica's push-off was too strong, which sent them spinning in orbit around Jonathan. They skated to an ungainly stop across the salt.

"Start small," he said. Jessica remembered when she'd first learned to fly, building up from easy steps to house-clearing leaps.

They pushed off again, a jump of about ten yards, then doubled it the next time into the air. Soon they were eating up the desert below them, headed toward the frozen plume trailing from Melissa's car.

"That's not good," Jonathan said.

Jessica squinted into the darkness. "What isn't?"

"Her dust trail isn't nearly as big as ours," he said. "It's like she didn't. . . ." His voice trailed off as their next leap took them through the stinging cloud of salt, a shower of needles that forced her eyes and mouth shut. When they cleared it, Jessica could finally see the car itself, a black shape on the glowing blue expanse.

"She didn't," Dess said.

"Didn't what?" Jessica asked.

"Brake in time."

A sparkling wedge spread out from the front of the car, a glittering spray of safety glass from the gaping hole in the windshield.

Twenty yards farther on, a dark figure was sprawled on the salt.

31 | 12:00 A.M.
CONCUSSION

Midnight didn't feel so good.

It hadn't brought its usual awesome silence. Instead there'd been a sudden burst of noise and mind-wrenching pain that had left her here, swimming in this dark place.

Melissa remembered driving fast, glancing at her watch, letting her foot off the accelerator, slowing as she waited until the last moment to put on the brakes.

Oh, yeah. Really important to put on the brakes ...

With an effort she opened her eyes. There were stars in front of her, pinpoints of light dancing against a cold black sky.

Can't get distracted. Brakes ...

380

Melissa moved her arm painfully, bringing her wrist in front of her eyes. She had to fight to bring the numbers into focus.

The watch face was cracked, the hands stopped at eight seconds to midnight.

She let it drop back to the salt, finally understanding.

"Stupid cheap quartz watch . . . ," she muttered.

Then her head began to pound. Melissa knew all about headaches. She'd felt her own and everyone else's since the day she was born. Totaled up, she'd probably spent years of her life with a headache. But this one . . . this was the worst *ever*.

She swam in the darkness for a while, the pain spreading like a bruise all the way to her fingertips. Then she heard footsteps pounding across the hard desert floor.

"Melissa!"

Stupid noisy flame-bringer. Jessica's buzzy brain tasted like a nine-volt battery pressed against Melissa's tongue.

"Quiet," she commanded, wondering if her eyes were shut. Open or closed, there were stars in front of her.

Loud as a car alarm.

"Don't move her."

Maybe that was Jonathan's voice. His bouncy Flyboy taste was around here somewhere.

Melissa decided to open her eyes. The voices weren't going to go away until she glared at them. Glaring was good for making annoying people shut up.

Jessica's blurred, concerned face appeared.

"I'm fine." Everything was fine . . . except for the dizziness and the feeling like she was going to puke and the headache. Anyway, there was a bottle of aspirin in her glove compartment, like always. Where was her car, anyway? She lifted her head to look. Jeez, it was *miles* away.

"Lie still," Jessica advised.

Yeah, I was just about to start dancing, Melissa thought.

Then a piece of memory fell out of the starry sky—why she'd been driving so fast. And even though speaking hurt, she said, "Go get Rex, you morons."

The three of them looked at each other, and no one said what they were all thinking, while precious seconds ticked away.

Finally Dess said, "All right. I'll stay here."

Melissa closed her eyes. Poor Dess, always the odd one out. Couldn't fly, couldn't flame-bring. They should all three go, leaving her for the darklings. Being eaten couldn't hurt worse than this headache.

But arguing would hurt too.

Their voices and thoughts got even louder. Dess kept telling Jessica which direction to go. Flyboy was anxious to get started and also quietly relieved to have only one passenger to carry. And all the while, not even a mile away, the arid taste of dark things was gathering.

"Go," she tried to say.

If Rex was out there, he wasn't conscious; Melissa couldn't taste him. But she'd driven ahead following the flavor of a familiar mind. Angie wasn't far away, her brash confidence silenced now by midnight.

Oh, if only Melissa could crawl that mile, the things she would do to Angie. Rex's dad could tap-dance around her after Melissa was done.

But lying still was better. So she lay still for a while longer.

★ ★ ★

383

"Wake up."

Only Dess now. The other two had faded, finally flying off to help Rex. Polymath thoughts filled the air as Dess pounded stakes into the ground, protection from the dark things all around them.

"Wake up! You've got a concussion. If you go to sleep, you could die."

Melissa groaned. "Fine with me."

"What a coincidence. Fine with me too."

She opened her eyes, looked at poor lonely Dess, tasting bitter as burnt rubber. Dess thought she'd been robbed of her secret friend. Didn't she see what Madeleine was? What she had done to them all? Abandoned them. Left them pathetic orphans, when she knew all the tricks.

And anyway, Melissa had had no choice.

She licked her lips, desperately wanting a drink of water. "I'm sorry I touched you, Dess. But they took Rex. . . . I had to find him."

No answer, just the pounding of stakes into the hard ground. Every stroke was like an ice pick through Melissa's brain.

Finally the hammer paused. "They know about her now, don't they?"

"They already knew." Melissa closed her eyes. Here, half conscious in the middle of the desert, she was awash in darkling thoughts, their slow rhythms easier to take than those of buzzy, headache-making humans. It hadn't been Madeleine's first slipup when she'd popped directions into Jonathan's and Jessica's brains. Over the years the darklings had sniffed her existence. They could hardly miss the spate of young midnighters appearing in Bixby. And the oldest, most paranoid ones had always suspected that someone had survived.

Then she realized the obvious.

"That's why they let us live," she croaked.

The pounding stopped.

"What?"

Talking hurt, but at least Dess wasn't driving tent stakes while she listened. Melissa lifted her head a bit and rolled painfully onto one side, feeling bruised shoulders and salt-scraped hands.

"We weren't a threat, not until Jessica came along. So the darklings were clever: they let us survive. To find Madeleine."

And to let Rex mature, she thought. They'd taken Anathea too young; that was why she was dying after only two years of darkling time.

They wanted Rex to be their slave for centuries. . . .

Melissa groaned, her head sinking back onto the salt.

"Can you sense her?" Dess asked.

Melissa sighed. Casting that far would hurt her head, like everything did. She could feel blood trickling down her face now, its progress as slow as thick oil. But she owed Dess an answer.

She sent her mind past the edge of the desert into the silent town, searching for the null spot that Dess's numbers had uncovered, hidden behind the contortions of midnight.

Just in time Melissa felt them watching and realized what she'd almost done. The darklings were all around, leery of the barrier Dess had made but paying close attention. They had almost followed her thoughts to Madeleine.

Melissa smiled and let the knowledge she'd taken from Dess scatter like shattered safety glass. One thing about going through a windshield, it made it easy not to think. They would sift Madeleine's secret place from her mind eventually but not tonight, not with this concussion raging in her head.

"Madeleine's fine," she said. *For now.*

Dess started pounding stakes again. The protection might not even be necessary—the darklings had bigger fish to fry. A dark mass of them boiled furiously nearby, excited by something in their midst. . . .

"No," Melissa murmured, and her head sank back to the hard ground. She let herself be overwhelmed, drifting in and out of the merciful sleep that might kill her, consciousness too painful to bear.

Of course, she really ought to remind Dess about the car poised sixty feet away. It was frozen now, but the old Ford was still doing better than forty miles an hour and headed straight toward them with no one at the wheel.

But the words of warning couldn't seem to form in the jumble of her mind. Amid the gathering darklings was a distracting flavor, the most familiar taste she knew . . . but different now.

Not far away, Rex was waking up.

32 | 12:00 A.M.
DEFENSELESS

The world was spinning, his heart beating out a panicked rhythm. He wanted to run, but his legs felt like they were sunk in something dense and bitterly cold. Then he remembered it was too late—they had already taken him.

Rex feebly moved his hands, clawing at the wall that pressed against him. Then the world tilted again, and he slowly realized that the hard expanse was the ground. He was lying flat and facedown. His lungs labored against some terrible weight as if a huge, unconscious body lay on top of him.

And he was blind.

He coughed, tasting salt and blood in his mouth. Breathing wasn't easy; whatever his kidnappers had used to knock him out still filled his head.

Rex tried to force open his eyes, but some sort of muck clung to his face. He also felt it smeared across his chest and between his fingers. Viscous, warm strands of the stuff tugged at his lips when they parted to let out a groan, as if he'd been dropped in a ditch filled with fresh entrails from a slaughterhouse.

Images of spiders filled his mind, and Rex remembered the old darkling at Constanza's spitting steaming mucus as it died. His heart began to pound again, panic welling up and his hands clawing blindly. But real tarantulas didn't shoot webs, he reminded himself.

He pulled one heavy hand toward his face and felt it drag across fine sand. Turning his head seemed impossible—as if it were trapped in a vise—but he forced his fingers to scrape at one side of his face until his right eye managed to open a slit.

Rex glimpsed blue light and for the first time noticed the silence. Only his own heartbeat

pounded in his ears. He must have been unconscious for hours; the blue time was here.

A glimmer of hope passed through him. His
kidnappers' understanding of the secret hour
couldn't be perfect. They had never read midnighter lore, only taken orders from their "spooks"
blindly, without real comprehension. Maybe they
didn't realize that Rex would still be awake while
they were frozen. Maybe they'd made a mistake.

But he had to get moving, had to stand up.
The blue time might be just beginning or almost
over. And this sticky stuff all over him probably
wasn't a good sign. . . .

Rex pawed at his face with two hands, tearing
at the clinging muck until he could open both eyes.
Blue desert floor filled his view through blurred
vision; he still couldn't turn his head. He tried to
push himself up, but his chest only rose a few
inches from the ground before sinking back
again. Scrambling to turn over, he tore with his
fingers at the dirt, but the vast weight atop him
pressed him firmly against the ground, almost
paralyzed, breathless with the effort of struggling.
He couldn't feel his legs at all.

What was on top of him?

With his face squashed against the dirt, Rex tasted salt. This was the flats, he realized. He'd been dumped far out in the desert, miles from humanity. Even if midnight had only just fallen, they would be here soon.

Then he heard something, a muffled cry.

He listened, and distant sounds reached him from every direction, shrill and inhuman. He weakly clawed at his ears to scrape them clean.

And suddenly the noise became deafening. The silence had only been because of the muck in his ears.

They were already here, all around him.

Rex felt his breath catch in fear and reached for Glorification around his neck. But the links of steel were gone, along with his jacket and shirt. He felt nothing against his skin except the clinging slime and the oppressive weight that pressed him down against the salt.

Something black and glistening slithered into view.

A small face, inches from his, looked up at Rex. A crawling slither, its soulless jet eyes peering at him curiously.

As his mind struggled to come up with a

tridecalogism, he wondered what a slither strike to the eyeball would feel like.

"Decompression," he croaked.

An invisible fist struck his stomach, forcing the scant air from his lungs, as if the desert had bucked angrily under him.

The slither wriggled out of sight. Buoyed by this small victory, Rex pushed against the desert floor again.

Suddenly the weight lifted from him, his whole body rising into the air. Rex's arms flailed weakly and whatever carried him staggered, the blue horizon tilting.

Through his blurred vision he glimpsed the shapes of spiders and worms, giant snakes and hunting cats, and things he didn't recognize, nightmarish beasts that mixed reptile and mammal and bird of prey. More darklings than he'd ever imagined, weathered and ancient. The ground beneath him seethed with slithers, writhing among the ankles of three frozen humans. Rex recognized Angie's motionless face, Ernesto Grayfoot with his camera.

A human sound came through the darkling

chatter, like a child sobbing.

He forced his eyes to focus and saw a young girl among the dark shapes. She lay huddled on the ground, naked, a thin, strangled noise coming from her.

Another victim out here in the desert.

But Rex had no metal, no weapons of any kind, not even clothes, nothing but words to fight with. He pulled a painful breath into his lungs.

"Magnification."

Another blow pummeled him, and he staggered backward, wobbling too high off the ground, like an amateur on stilts. But balance returned, and he finally saw the great wings gathering the air on either side of him, pulling him upright. A glistening, viscous slime still clung to them.

He let his eyes close, finally understanding. Who the girl was; what he had become.

"Disappearance," he whispered.

The sharp and awesome pain struck again, as though he were vomiting up something spiked and huge. The thirteen-letter words were poison in his mouth, of course. Even thinking them made his mind split in half, tearing at the part of his brain that still could not believe what had happened, the part that was still human.

It was too late to run, too late to fight.

Rex was one of them now.

33

12:00 A.M.

SEERS

The first slither hit without warning.

A swarm hovered in the distance, marking the spot where Rex must be, but the flying snake seemed to come from nowhere, glancing off Jessica's arm and leaving it buzzing like a hammer to the funny bone.

Her hand half numb, Jessica pulled her flashlight out.

"Unanticipated Illuminations," she whispered, and turned it on. Power surged through her, and another slither flared up in its beam, filling the darkness with red flame and a shrill cry. Jessica swept white light across their path, igniting a handful more slithers before them.

"What's this thing called?" Jonathan asked, squinting from the light and gesturing with his shield.

"Uh . . . Dess said to call it Brobdignagian Perambulation."

"Is that English?"

"Yeah, it means 'walking tall,' sort of." She touched the shield and said the name again.

As they descended, Jessica caught movement on the desert floor below. She pointed the beam downward, igniting a nest of crawling slithers that had been waiting for them. "They're everywhere!"

"Trying to slow us down," he said.

Something fluttered behind them, and Jonathan cried out as a slither struck him in the middle of the back. He stumbled as they landed, dragging Jessica down into the salt before she lost her grip on his hand, normal gravity draping over her like a lead blanket. She fell onto dead slithers, the reek of burned flesh filling her lungs.

Jessica rose to one knee and spun around, trying to point the flashlight in all directions at once. Things lit up in the sky around her, but she saw another flying streak hit Jonathan on his leg before bursting into flame.

"The flare!" he called, deflecting another slither with Perambulation.

She pulled Explosiveness from her pocket and tore it in half, crying its name. The flare burst to life, half blinding her and filling the desert with jittering shadows. Screams rose up on every side as she thrust it over her head.

Leathery wing beats faded all around them, carrying the screams away.

Jonathan shielded his violet-flashing eyes from the flare. "How long does that thing last?"

"Half an hour, I think. But it'll go out if I drop it."

"Don't. I can't see a damn thing, but it's better than getting chewed to pieces." He held out one hand, keeping the other across his eyes, favoring his right leg. "You navigate. Tell me when to jump."

Jessica took his hand. Jonathan's lightness buoyed her, mixing with the wild energies flowing up through her body and into the hissing flare. She calculated their next jump, tugging at his hand to indicate the direction.

"Three, two, one . . ."

They leapt, but Jonathan's bitten leg buckled,

sending them spinning around each other. Jessica corrected their flight with a twist of her shoulders, the second law finally and mystically becoming clear in her mind. Too late for any physics test, but maybe in time to save Rex . . .

They arced high above the desert, headed toward the swarm.

"Landing in five, four, three . . ."

Their feet touched down, and she pulled Jonathan into the next jump, perfectly this time. In midair she drew him close so that he wouldn't cast a wedge of shadow into the desert sky and open up a line of attack. He buried his face against her shoulder, flinching from the sparks of Explosiveness that swirled around them.

"One more and we'll be there," she said at the peak of their jump. Already the cloud of slithers and darklings ahead was scattering, terrified of the brilliant flare bounding toward them. Jessica smelled her own hair singeing in the veil of sparks, but, like soldering at Dess's house, the scent of combustion only thrilled her.

"Two . . . one . . ."

They landed and jumped again in perfect tandem, flying straight into the swarm.

It was like falling through a chorus of screams.

Flames spread in every direction as slithers too slow or too stupid to get away were ignited by Explosiveness. These flailed their burning wings and careened into others, carrying the inferno outward in an expanding sphere, like a great blazing eye opening around them. A darkling in the shape of a winged panther was caught by the spreading conflagration. It whirled in circles, trying to put itself out before tumbling from the sky.

"This sounds pretty intense," Jonathan said, his eyes glued shut.

"Pretty," Jessica answered. Her entire body hummed with the sputtering hiss of the flare.

They fell through the mass, a ring of fallen, smoldering beasts lighting the desert floor below them.

"We're coming down," Jessica warned, seconds before they landed and staggered to a halt.

At the center of the burning slithers—right at the spot Dess had predicted—stood three stiffs, frozen by midnight. One was Jessica's stalker, handsome Ernesto Grayfoot, camera in hand. Another was a tall woman with blond hair, the third an old man, elegantly dressed in clothes that seemed decades out of date. Even from a distance Jessica could see the resemblance between Constanza and her grandfather.

A fourth figure huddled on the salt between them, small and naked and pale.

Jessica dropped Jonathan's hand and ran to the trembling figure, carrying Explosiveness over her head, spitting demonic shadows in every direction.

It wasn't Rex.

The girl was sickly and withered, her legs too thin to stand on. Clumps of leathery skin clung to her human flesh, which shone albino white from years in darkness.

"Bright . . . ," she said with a dry throat, as blinded as Jonathan by the flame.

Of course, she was a midnighter still. A seer, Rex and Melissa had said. Jessica hid the flame behind her, and the eyes crept open a slit, flashing purple.

"You finally came for me."

Jessica blinked. Finally—after fifty years. The girl couldn't comprehend how long it had been.

"Yes. You're okay now." She didn't look okay. She could barely hold her head up, her muscles wasted from years imprisoned in darkling flesh.

"I don't know you," she said softly. "I'm Anathea."

"We're new in town," Jonathan said, limping up behind Jessica. "Anathea, we're looking for a friend. . . ."

"The other seer," she said, nodding sadly. "They changed him and left me here."

"Do you know where they took him?"

"I can look." She pointed a thin finger at Explosiveness. "But put that out."

Jessica turned and threw it into the darkness. The moment it left her hand, the flare sputtered, dying before it hit the ground. She pulled out Unanticipated Illuminations again, in case any slithers had dared to stick around.

The girl sighed with relief in the sudden blackness and opened her eyes wider. She swept her seer's gaze across the horizon, then nodded.

"He's flying that way."

"Flying . . ." Jessica could barely make out a flock of shapes against the rising moon. Rex and his new entourage.

They were too late.

"We have to follow him . . . ," she said desperately. "Try to save him."

"If you can keep him aboveground until the sun comes up," the girl said, "the darkling flesh will burn away, I think."

"I've got my own sun," Jessica said, her hand clenching Unanticipated Illuminations. "Come on, Jonathan."

He paused, looking down at Anathea. "Are you going to be okay?"

The girl shook her head. "I know why they let me go." She sank back to the ground, exhausted.

"Come on!"

"What if they come back and hurt her?" Jonathan said.

"They don't want my flesh," Anathea answered. "I'm one of them now."

Jessica looked up at the retreating swarm, chilled by the words. If that were true, then Rex was one of them too. "We have to go, Jonathan."

Jonathan paused, then took off his jacket and wrapped it around the girl's frail shoulders.

"We'll be back," he said to Anathea, and then took Jessica's hand.

Unanticipated Illuminations swept the night sky nervously, its beam clearing a path before them.

A few flocks of slithers challenged the light but burst instantly into balls of flame, consumed as they streaked toward the ground.

Even with Jonathan half blinded, they gained on the swarm quickly. Soon Jessica could see why. At its center flapped a darkling in almost human form. Its flight was ungainly, the wings uncoordinated and the body twitching horribly, as if it were at war with itself. Its long spiked tail swung like a nervous cat's through the air.

"Rex," she whispered.

They grew closer, and the flashlight began to tear at the trailing edge of the swarm, igniting slithers and driving the rest into mad vortices.

Two darklings descended to join the thing in the center, taking positions on either side and trying to coax it forward, but Jessica saw its human arms flailing, fending them off.

At the peak of their next jump she pointed Unanticipated Illuminations directly into the swarm and said its name again, willing every ounce of her power into it.

The beam lanced through the mass, and the two darklings shrieked and veered away, the halfling bursting into flame.

"Rex!" she cried.

The blazing shape tumbled, gyrating toward the ground like a crumpled paper airplane. At the last moment it managed one billowing flap of its burning wings, bringing itself softly to earth before collapsing.

The swarm twisted around, transforming into a whirlwind that surrounded the fallen creature. Slithers broke off from the spinning mass, launching themselves into the path of her flashlight, disintegrating as they flew. The stench of the screaming, burning animals began to choke her.

Then one struck Jessica's right shoulder, streaking in from below and sending an icy bolt of pain through her arm. She twisted the flashlight around, igniting burning slithers in all directions.

But there were so many of them, and she didn't have another flare.

"Stop here!" Jessica cried as they landed, and Jonathan stumbled blindly to a halt. "There are too many!"

A shape loomed up before her, and Jessica reflexively brought her hand up to protect her face. The slither bounced from her wrist with a screech, leaving the charms on Acariciandote glowing.

Through the darkness she saw sleek forms bounding across the desert, hunting cats carried toward them in thirty-foot strides.

She could burn them all one by one, Jessica knew, but in the meantime the swarming slithers would cut her to pieces. The darklings, however cautious and fearful after their long lives, were willing to sacrifice themselves to save their new halfling.

And kill Jessica Day in the bargain.

"What do I do?" she murmured.

"I've got you," Jonathan said. Eyes squeezed shut against her darting white light, he wrapped himself around Jessica, protecting her back. "Just keep fighting."

She felt his body jerk as a slither hit him from behind.

"Jonathan!"

He groaned. "Just fight!"

There wasn't time to argue. She turned Unanticipated Illuminations on the nearest darkling, which stumbled and howled as flame skated across its fur. She swept the light across a flock of slithers to reach another great cat. The beast leapt sideways, but she followed it with a flick of her wrist until it was reduced to a scattering of bright motes tumbling across the salt.

Jonathan flinched again as something struck him, pulling her off balance as he swung Perambulation blindly. Jessica clenched her teeth and ignored his cries of pain, aiming her flashlight at another panther, whose purple eyes flashed, then boiled from its head. The thing screamed, launching itself up into the air, wings bursting into flame even as they sprouted from its back.

It crashed to the ground close enough to shake the desert under her feet, thrashing up a cloud that rolled across them, filling Jessica's eyes with stinging salt.

Another slither flared behind her as Jonathan fended it off with his shield.

A whistling sound came from overhead, a huge darkling plummeting through the air. But Illumination's beam transformed it into a bright, shrieking meteor tumbling to the ground. It was headed right toward them, a flaming pinwheel of claws and teeth and wings. Jessica struggled, trying to move out of its path, but Jonathan was wrapped around her, still blinded by the white light.

"Jonathan! Incoming!"

He grunted and dragged her backward while Jessica kept the light focused on the beast. The creature burned away as it fell and crumbled when it struck the earth before them, scattering glowing embers around their feet, like the remains of a dying campfire kicked across the desert floor.

Howls came from all around them then, awful sounds of defeat and terror.

Jessica cast around for another black shape in the air or on the ground, but her beam found nothing but a few stray slithers. The other darklings must have given up, their age-old fearfulness finally driving them back into the night. In the distance she could just make out the tattered remnants of the swarm fleeing across the flats.

"I think that's it," she said in the sudden silence.

Jonathan's arms slipped from around her, and he fell to his hands and knees.

Jessica whirled around. His sweat-streaked face was twisted with pain. "Jonathan!"

"I'll live," he panted. "Go get Rex."

He raised his head and squinted across the desert, pointing to the crumpled, smoldering heap where the halfling had fallen.

Jessica bit her lip, scanned the sky again. Nothing.

"Okay. Stay here."

She fell into a dead run across the salt, playing the flashlight's beam across Rex as she drew closer. The remains of his darkling body burned away in great gouts of white fire, the wings disappearing into sheets of flame, the outer layer of skin blasted from him like dirt under a fire hose.

When it was done, she turned the flashlight off and ran to where he lay crumpled on the salt.

"Rex!"

He looked up at her with wild eyes, hissing at her through clenched teeth.

"Rex, are you . . . ?"

A shudder passed through his body. He looked down in amazement at his arms, pale and bare. His hair was half burned away, but his skin looked unhurt, as if Unanticipated Illuminations's white fire had stopped at the limit of his humanity.

"Rex?"

"Did you see her?" he croaked. "The other one?"

"Anathea? Yeah, she's back there."

"Take me to her."

Jonathan ran up, limping horribly. "Are you sure you can . . . ?"

Rex rose, not a stitch of clothing on his body, and said, "Quickly. She's dying."

34 | 12:00 A.M.

ANATHEA

Freedom was killing her, she knew.

She'd thought of nothing else all this time, nothing but getting *out* of darkling flesh, back to Bixby, to Ma and Pa. In her tattered dreams Billy Clintock always came flying across the desert to save her, clinging to her as the sun rose up over the desert and set her free.

But the reality had turned out to be a grim one. She had grown too weak inside that other body. They hadn't left enough of her to survive without her other half.

Still, it was good to be herself again. Human, more or less.

Anathea curled up on the salt, hoping she'd

make it to sunrise or at least until the dark moon set.

When they came back, as the young acrobat had promised, there were three of them.

They landed hard, the other seer stumbling. He was naked until he put on his long coat that had been discarded on the salt, but the darkling flesh had been stripped away from him somehow.

Anathea found herself both angry and glad that they'd saved him, as no one had ever saved her.

The redheaded girl had said she'd brought her own sun. Anathea wondered again at the strange, intense Focus that clung to her. She carried some sort of metal shaft in her hand, a weapon that Anathea had watched cut through a whole swarm to rescue their friend. And her eyes were wrong.

What talent was she? And why didn't Anathea know *any* of them? Had it been that long?

"You're Anathea?" the other seer asked her.

"Yes," she said softly. Her voice had grown weak after all that time inside the darkling.

"What year is it?" he asked.

She frowned.

"What year do you remember, I mean?"

She hadn't thought of years and months for so long. . . . Darkling reckoning in twelves and gross counts seemed more natural to her now. "Nineteen and fifty-two?"

He nodded, as if glad for the information. She let her eyes drift closed.

"Do you know what happened?" he said. "To the rest of your people, the midnighters of your time?"

"My time?" She shivered, remembering now. There had been orders given by her own hands long ago, arranged out on the spelling blocks for villainous daylighters to read. But that had been so long ago, too long to recollect. She shuddered. "Terrible things. But it wasn't my fault. She gave up the secret. Not me."

"The secret?"

"No one was supposed to tell." She shook her head. "That's what started it all, that Madeleine Hayes telling secrets. Those Grayfoot boys knew what they were doing when they brought me out here. . . ."

Anathea let herself sink back to the ground. Thinking about things that had happened before the transformation hurt her head. Maybe she wasn't so human anymore after all. And talking stole her paltry breath. She felt herself slipping away.

The acrobat, the pretty Mexican boy, spoke up. "Can we do anything for you?"

She smiled then and held out her hand. All this time she'd had wings, but it was hard work, laboring inside that horrible other body. Nothing like when Billy Clintock had taken her soaring, what seemed like years ago. "Please?"

He understood and took her hand, and that lightness filled her. It had been so long. . . .

35 | 12:00 A.M.

FLATS

They decided to leave her there on the salt flats. The three darkling groupies—Angie, Ernesto, and the eldest Grayfoot—still stood frozen, looking at the spot where they had left Rex for the darklings. Maybe the appearance of a dead girl in his place would give them something to think about.

Jonathan turned away, unable to watch as Rex arranged dominoes around Anathea. Rex had dressed, finding his clothes untouched where the darklings had discarded them, and he looked eerily normal. All that was different was his burned hair and his hands, which trembled just like his father's now.

Jessica also didn't look. She pressed against his

chest, crying, but Jonathan found he didn't know how to grieve for Anathea, born in 1940 but dead tonight at only fourteen. Her wasted body looked hardly twelve, the age she'd been when she was taken.

And what had she said about a Madeleine Hayes, right before the end? Was the old mind-caster the one who had betrayed her generation so long ago? He would have to ask Dess about that.

"Okay, let's go," Rex called.

Jonathan turned and saw what Rex had left for the groupies, and a chill traveled down his bruised and battered spine. He stared into the seer's eyes: no tears for Anathea, just a fierce, haunted expression, as if Unanticipated Illuminations hadn't burned all the darkness out of him.

Rex had ignored the lore meanings of the dominoes, arranging them into letters a foot high. Around Anathea's body they spelled out in simple English:

YOU'RE NEXT

It made an awful picture, but that was the point, Jonathan supposed. It might convince Angie and the others to pursue a different career path. With no halflings left, this terrible message would be the last the darkling groupies ever received.

Jonathan took Jessica's hand and kissed it, tasting the salt from her tears. "Don't look," he said.

She shook her head.

The slither strikes across Jonathan's back were fading together into one giant bruise, and he winced as he held out his other hand for Rex, whose trembling didn't stop when midnight gravity connected them.

They hadn't told him yet about Melissa going through her windshield. As they flew, the seer's leaps weak and tentative beside him, Jonathan wondered if Rex would make it if she hadn't survived.

They reached the car as the dark moon was setting.

Melissa stood shakily as they landed, her face streaked with blood but managing a smile. Rex pulled his hand from Jonathan's and stumbled toward her across Dess's pattern of stakes and wire, gathering Melissa into a hug.

"I knew it," she said. "You tasted human again."

Jonathan glanced at Dess, who rolled her eyes. She seemed better than when they'd left her.

"Help me with this?" she said, stooping to pull a tent stake from the hard ground. "With Jessica around, we can clean this up before that monstrosity gets rolling again."

Jonathan followed Dess's gesture to the old Ford, pointed at them and trailed by a cloud of dust. "Oh, yeah. Good call."

He held Jessica's hand for a moment longer, and then they set to work, Jonathan's slither bites aching as he bent to pull up the metal stakes. His left leg and all of his back felt like they'd been hit with line drives and then sunburned extra-crispy. And he was starving. He couldn't wait to get back to the peanut butter on banana bread sandwich stashed in his glove compartment.

"You believe those two?" Dess whispered as she wound a spool of wire.

Rex and Melissa still embraced, their faces close, eyes flashing purple from the setting moon.

He shook his head.

"Do we *have* to tell them about the car?" Dess said quietly, a smile playing on her dirt-streaked face.

Jessica didn't smile back, just bent to pull up another stake, and Jonathan reached out and touched her arm. Death was too real to joke about tonight.

They stood back a good hundred yards to watch the two cars jump to life again, streaking across the desert in sudden tandem as the blue light swept from the world. Jonathan's whirled to a quick stop, but the old Ford rattled across the salt for half a mile. He'd already reached inside to turn the engine and headlights off so it disappeared into darkness, only a dust cloud marking its passage.

"I'll get it tomorrow," he promised Melissa again. It was the weekend, and nobody would be out here for a couple of days. As if anyone would steal that crappy old wreck with its busted windshield anyway.

"I hate the hospital," Melissa whined again. "All those sick people. And doctors touching me."

"You need stitches," Rex said. "And you could have brain damage."

"*Could* have?" Dess muttered.

Jonathan sighed and limped toward his car. It was going to be a real treat driving back into town. Finally it was just like Rex had planned, all five of them together again.

But at least they were all still alive. More or less.

Melissa's face had stopped bleeding, but she was going to have scars on her forehead and left cheek for a while, maybe forever. Rex's hands still trembled, and he twitched at sudden sounds. He walked carefully, half blind, his glasses lost somewhere out in the desert. Jessica hadn't said a word since Anathea had died; she clung to Jonathan's arm, exhausted by the fight and by everything they'd seen.

Only Dess seemed herself.

"Is Madeleine okay?" she asked as they walked toward Jonathan's car.

Melissa tipped her head back into the air, and nodded. "She made it through the night. But she knows what's happened; they'll find her soon."

"You are in so much trouble," Dess said.

"You're the one who's crap at keeping secrets."

"You're the one who can't keep her hands to herself!"

Jonathan tuned the argument out, pulling Jessica closer, glad of her support as they made their painful way to his car. He needed her touch, especially here on the salt flats, the flattest stretch of Flatland there was.

36

PARAGON OF SANITY

His vision came and went, sharp details fading into a blur and back again. On his way to the hospital the morning light had been viciously bright, metal-reflected sunlight leaving streaks across his eyes.

The walls of the hospital were riddled with Focus, but not the marks of midnight. Rex could see new things now, traces of daylighter hands, the impressions left by their minds as they solved problems, worked their tricks with numbers and alloys and clever machines.

It had taken all morning for him to realize what these new visions were: tracks of prey.

For a hundred thousand years darklings had

pursued humans, learning to track them, to read their places and their paths. As the last predators to dare hunt them, they knew humans better than any other beast alive, better than the half-blind bipeds knew themselves. Rex could see these signs now, could feel the manifestations of everything the darklings hungered for . . . and feared.

An intercom overhead barked out some emergency call, and he flinched. There were machines everywhere in this place—bright fluorescent lights, devices for measuring blood and flesh, thousands of clever tools. Rex longed to run for the door and into some open field, away from all these overwhelming signs of human ingenuity. They made his hands shake, the fear strung tight across his shoulders.

But he had to see Melissa and show her what the change had done to him.

He looked up at the number on the door he was passing, and the world blurred again momentarily.

He hadn't brought his spare pair of glasses; he didn't seem to need them anymore, now that the Focus clung to almost everything. But there were moments when his vision faded. They hadn't changed him all the way after all. He was still a human, still Rex Greene—a seer, not a beast.

An X-ray machine flashed nearby, its violet flare reaching his eyes through the walls of the hospital, and Rex flinched again, hissing through his teeth.

He had to find Melissa and share this with her. He needed her touch to make him feel human again.

Around another corner he found her hallway, the code of numbers and letters finally making sense. He hoped he wasn't losing his ability to read human symbols. It was probably just exhaustion from waiting for three hours in the emergency room last night. It had taken that long before they'd admitted Melissa and sent him home, finally believing their story—that she'd lost her ID in the accident, was eighteen, and had no parents to call.

As he made his way down the hall, something sharp caught Rex's eye ahead, a figure glowing with Focus.

An old woman, leaving Melissa's room.

Rex came to a halt. The marks were deep on her, detail worked into every line on her face.

She was looking at him with an expression of recognition, a smile playing across her aged, pale features.

"Rex! My boy." She held out a gloved hand, and he shrank away. What trick was this?

She shook her head. "Poor Rex. Still jumpy, of course. It was a near thing last night. As near as anything I've ever seen. And I've seen a lot."

"Who are you?"

"I'm . . . Melissa's godmother. Madeleine."

He shook his head. There was no such person, not that he could remember. But remembering was hard today. Rex had tossed and turned all night, trying to untangle everything in his head, all he'd learned from Melissa when they'd embraced on the salt flats. And later when they'd touched each other in the emergency room, swapping their pain back and forth like two kids with something too hot to hold . . .

But this morning he'd hardly had time to sort through the changes in himself, much less everything Melissa had shared with him. This woman Madeleine had something to do with Dess's calculations and with the lost generation of midnighters, that was all he could remember.

"I thought I'd visit her," she was saying. "You see, I may not have much time left. And I've always wanted to get to know her better." She shook her head. "My fault, really, leaving it so late like this."

An X-ray flashed again, and Rex spun toward it, a tremor running through his body.

She didn't notice the animal reaction or pretended not to and repeated softly, "All my fault, really. I was so scared, so horrified by what I'd done."

He stared at her again, and a measure of his old vision returned. Rex realized that her Focus was the most familiar kind, the mark of midnight.

"You're one of us," he said.

"Yes, Rex. But Melissa will tell you all about it. We've been visiting, you see, getting to know each other. She's waiting for you."

The woman brushed past him, and as she strode away down the hall, Rex saw that she was wearing only one glove.

He turned and ran toward Melissa's room.

Her eyes were closed, her face pale in the buzzing fluorescent light. The wounds, two on her forehead and one stretching down her cheek, were stitched now, crosshatched with pink thread binding the skin together. The stitches were made of some synthetic; Rex could sense its awful, clever newness.

She had the same Focus as the woman in the hall.

"Melissa?" he called softly. Wondering what the old mindcaster had done to her in her sleep.

Her eyes opened, and she smiled. "Looking good, Rex. Like the hair."

He sighed with relief and exhaustion. Melissa seemed like her old self.

The other bed in the room was empty, and he sat down on it, rubbing his palm across his shorn scalp. He'd buzzed it down to half an inch, cutting all the burned locks away. "Thanks. Looking good yourself."

She snorted. "Thanks, Rex. And I was worried that these scars would tragically affect my popularity at school."

He laughed, but the sound was hollow. There were too many machines in here—call buttons and intercoms, special wall plugs for heart monitors, a whole infrastructure of cables and steel around them. And suddenly Melissa was rising toward him like a mummy, the bed's tiny, clever motors making it flex at its center.

"You taste weird, Rex."

He looked at his shaking hands. "You think?"

"Kind of . . . psycho-kitty. They changed you, didn't they?"

He blinked, then nodded. There was so much in his head, new species of tastes and visions, wild thoughts bubbling up from some animal buried inside him. But one question made it through the confusion.

"Who was she?" he asked.

Melissa smiled. "My godmother, like she said. The godmother of us all." She sighed. "Until they find her, anyway. They'll be looking now."

Rex closed his eyes, his head racked with too many new sensations and now more information crowding it. Coming here had been a bad idea. He needed to head to the badlands, to find some place bleak and empty to sit and think.

"Come here, Rex."

He shook his head. "You're too weak. You won't be able to take what's in my head." He looked around at the walls, marked with handprints of sick and dying humans, easy prey to cut from the herd. "Especially not while you're in this place."

She laughed. "Not a problem."

"I thought you hated hospitals."

"I hated everything, Rex."

He frowned, some part of his mind recalling the intricacies of grammar. "Hated?"

"Not anymore." Melissa reached out, taking him by the arm. She drew him toward her and, for the first time, pressed her lips against his.

She came into him—not with the usual mad flood of emotions, but in a fashion measured and controlled, shaped by the technique of a hundred generations of mindcasters, an artistry passed from hand to hand across the centuries. Dess's numbers had found it, the thing Rex had always searched for, the connection to their past that the severed lore had never offered. And Melissa had been given it here in the flesh, this morning, by Madeleine and the host of predecessors in her memory. Finally a bond with living history; at last, for Melissa and the rest of them, the human touch.

Even carrying those centuries, the kiss was between the two of them alone, their old friendship turning suddenly and completely inside out, overwhelming him almost as much as his trans-formation in the desert.

And Rex knew he would survive.

He might be half a beast, afraid of the marks of humanity all around him, wounded by the darklings that had reached inside and turned one part of him against another, but he had her to carry him.

Nothing had ever tasted this sweet.

37 12:00 A.M.

INTRODUCTION

"It wasn't that hard, really. Dess brought her GPS thingie, so we knew exactly where the car was. Close enough, anyway."

"And you drove it all the way back to Melissa's?"

"No way. Just to the roadside. Melissa can get it home herself. That'll teach her not to wear a seat belt." Jonathan smiled. Even in the blue time his dark face showed that he'd caught some sun on the trek across the runway this afternoon. "Driving back across the flats with no windshield was the worst part." He licked his lips. "I can still taste salt."

Jessica laughed, gazing down into the back-yard, regarding the frantic progress of her father's gardening. She felt safe sitting up here on her own

430

roof, staying close to home tonight.

"You guys didn't see . . . Anathea, did you?"

He shook his head. "We didn't go over there."

The tugging pain she'd felt all day shot through Jessica once more. "Maybe we should have buried her."

Jonathan sighed. "We didn't have a shovel, we didn't have time. And someone had to get Melissa to the hospital. Besides, the darkling groupies most likely took care of . . ."

He didn't finish the sentence.

"Oh, I didn't get a chance to tell you," she said. "Rex called. Melissa was released today. Her X rays didn't show anything. He said she's really . . . in great shape."

"Melissa, in great shape?" Jonathan laughed. "Whatever. Wonder how she's going to explain everything to her parents."

Jessica rubbed her arm where last night's slither bite had turned into a purple-yellow blotch. "I don't think Melissa has to explain things to her parents."

"Oh, right." Jonathan looked down.

Jessica had told him about Melissa's powers—the truth about Rex's father and what she'd done to Dess in the backseat of the Ford—but Jonathan didn't seem to have taken it all in yet. He only wanted to talk about what Dess had told him about Madeleine or about rescuing Melissa's car, not about terrible things done in the past or even the night before . . . or about Anathea, dead out in the desert.

"How was Dess?" she asked.

He shrugged. "She was talking about darkling-proofing Madeleine's house. She seemed good."

"She wasn't good last night." After they'd finally gotten back to Dess's house, she'd slept, but only to have nightmares every hour, most of which had involved screaming the name of her Ada Lovelace doll for some reason.

"Well, now that she's got a new project, she'll be okay."

Jessica shook her head. "You should have seen it, Jonathan. It was like Melissa . . ." She couldn't say the word. "You just don't know."

"I do know, Jess. Melissa touched me too."

She looked at him. "What?" A stab of something sickening went through her, a mixture of jealousy and disgust. "When? *Why?*"

"The night you found your talent, I had to jump with her and Rex."

Jessica swallowed. She remembered them soaring across the desert together, into the snake pit, but she'd never realized. . . .

"God, that's right. I didn't even know back then."

"None of us did, except Rex and Melissa."

She realized she'd pulled away and reached out again for his hand. "I'm sorry, Jonathan."

He shuddered slightly. "Don't be sorry for me. Be sorry for Melissa."

"I'll save it for Dess, actually." She looked down into her dad's garden again. "I wonder if she ever did anything to our parents."

"Melissa? Nah. I doubt she'd bother with my dad. He's never given me that much trouble."

She nodded. "Yeah, but what about when my parents let me go to that party . . . just when Rex needed me there."

"But you're still grounded, Jessica, six nights a week, anyway." Jonathan spread his hands. "Wouldn't she just get you off completely?"

"Unless she was trying to be subtle."

"Melissa? Subtle?" Jonathan laughed. "Come on. We can't start being paranoid about every single thought in everyone's head, you know?"

"I guess." She sighed. "I don't know why I'm this way. Maybe because . . ." She turned to him, and the tears that had been ambushing Jessica all day blurred her vision again. "I just never saw anyone die before."

He put his arm around her. "Me neither."

"She was about the same age as Beth when they took her."

"Oh, yeah."

She shook her head, repeated the words that had been in her head for hours. "I'm sorry."

"For crying? Don't be. But . . ." Jonathan chewed his lip, which meant he didn't want to say the wrong thing.

"Go on."

"Well, it was horrible what they did to Anathea, but that was fifty-three years ago, like something in an old newspaper clipping. To me, it's like the girl we saw last night was a ghost, and we finally put her to rest."

Jessica stared at the dark moon; it didn't hurt her head so much these days to look at it. Maybe she was becoming more of a midnighter. "I guess that's one way to think about her, like a ghost that's free now."

"*And* you saved Rex, so the same thing didn't happen again."

She squeezed his hand. "I had some help with that."

He shook his head. "Just imagine old Grandpa Grayfoot standing there when midnight ended. Looking down at the girl he kidnapped back when he was a boy. He probably died of a heart attack."

Jessica flinched, not wanting to imagine any such thing. She didn't want anyone to die, she knew now. Not ever. She was glad that the other three were over at Madeleine's tonight—Melissa hiding in the contortion to protect the secret of its location, Dess working to darkling-proof the house, Rex beginning the task of reading through its archive, adding to the lore, maybe one day finding something to keep them all safe at midnight forever.

"Sorry," Jonathan said, having felt her pull away.

Jessica shook her head silently and looked across the street to the row of bushes where Ernesto

Grayfoot had hidden with his camera. "I can't believe it's only been a week since my stalker showed up."

"Yeah, really." Jonathan laughed. "Shows how much you can get done with an extra hour every day."

She smiled weakly. "Yeah. And what can get done to you."

They were silent for a while, the dark moon setting before them, before Jessica got up the nerve to ask. "I don't want to be alone, Jonathan. I keep seeing Anathea, dead, where we left her."

He took her hand again. "I'm right here."

"I mean tonight. Later."

Jonathan looked up at her. "Are you sure that's a good idea? Your parents . . ."

"Are sound asleep," Jessica said. "Mom was at work all day, and Dad was digging up the backyard. He's going to grow all our vegetables from now on, he says."

Jonathan laughed. "Beats working, I guess. Sure, I'll stay with you."

"There's just one catch."

"Hey, no problem. I'll sleep on the floor."

"No, you won't," said Jessica softly. "The catch is . . . there's someone I want you to meet."

Ninety seconds before midnight ended, they alighted outside her window.

Jessica hauled herself in and extended her hand back to Jonathan. He was still limping from his slither bites and reached up to let her pull him in. But when he got inside, Jonathan stammered, "Uh . . . Jessica?"

"That's the catch," she said. "Just for a few minutes. She's been wanting to meet you."

"Yeah, but . . . are you sure this is a good idea? Me just appearing out of nowhere?"

Beth sat on the bed where Jessica had left her an hour before, hands over her eyes, an annoyed expression clearly visible on her motionless face.

"Yeah, I'm sure." Jessica smiled. "Surprises are good for her."

"But . . . won't she wonder where I came from?"

"I already told her: Pennsylvania." Jessica giggled. She checked her watch, excitement building in her. Maybe this was a crazy idea, but she wanted to give Beth some small measure of the blue time—Jonathan, here and now, just as midnight ended.

Jonathan stood still, looking at the open window as if contemplating a mad leap in the remaining seconds.

"Listen," Jessica said, "I told her I had a surprise for her, and she really did want to meet you. Just for a few minutes, then she'll go to bed."

Finally Jonathan laughed nervously and sat down on the windowsill, one leg up as if he'd just darted through. "Okay, sure. I'm glad to meet her. Just one question."

"What?"

"What is it with you and your little sister, anyway?"

Jessica smiled. "It's a work in progress."

Seconds later the world shuddered. The blue light faded, and rich colors settled over everything. Her room looked alive again, set free from the arresting paleness of frozen time.

"—is *so* retarded," Beth finished.

"Okay," Jessica said. "You can look now."

Beth dropped her hands, a resolutely unimpressed expression already fixed on her face, one that lasted about half a second.

"Jesus!" she cried, half jumping up from the bed. "Who the hell . . . ?"

Jessica started to say something, but laughter snorted out of her instead of words. She struggled to suppress more giggles and felt her face turning red.

Jonathan smiled, holding out his hand.

"Hi, Beth, my name's Jonathan," he said politely. "It's nice to finally meet you."

The dark creatures are gathering for battle in
Midnighters vol. 3: **BLUE NOON**

Melissa noticed Rex sniffing the air, eyes twitching as his nostrils flared.

The pep rally chant was making him anxious.

"It's like a hunt," he hissed. "This is how they got themselves ready in the old days."

Melissa touched Rex's hand and for an awful moment felt the crowd as he did. Little humans, weak and frail—but *so many of them*. It had been rituals like this that had helped them conquer their fear of the darklings. One day they had begun to hunt their own predators, packs of humans armed with fire and their sharp, clever stones.

Finally a band of them had gotten lucky, taking down a young darkling. And some of the dread that the master species had always depended on was lost forever.

Maybe this pep rally wasn't such a joke. After all, high school was all about the oldest human bonds—the tribe, the pack, the hunting party.

She firmly took his hand and reached inside herself for a place that Madeleine had shown her.

She felt Rex relax, his fear of the crowd—and

of the beast inside him—slipping away.

"Whoa," he said softly. "Thanks, Cowgirl."

"Any time, Loverboy."

"Maybe we can—" Rex's voice choked off, his grip suddenly tightening. "Something's coming."

"What—?" she started, but then she felt it too and slammed her eyes shut again.

A taste was thundering toward them across the desert, vast and ancient, tumbling over itself in a wave. It grew stronger as it advanced, like an avalanche pulling down more snow from the mountainside, burying everything in its wake.

Then it struck, washing through the gymnasium, obliterating the surrounding mind noise of Bixby. Only Melissa's connection with Rex remained, his shock and alarm reverberating through her like the echoes of a gunshot.

She opened her eyes and saw what had happened. The blue light, the frozen bodies, a leaping cheerleader hovering suspended in the air. The whole world struck by . . .

Silence.

Melissa looked at her watch in amazement. It was just after 9 A.M.

But the blue time was here.